# ACROSS THE BRIDGE

Loved Grace,

Kristi Neace

Books by Kristin Neva

Copper Island Novels:
*Snow Country*
*Copper Country*
*Across the Bridge*

Children's:
*Toothella — Tooth Fairy in Training*

Memoir:
*Heavy — A Young Family's First Year with ALS*

# Glossary
## of Finnish and Yooper Words

*chook*— Yooper for a knitted winter hat, most likely from the French-Canadian *toque*

downstate— the Lower Peninsula of Michigan, below the Mackinac Bridge

hey— generally used to attract attention; in the UP this word is also used at the end of sentences to elicit an affirmative response or to add emphasis to a statement, also eh

*hyvää päivää*— Finnish for good day

*kantapää*— Finnish for heel, used by Finnish-Americans for heel of a loaf of bread

*kävellä*— Finnish for walk

*makkara*— Finnish for sausage, generally summer sausage

*nisu*— Finnish for sweet cardamom bread

*päivää päivää*— a Finnish greeting, literally day day

*pannukakku*— Finnish for oven pancake; a bready, custard-like dish baked in a pan

*paska*— Finnish for excrement

pasty— a regional dish of cubed potatoes, carrots, rutabaga, beef, and pork stuffed in a flour shell and baked

| | |
|---|---|
| *popple—* | colloquial term for poplar trees, specifically *populus tremuloides* (quaking aspen) and *populus grandidentata* (big-tooth aspen) |
| *ravata—* | Finnish for trot |
| *riisipuuroa—* | Finnish for sweet, creamy rice porridge |
| sauna-swim— | repeated sauna warm-ups followed by swimming |
| *sisu—* | the Finnish spirit of resilience and determination in the face of adversity; a word with deep cultural significance to Finns and Finnish Americans |
| UP— | the Upper Peninsula of Michigan, spoken as each letter *U – P* |
| Yoop— | a nickname for the Upper Peninsula of Michigan |
| Yooper— | a resident of the Upper Peninsula of Michigan |
| yous— | plural of you, found in some Northern US dialects, also spelled youse, rhymes with news |
| *voi—* | Finnish-American exclamation |

# KRISTIN NEVA

## ACROSS THE BRIDGE

A Copper Island Novel

THE
CHRISTMASTREE
HOUSE

*for persons with ALS*
*and their caregivers*

# *Prologue*

*T*he room seemed bigger now that it was empty. The hardwood floor was bare except for a rectangle of dust where the bed had been. Tiny holes from nails and thumbtacks dotted the walls. AJ rifled through his backpack. It contained all the necessary distractions for the three-and-a-half-hour ride to the Copper Country. A Star Wars book. A notebook. Pencils. And most important, an iPad with games.

He pulled out the device and pressed the home button. A screen saver flashed a picture of him and Mom. He put on his headphones, even though he only had a few songs and there'd be no internet to watch YouTube. But at least he could pretend not to hear his dad and all his stupid questions.

Dad was just trying to cheer him up, but asking pointless questions in a chipper voice wasn't the way to do it. If he wanted him to be happy, they wouldn't be moving. He'd said he needed help. It was too much to be a single dad and work full-time. He should've thought of that before kicking Mom out of the house.

Now AJ was losing his home, his school. And his dad's stupid jokes weren't helping.

"Ready, Freddy?" Dad called from downstairs.

AJ could feel his eyes roll in their sockets. He slung the backpack over his shoulder.

Though he usually didn't, he closed his bedroom door behind him when he left. It was still his space, the only bedroom he could remember in his ten-and-a-half years. They had lived in Quincy when he was little, but he didn't remember it.

"There you are. Are you ready, Freddy?"

"I'm not Freddy."

"You're supposed to say 'Sure, Betty.'"

"You're not Betty."

"That's the joke." Dad tousled his hair.

AJ pulled away. "Jokes are supposed to be funny."

Dad laughed. "Okay. Let's go. The Smith boys will conquer the Yoop."

Just past noon, Wausau felt like a sauna. Dad opened the driver's door of his truck and then the small door that opened backward so AJ could get in to the back seat. AJ strapped himself in the middle. Mom always made him sit on the side with the shoulder belt, but Dad was cool with him sitting in the middle with the lap belt. He could put his feet up between the front seats and look out the windshield.

Dad put the truck in reverse, backed up, and paused at the end of the driveway. "Say one last goodbye, AJ."

"I don't say goodbye to things I love."

"Hey, you say goodbye to me all the time." Dad laughed. He must have known AJ was talking about his mom and house, but Dad would rather make jokes.

"I don't understand why we have to leave."

"I told you. I need help. We'll be near Grandma and Grandpa, so you'll have a place to go after school and someone to watch you if you get sick. It was either move to the Keweenaw or to the Detroit area near my folks, but Granny and Pops are getting a bit too old to chase around a rug rat like you." Dad looked at him through the mirror, as if waiting for a smile.

He wasn't going to get one.

AJ pressed the home button, hit the music icon, and played

the first song. He opened the camera roll and pulled up the screen saver picture. His mom was beautiful with long blonde hair and soft blue eyes. He wished he had her eyes.

He didn't know why he cared. He just wanted more than a picture on his tablet to remember her by. He was eight when she died, and now he had a hard time remembering how she laughed.

Dad grabbed his ankle. "It's already been five minutes, and you haven't asked 'are we there yet.'"

AJ turned up the volume.

# Chapter 1

"*I* wish I could see you off at the airport, but you understand." Marcella Seppa gingerly stepped down her gravel driveway, walking her vacating tenants to her own vehicle.

"Are you sure it's okay?" Achara held Marcella's arm. "We can take a taxi."

"It's no problem." She brushed jagged rocks away with her bare feet and stood on a sandy patch. "Just leave the key above the visor. I'll bike up there after I meet the new potential renters."

Achara shook her head. "You are so—what's the word—hard heart."

Marcella laughed. "Hard core?"

"That's it. It's uphill the whole way."

Marcella shrugged. It would be slow going, but she liked the exercise, liked how biking cleared her mind. She handed a gift to Achara. "This is for you and Aat to remember Copper Island."

"Thank you." Achara's face lit up.

"I knew you wouldn't have room to bring much with you on the plane. It's more sentimental than valuable." Marcella had printed a dozen pictures from their adventures in the

Keweenaw. A Lake Superior sunset. Hungarian Falls. A sledding party with international students. The northern lights. She put them in a small plastic album.

"And we got this for you," Achara said.

Aat bowed his head and held out a wrapped present with both hands. "More valuable than expensive."

Marcella took the gift that had a distinctive bend in the middle. A thick book with a soft cover, she surmised. She cringed inwardly guessing what it was, but forced a smile. "Thank you. You two are so sweet, and I love how you care for me." She did appreciate them. They weren't pushy at all about their religion—just passionate. A passion she didn't share, not since she was a teen.

Achara hugged Marcella. "We'll miss you. You were a good landlord."

"You were good tenants." Marcella wondered who'd be next to occupy the lower level of her dad's duplex. "You and Aat have been such good neighbors."

"You are a good friend," Achara said.

"Have a safe flight home to Bangkok. You two are going to make excellent professors."

"I pray so." Achara giggled.

Aat circled around to the driver's side, and Achara got in the passenger seat and rolled down her window. "I'll miss you."

Marcella smiled. "Watch out behind you when you back up. Someone's on the sidewalk."

Hearing her, a man and boy, who were gawking at them, moved over.

As her friends drove off, she felt a sense of loss. She already missed them. The doctoral students had been a welcome relief from the typical college renters. No parties. No loud music. A wave of apprehension washed over her. Who would her next tenants be? She took a calming breath and walked to a large oak which provided shade from the mid-morning sun. She set down the gift, flipped her blonde hair over her shoulder, and wrapped her arms partly around the massive trunk, pressing her cheek to the rough bark. She felt the solidness of the earth, grounding her, beneath her bare feet. She breathed in the musty bark. "Please let me get good renters."

"Is she talking to the tree?" A boy's voice startled her.

Marcella let go, and the man next to the boy chuckled. Marcella picked up the gift and took a step toward them. "Trees are good listeners."

"But not very good huggers." The man's eyes twinkled. "I'm looking for a Mr. Larry Seppa. We're supposed to look at a rental."

"I'm Marcella, Larry's daughter. He asked me to meet you." Marcella matched his smile. A family. Not partiers. No beer cans in her garden. She looked toward the sky. *Thank you!* She exhaled. She hadn't been praying—not really. Asking a divine being to intervene didn't make sense to her anymore, yet she still found herself talking to someone or something. "I wasn't expecting you quite yet, not for..." She looked at her phone. "... half an hour."

"I was hoping it would work out to come a little early. We have another appointment after this." The man moved forward and held out his hand. "I'm Drew." He had red hair in a classic short cut. And though he wore jeans, they were clean, and he wore a collared shirt. A business guy. "And this is my son, AJ."

She let go of Drew's hand and bent at the waist to meet AJ's eyes. She shook his hand, too, and he lifted his chin. "I can show you the place now." Marcella tossed her hair over her shoulder and led them into the glass-paned porch where there were two doors marked A and B. "Are you just moving to town?"

"We drove in last night from Wausau. I got a job at Douglass State."

"There's an entrance in the back, but this is the main door." It made a better impression to come in through the living room rather than the kitchen. She turned the knob on door A. "I wasn't thinking. It's locked. I'll go around and open it up. You can wait here."

Marcella hurried around the house. She had planned to do a quick check of the apartment before the potential tenants arrived. Not that she was worried about its cleanliness. Achara was a fastidious housekeeper.

As she walked through the kitchen, she set her gift on the counter. She passed through the dining room, glanced into the first bedroom, the bathroom, the second bedroom, and then made her way into the living room.

The brown-haired boy was peering through a window. She waved, and he smiled, showing a cute gap between his front teeth.

She opened the door. "I'm sorry. My friends just moved out, and I wanted to give it a quick look over."

"It looks great." Drew scanned the room. "It comes furnished?"

"Kind of. The Puntasrimas, the couple who just left, are going back to Thailand, so they asked if they could leave some stuff they weren't able to give away or sell." Marcella's phone dinged, but she ignored it. "Most of my renters appreciate free furniture. Whatever you don't want, we can put on the curb. Someone will snatch it up."

"I might have to do that. I already have a houseful of furniture in storage that I'll need to squeeze into this one level." The man crossed his arms, putting his hand by his chin, and scanned the room. He wore a wedding ring. "And it has a fireplace. Does it work?"

"Yes, of course," she said. "It doesn't do much to heat the whole house, because it'll suck all the warm air out, but it'll make it cozy in this room on a cold winter night."

The boy walked toward the bathroom and bedrooms.

"The bedrooms are back here." Marcella led Drew to the larger of the two rooms where AJ was exploring. "This is the master."

AJ turned to them with a broad smile. "Can I have this one?"

"Good luck with that," his dad said. "You'll get the smaller room."

"Will it be you, your wife, and AJ?"

Drew flashed a pained look. "Just me and my boy. I'm not

married."

"Oh, sorry. I thought… I saw the ring."

"I suppose it's time to take it off." He twisted it on his finger, but left it there.

The boy walked out of the room with his head drooping. Drew followed him into the smaller room.

It looked like something was going on, so Marcella let them be and returned to the kitchen.

She checked her text messages. A message from her friend Beth. *Visiting Grandma. Could you work her in for a massage this afternoon? She's got a lot of discomfort. Can't sleep.*

Marcella exhaled. She looked at her watch. She'd have to bike to the airport to retrieve her SUV so she could transport the massage table, and after that trek, she'd have to hit the shower. She could do it, but that would eat up her afternoon and she wouldn't have time to tend her garden as she had hoped. But she wanted to help.

*Later this afternoon? After dinner?* She replied, and then set her phone on the counter and picked up the gift. She unwrapped it. A Bible. She knew it. She opened to the title page where Achara had written a note.

*My dear friend, Marcella, I will continue to pray that you will find peace with God. With Much Love, Achara and Aat*

So sweet. She'd treasure it because of the note. They didn't know she had several Bibles in a box in her dad's attic. The one her parents had given her on her tenth birthday. A teen study Bible they had given her on her fourteenth birthday. Her mom's Bible—well-read, well-marked. Maybe someday, if the ache subsided, she'd bring them down.

Marcella's phone dinged, and she quickly read the message from Beth that flashed on the screen. *See you around 6?* She quickly texted an affirmative response.

Marcella closed the Bible and held it in front of her, staring at the cover. They had even had her name embossed in the bottom right corner. She exhaled. She did have peace, some of the time, as long as she didn't think too much about God and faith. When Achara had tried to probe into her thoughts on the subject, Marcella felt herself closing up. Sweet Achara backed off.

"And there's a nice kitchen." Drew nodded approvingly as he entered, his hand on his son's shoulder. "A Bible?"

"It's a gift."

"Thank you, but I don't know if we're going to take the apartment yet."

"I meant it was a gift someone gave me, but you can have it if you want." She regretted offering it as soon as she had said that, given the note inside and her name on the cover. Why had she said that?

"That's okay. I have a Bible on my phone," Drew said, as he opened and closed the refrigerator. He inspected the stove. "No dishwasher?"

"No, unfortunately."

"Not a big deal. I have my own." He pointed at his son.

AJ rolled his eyes.

"Do you have laundry hookups? I kept my washer and dryer."

"There's a washer and dryer in the basement that we'd share. You can use them for free, just buy your own soap. Follow me. I'll show you." Marcella led them through the back kitchen door which opened to a vestibule with one staircase leading to the upper unit and another leading to the basement.

As she descended the stairs, she wondered what he'd think of the old cellar. It was clean, but there wasn't much she could do with the space because it got wet in the spring.

"Whoa," AJ said, looking around. "This is cool. It's like a cave."

A newer high-efficiency furnace sat in the middle of the basement next to a water heater. The washer and dryer were off in the corner next to a laundry tub.

"Look at this, AJ." Drew pointed to a hatch on the driveway side of the basement. "That's an old coal chute. Our house in Wausau used to have one like that, but it was replaced with glass blocks."

"I like the walls." AJ ran his hand along the basalt rocks

fitted together with liberal amounts of mortar.

"Those are from an underground mine," Marcella said, coming alongside him. "Barren rocks, but you can see flecks of copper in some of them." She pointed to one. "Like this."

"Could I put my weight set down here?" Drew asked.

"Sure, as long as I can use it." Marcella said, half-joking. Drew nodded.

This was a good sign. They seemed to be liking it. "Although you need to be careful about putting anything on the floor in the spring when the snow melts."

"Well, we've probably seen enough. Come on, AJ. We should be going." Drew walked toward the stairs and his son followed him. He went right out the back door.

Standing on the back deck, Marcella asked, "Is something wrong with the apartment? I know it's old, but it's well-maintained." It had been built in the 1890s when Quincy was a bustling, prosperous city. It was one of several properties her father owned, and he had renovated it before the Puntasrimas arrived four years ago for their master's programs. Prior to that, it had been trashed by bad renters.

"Oh, it's great. This place looks better than most in Quincy. And it's walking distance to my in-laws."

"And to the elementary school." These guys would be great tenants. "What grade will you be in?" Marcella bent at the waist.

AJ stood up straight. "Fifth."

"Seriously, you don't need to sell us on it. The property looks great." Drew checked his phone. "We have one more to look at up on the hill, and then AJ and I will discuss it and make a decision."

The boy lifted his chin, as if proud to be included in the decision-making process.

"Hey, if you're going up the hill, would you mind giving me a ride to the airport?" she asked, wanting to have time in her garden.

"That'll be no problem at all." Drew smiled, softening his features, which otherwise looked pretty chiseled, probably from frequent exercise.

Or maybe he hadn't been eating enough. Marcella wondered if that was the case, because of circles under his blue-green eyes.

"I'm happy to help out," he said. His eyes remained fixed on hers.

She looked away. Intense guy. Maybe it would be better if she'd forgo her gardening instead. "On second thought, I think I'm going to bike to the airport." She gave Drew a polite smile.

"That's quite the ride."

"It's only eight miles."

"Uphill," he pointed out.

She did want to have energy left to give Louisa a deep massage and time to pull weeds. She smiled at the guys. "Let me get my purse."

"And shoes," AJ blurted.

"What?"

"Shoes." He pointed to her feet with a cheeky grin.

Laughing, Marcella looked down over her silky culottes and wiggled her toes. "The great thing about growing up is that you can break all the rules. I'll meet you out front." She ducked out the back door and up the stairs that led to her kitchen.

She set the Bible on her counter, grabbed her purse, slipped on sandals, and left to meet the guys.

Drew opened the passenger door of his truck and cleared off the seat, stuffing Craigslist ads for rental properties above the visor. "Climb in."

He didn't know why he was so pleased to be helping her out. He wasn't at all ready for another relationship. He had his son to consider. In fact, AJ was the *only* thing that mattered to him, and he was determined to be a good father, to give him a great childhood in spite of the circumstances.

Marcella grabbed the assist handle and pulled herself up into the truck. She wore an airy, wide-legged split skirt, a hemp fabric peasant top, and Birkenstocks. She possessed an ethereal beauty. He was surprised by how he was drawn to her, but it would be best to put it out of his mind.

She flipped her shoulder-length hair back. "Thank you." She smiled, showing perfect teeth.

He studied her profile as he opened the rear passenger door. AJ climbed in and onto the jump seat.

Drew closed the doors and rounded the truck. Struck with a bittersweet memory, he shuddered. How many times had he helped Kristine into the truck and then AJ jumped in the back? Was a year and a half too soon to even entertain ideas of dating again?

He hadn't dated for over eleven years, not since he married Kristine. She was fresh out of high school, and he was entering his junior year at Douglass State. Now AJ was ten-and-a-half. He chuckled to himself. Whenever new friends asked how long they had been married and how old AJ was, their minds started working. He could see them do the math in their heads.

Yup. But he made it work as long as he could.

In the driver's seat, Drew started the truck. AJ kicked his feet up on the center console.

Marcella turned to him. "You get to sit in the middle? How cool is that? My mom hated it when my dad let me sit in the middle."

"Mine too." AJ beamed at the attention.

Drew glanced at the dashboard clock. "Are you in a rush to get to the airport? Time's got away from us, and I need to meet the landlord for the other property in ten minutes." Drew drove down a sloped side street that connected to US 41. "Do you mind if we stop? It won't take long."

"I'd love to check out the competition."

"They're no real competition. I'll go with your place, if it's all right with you, but I don't want to be rude and not show. So we'll make a super quick stop to see the other place, drop you off at the airport, and then AJ and I will head over to the Heikki Lunta for lunch. How does that sound, buddy?" Drew looked to AJ in the rearview mirror.

AJ smiled.

"Yay," Marcella said enthusiastically. "You're welcome to move in anytime. I'd love to have you as neighbors. I hoped the universe would be kind to me today."

"Your sales pitch worked, too. AJ and I had a chance to talk when you were grabbing your purse, and he likes the place." Drew turned onto the highway to head up the hill. "It's well-maintained. The neighbor seems nice." He glanced over at her, pleased that she smiled. "And it's walking distance to school and his grandparents."

"Who are his grandparents?"

"Ron and Patty Hiltunen."

"Oh." Marcella's voice had a knowing tone.

# Chapter 2

*I*n a red, wood-clad diner on a sloped side street of Douglass, Danny Johnson took a stool next to Mak. "It's noon, what are you doing here?"

Mak peeked over the trade paperback he was reading. "*Hyvää päivää*," he mumbled the Finnish greeting and put his nose back in the book.

Tammy topped off Mak's coffee. "If he stays here any longer without ordering something else, I'm going to charge him rent." She flipped a cup over in front of Danny and filled it. "What can I get you, hon?"

"A BLT."

"And for you?" Tammy gazed at the old man.

"*Pannukakku*," he said, without looking up from his book.

"You ate the last of that this morning." Tammy shook her head and took Danny's order to the kitchen.

Mak picked up his coffee, which sat next to a stack of books. Atop the stack was *Greta's Dream* with a picture of a young woman in a bonnet in front of a golden wheat field.

"Amish fiction?" Danny laughed.

"Research." Mak took a drink.

Danny removed his Michigan State Police hat and set it on

the counter. "Research for what?"

"I gots to put a bonnet on it." Mak splayed the book on the counter. "Iris MacDowell found a publisher for her Western romance, but I gots to turn it into an Amish fiction."

"Who's Iris?"

"I'm Iris. That's my pen name."

The bell above the door to the Heikki Lunta chimed. Danny turned his head to see if it was a familiar face entering. An older couple he had seen before, but didn't know.

"You found a publisher for that book you're writing?"

"Yah, a small publisher, but it's a start. Da big houses won't even consider you unless you got a platform. And I'll need a book or two under my belt to build a platform."

"What's it about?" Danny took a sip of coffee.

"A young woman falls for a cowhand, but come to find out he has a past—a son from a prior relationship—and she's got to come to terms with that."

Danny slammed his cup on the counter. "I said you couldn't use that."

"What? Any resemblance to actual events or persons, living or dead, is entirely coincidental." Mak smirked. "It'll say that on the copyright page."

"There's no proof that that boy's mine."

"Calm down." Mak sipped his coffee. "Names, characters, and incidents are products of da author's imagination or used fictitiously."

Tammy wiped spilled coffee off the counter with one hand and plunked the plate with chips and a BLT in front of Danny with the other. "What's the disturbance here, Officer Johnson? You're going to make me call the cops on a cop?"

"It's nothing." Danny pulled the toothpick from one of the sandwich halves. He popped a chip in his mouth. "I can't believe you got published."

"It took a while. A year to write it, months of editing, dozens of submissions."

"Who's going to want to read a romance written by an old Finn?"

"It's written by Iris MacDowell. She's Irish, I guess. They'll want to read a book by Iris."

"And how can you write when you can't even speak properly?"

"What you talkin' about? I speak perfectly good."

"You say Ds for Ts, or you just skip them. You drop your prepositions." Danny shook his head.

"You been hangin' around Beth too much. She's a grammar Nazi." Mak swiveled his chair to face Danny. "How is she, anyhow?"

"If I tell you, are you going to put it in the book?"

Mak laughed, showing his yellowed, coffee-stained teeth. "No, I'm just curious. How's she gettin' along in snow country?"

"It's not snow country now. It's blazing hot out there. It's got to be seventy-five. And she's loving summer, or at least what's left of it."

"I ain't been seein' much of you in the mornings now that you're married. She got a bun in da oven yet?"

"None of your business."

"I take that as a yes." Mak swiveled his stool back around and opened his journal. He jotted down a note.

"I told you not to use my life for your chick lit books."

"Ahh." Mak flapped his hand dismissively. "Everything's material."

Danny started working on his sandwich as his mind wandered to the past year. He and Beth got married the prior Christmas Eve, and she was pretty eager to start a family. After six or seven months of trying—a lot.

"What's so funny?" Mak asked.

"None of your business." Danny returned to his thoughts. After months of trying, they started to get worried, but then it happened. It was still too early to announce anything. Beth was ecstatic, but then concerned because she'd already purchased the bridesmaid dress for Aimee's wedding. It would be a mid-October wedding, so Beth didn't think she'd be showing, but she wasn't going to try keep her weight down. She hoped the dress would still fit. "Hey, Mak, have Russ and

Aimee figured out where to have the wedding?"

"They figured out where not to have it. Aimee don't wanna convert to Lord's People, so da Traprock or Quincy assemblies are out of da question. Russ's family won't feel comfortable at Pinehurst. Senja's lookin' for an outside venue."

"An October wedding outside in the Keweenaw. It could be beautiful or blustery. They better start praying for good weather, hey."

Mak laughed. "Yah, eh."

The door chimed again. Mak and Danny swiveled their heads around. A redheaded man entered with his brown-haired, doe-eyed boy. Danny dropped his half-eaten sandwich on his plate and stared at the crumbled bread and strips of bacon.

"You look like you seen a ghost." Mak pulled his journal toward him and scribbled a note. "This'll be better than da first one."

Danny pushed his plate aside and donned his cap. He threw a ten-dollar bill on the counter. "Tammy, this should cover it, hey?"

"If you want to be a cheap tipper." She pulled his tab from her apron pocket and set it in front of him.

Danny added a dollar. "I've got to go."

Up on Quincy Hill, Beth Johnson drove down the county road past her grandma's old farmhouse. Vacant since the beginning of the year, it still looked lived-in because her husband mowed the grass and they had planted the garden together in the spring.

The garden looked green and luscious from a distance, but on closer inspection it was mostly weeds. She hadn't much time to keep up on it given her full-time work at Douglass State and spending her off hours with Danny or visiting Grandma at High Cliff.

She parked in front of the little blue house next to Danny's

Jeep. Even after eight months of marriage, Beth still felt flutters before seeing him.

"I'm home," Beth yelled when she opened the door.

No response, likely due to the thumping music coming from the bedroom. Danny listened to "Torn for You" and other Christian rock when Beth wasn't home. She'd surprise him. She slipped off her shoes and walked down the hall.

"There you are," she yelled over the music.

Danny shut off the computer monitor. He stood with eyes wide. "Hey, Beth." He turned the volume down on his music and then wrapped his arms around her, lifting and squeezing her tight. "Oh, I should be careful." He set her down.

Beth laughed. "I'll be fine. I can't be more than six weeks along." She pulled on his arms and fell back onto the bed.

Danny laughed. He pulled back and sat on the edge of the bed.

"What's wrong?" Beth sat up and examined his face.

"It's nothing. How was work?"

"Work was fine. What's wrong? Whenever you're upset, you lose your appetite for food and—"

"Nothing's wrong." He sounded annoyed as he grabbed her hand and stood. He smiled, showing that adorable gap between his teeth. "Let's go make dinner."

"What are you keeping from me?"

"I'm not keeping anything from you."

"Daniel Walter Johnson, you said you'd never lie to me again."

"I'm not lying."

"Withholding information is like lying." Beth had heard stories of men addicted to nasty stuff on the internet, but she hadn't thought Danny was the type. But then again, what was the type? "What were you looking at on the computer? Why did you turn the monitor off?"

"I was just on Facebook."

"So why did you shut off the monitor? You never turn off the monitor." Beth stood and gave him the stare.

He crumbled every time he saw it. "Don't look at me like

that."

Beth folded her arms, doubling the intensity.

"Okay, fine." He went to his desk and turned on the monitor. "I was looking at pictures of AJ."

"Oh, why didn't you just say so? You know that I'm okay with it, right? I've come to terms with your past. He's a gorgeous boy, and if we have a boy, I hope he looks like him."

"I saw him today." Danny mumbled the words, resting his arm on his forehead and turning away.

"You mean for real? Like you actually saw him in person?"

"Yeah."

"Where?"

"At the Heikki Lunta. He came in with his dad, but I ducked out."

"That's awkward. But he still doesn't know who you are, I mean that you're his dad. So what's the big deal?"

"This is a small town. He's ten now, and he's looking more and more like me. It's only a matter of time before someone says something stupid. Someone like Mak. He's got a big mouth, especially for a Finn."

"Would it be so bad if he knew the truth?" Beth searched his eyes.

Danny exhaled loudly. "He has a dad."

She squeezed his arm. "You'll never be that, but maybe you could be..." She paused in thought. "...something else." She shrugged.

Danny looked at her quizzically, as if wondering what that something else might be.

"Let's grab something out and then go see Grandma." Beth held his hand and led him out of the room. "Marcella's coming at six to give her a massage. I need your help to get her on the massage table."

# Chapter 3

"You're pretty." Marcella dug her fingers in the dirt and yanked out the weed, root and all. "But you don't belong here."

She threw the weed into a pail and then rocked forward as she remained on her haunches. Her bare toes squished between soft, black soil. Over the last few years, she'd worked hard to develop the soil. Compost. Mulched leaves. Chicken manure.

Of course, the latter was the end-of-year treatment, so by the time the warmest days of summer allowed her to be barefoot, the manure had become beautiful, rich gardening soil. She'd like to have layers herself, but chickens weren't permitted in the village limits. Her garden kept her busy enough and she had a client with chickens and no garden, so she had access to the good stuff.

"You, too." She yanked out another weed. "Are you feeling less crowded, Basil?"

A taut, pink string ran between stakes marking her rows of carrots, tomatoes, and a few leafy greens. It was hard for her to differentiate between plant and weed at the beginning of the year, but now she knew her friends well. She could tell who belonged and who didn't. She also grew herbs—peppermint, lavender, and both sweet and Thai basil. She started growing the Thai basil after Achara taught her how to cook a few traditional Thai dishes. She used the lavender to make essential oil. She couldn't get much more than an ounce out of her plants, but it was worth it. And she made loose-leaf tea with the peppermint. She wished she could grow more mint but needed to limit her supply to one garden box to contain the roots. Otherwise, it would take over her garden.

Her backyard was pretty much all garden. Fortunately her house—rather her dad's duplex—was on the south side of the street, and being on a hill, the backyard was exposed to the southern sun. Her garden needed as much sun as it could get over the short growing season on the Keweenaw. She had to start several of her plants indoors, as she couldn't plant until the first week of June, and frost sometimes came as early as the first week of September.

"Marcella!" Her dad stepped into the backyard with Kandy. She offered a polite smile.

"We have some news." Dad's tone was serious.

Marcella's stomach tightened. "Are you sick?" Dad had said the exact same thing when Mom had gotten the cancer diagnosis.

He shook his head. "Don't look so worried. It's a change, but not a bad one."

Marcella fought back a laugh. She was having *déjà vu*. He had also said those words almost a decade ago when he told her she was going to have a stepmom. But now she was an established adult. As long as he wasn't sick, his news wouldn't affect her—whatever it was.

"We wanted to give you the news in person." Her dad grabbed Kandy's hand, and his face broadened into a giddy smile. "We're moving."

"What?" Marcella was sure she had misheard him. There was no way he could be moving. He had lived in the UP his entire life. He had been with his company for more than twenty years.

"We're moving to Madison." Kandy clapped her hands.

"Why?" Marcella rose to her feet.

"I'm being brought on as vice president of business development for an environmental engineering firm headquartered there." Dad looked again to Kandy.

She put her hand on his shoulder, aglow in approval.

Dad continued, "I just put in my two-week notice. I couldn't say anything to anybody until it was official."

"Not even to your own daughter?" She asked the question softly.

"We've been praying about this for months," Kandy said. "God's telling us this is the right thing to do."

"You asked God, but you didn't bother to ask me?" Marcella didn't know why she was so upset about it. She didn't see her dad often anyhow. She couldn't bring herself to spend time at the house with Kandy always there. She had dinner with her dad from time to time when Kandy was out of town or busy for the evening, and he'd stop by to check on the duplex. He did all of the maintenance himself.

"Listen, Marce," her dad spoke empathetically. "I'm going to be coming back quite a bit, at least over the next year while I get the house and rental units ready to sell."

"You're going to sell the rental units?" She felt the rug being pulled out from under her.

"I don't want to be an absentee landlord. And housing's quite a bit more expensive in Madison, so it'll take the equity from the lake house plus the other properties to get something decent."

Kandy let out a squeal of excitement. "I'm going to get my dream home."

"I have to go wash up." Marcella grabbed the bucket of weeds and headed toward the house. "I have a client at six."

"Good afternoon, Louisa." Marcella laid her hand on the woman's shoulder in the High Cliff dining room. A glass wall framed the Portage Canal valley, with the mine shaft sitting atop Quincy Hill on the far side. "Hi, Senja."

"Hello." Senja looked up, holding a forkful of mashed potatoes in front of Louisa's mouth.

Louisa remained facing forward, and Marcella came around her wheelchair.

"There you are, dear," Louisa said with a heavy tongue. Someone who didn't know better might have thought she was drunk, or perhaps had a stroke, but neither was the case. She had been diagnosed with ALS a year and a half prior.

Senja forked the potatoes into Louisa's mouth.

"Good grief!" an elderly woman at a neighboring table said, flashing a look of disdain toward Louisa. Her tablemate shook her head.

At other tables, dozens of residents of the senior home mostly ate on their own, but a few had private care. Several of Louisa's friends volunteered for different time slots, and she paid out-of-pocket for other caregivers.

Senja held up a cup of tea, and Louisa sipped from a straw.

Marcella sat at the table. "How are you feeling?"

"Tired. I hope I sleep better tonight after the massage." Louisa smiled. "You have gifted hands."

Marcella returned her smile. "I came early so I could work on you a bit longer. We'll start in the chair if you finish eating before Beth and Danny get here."

"Good. I—" Louisa's face tightened, and she strained to speak.

Realizing that Louisa's jaw was cramping, Marcella came back around and rested her fingers on Louisa's face. Then when the worst was over she began massaging lightly in small circles. *Let go. Relax. It's okay.* She thought the words first and then whispered, "You can let go." She felt Louisa's jaw relax and moved her hands down Louisa's neck, willing the tight muscles to release.

"Lou," the neighboring lady called.

Louisa slowly turned her head.

"This place is already looking too much like a nursing home with people being fed. It shouldn't look like a massage parlor, either." The woman turned her chair to face the other direction.

Louisa chuckled and then said softly, "Margaret hasn't changed since middle school. Thank you, Marcella. We'll continue the massage in my room when I finish."

So unfeeling. And sweet Louisa seemed to take it in stride. Marcella returned to her seat.

Senja held Louisa's tea again. "I made this from the peppermint leaves you brought for Louisa," Senja said to Marcella.

"It's very good," Louisa said after she'd taken a long sip. "And I understand there's more peppermint at my house that Beth hasn't gotten around to harvesting. You're welcome to it."

"I'll dry it so you'll have tea all winter." Marcella admired her elderly client. Even with a terminal illness, she still managed to appreciate the little things.

Louisa smiled her thanks. "Have you had any interest in your lower flat?"

"Yes, I *do* have new renters, and I think they'll be good tenants."

"Good. I've been praying that everything would work out for you."

"Thank you." She appreciated the sentiment, but cringed inside whenever someone told her that. Things always seemed to work out when one took a selective view of reality. She left unsaid the bombshell her dad had dropped. She still couldn't believe it. If he did find a buyer for the duplex, she doubted the new owners would accept the steeply discounted rent she paid her dad. They might even want to occupy the flat themselves.

"Who are your new renters?" Senja asked.

"It's a father and son. Kristine Hiltunen-Smith's husband and son," Marcella said.

"I heard rumors," Senja said. "Is it true the boy's the spitting image of Danny?"

"Now, now. That's none of our business." Louisa turned to Senja. "Are you excited for the new semester to start?"

"Hardly. I'm being pushed to the sidelines." Senja cut a piece of gravy-covered turkey with the side of the fork. "A new kid's starting on Monday. I need to train him on my job. I've been doing that job for forty years. There's no issues with how I do the job, and I'm not planning to retire anytime soon." Senja lifted the turkey to Louisa's mouth.

Louisa opened her mouth, but her nose caught the gravy.

Senja wiped Louisa's face with a napkin. "I'm getting increasingly frustrated with Douglass State. Last year they put in a new accounting system, and now it takes me twice as long to make my month-end entries."

Senja was getting worked up, and the negativity would not help Louisa relax during her massage. "Senja, how's the planning going for Aimee and Russ's wedding?" Marcella asked.

"It's going well. She's coming up Labor Day weekend for her bridal shower. We're going to have it at Lou's farmhouse. Can you come by to give chair massages? I'll pay you, of course."

"I'd love to, but you don't need to pay me. I'll do it as a friend, and maybe for some peppermint."

Louisa chuckled.

"I didn't know you were friends with Aimee," Senja said.

Marcella shrugged. Senja was always so blunt. "We were friends in middle school. She was one of the few who came to the funeral when my mom died." She and Aimee moved in different circles, but they were always cordial when they ran into each other. Besides, what was a friend? She knew Aimee and she liked her, so whether or not they did all that girly stuff together or had moments of deep bonding was beside the point. "And Beth's her maid of honor, right? And I'm friends with Beth, so I'd love to help."

"Well, thank you." Senja forked more turkey from the plate. "Louisa, have you thought about what you're going to do with the house?"

Louisa momentarily scrunched her face and shook her head. "I don't know. An old farmhouse isn't worth that much, and I don't need the money now. I guess I'll leave it for Scott and Rebecca to deal with after I'm gone," she said, referring to her son and daughter. Her chest rose, and she exhaled slowly, lowering her head.

"Have more turkey." Senja held the fork. "Without all that messy gravy."

Louisa lifted her head, took a bite, and chewed slowly.

"They'll probably sell it since they're in Chicago and LA," Senja said.

Louisa gasped. She made a futile attempt to clear her throat, sounding like a cat. "Water," she said in an airy yell.

Senja stood with a start and lifted a glass to her mouth. Louisa gulped as water spilled out the side of the glass. She swallowed hard.

"Thank you. It's too dry." Her eyes looked panicked, watering.

"Lou, it's time for a feeding tube." Senja dabbed water from Louisa's blouse.

"I want to eat on my own." Louisa's voice was firm.

"You're obviously not eating on your own." Margaret pushed her chair back from the next table. "It's spoiling my dinner. I'm going to talk to the staff about this." She stomped off.

"It wouldn't keep you from eating on your own on your good days." Marcella leaned forward in her chair, placing a hand on Louisa's knee. She hated seeing her dear friend struggle. Tears threatened to form.

Frowning, Louisa hung her head again. She was a stubborn woman, Marcella thought. The Finns called it *sisu*, an admirable trait when one is young and healthy and making wood for winter heat, but infuriating when stubbornness interferes with people getting needed medical intervention—like when Mom put off scheduling an appointment with her oncologist even after feeling fatigued.

"Have some mashed potatoes with gravy." Senja cupped her hand under the forkful to catch the dripping gravy.

Louisa shook her head. "I'm done."

"Hi, guys." Beth said, approaching their table with Danny trailing behind. "What's wrong?" Beth leaned over her grandma's shoulder and kissed her on the cheek.

"Louisa had another choking incident," Senja informed her.

"I wasn't choking. I just had trouble swallowing the dry turkey." Louisa said the words slowly.

"You need to get that PEG, and soon before your breathing declines any further." Senja looked to Beth, as if asking for backup.

Beth nodded but didn't say anything. Marcella resisted the impulse to give her opinion. She wasn't family.

"How are you, Danny?" Louisa's eyes brightened as he hugged her.

"Ah," he said dismissively. Leaving the empty seat for Beth, Danny asked a woman at a neighboring table if he could take a chair.

"These chairs belong to this table," the woman said.

"So sorry." Danny sat and then motioned for Beth.

Beth hugged Senja and Marcella, and then sat on Danny's lap.

"Beth," Louisa said with a sparkle in her eye, "you seem to have a glow about you. Anything new?"

Blushing, Beth put an arm over Danny's shoulder and kissed him on the cheek. "You'll be the first to know if anything's new. Marcella, have you found renters yet?"

"Yes, I did," Marcella said, amused her friend was so quick to change the subject.

"College students?"

"No. A nice family."

"Who's that?" Danny asked.

Breathe, Marcella thought. *Tree. I need a tree.* "From out of town. Moved here for a job at Douglass."

"How about we go upstairs and get on the massage table?" Louisa said quickly.

# Chapter 4

*M*arcella lugged her massage table down the hallway, following Danny and Beth as they held hands. Louisa led the way in her power wheelchair. Senja had gone home.

Louisa drove in a wide arc veering to the left until she approached the wall and then paused. Danny gently pulled on the joystick and drove her away from the wall, pointing her back to the right. Louisa continued again in a wide arc until she reached the left wall. After another correction and a few more yards, they reached her room.

Marcella slipped the strap off her shoulder and set the massage table on the floor. She unzipped the bag.

"I had better use the bathroom first," Louisa said. "Can you ring for a CNA?" She frowned. "It may be awhile."

"Danny and I can help you, Grandma," Beth said. "Is that okay?"

Louisa hesitated and then nodded.

"We'll drape the hospital gown in front of you." Beth reached down behind the back wheel of the chair and pulled out a lever, freeing the transmission. She rolled the chair into the bathroom.

Marcella set up the table. As she waited for them to finish, she sat in a chair and gazed out the second-floor window into the dense woods on the other side of the parking lot. The maples and oaks had turned a deep, matte green. That final green of late August before the trees give up and shed their chlorophyll.

She loved fall. She loved the cycle of the seasons. Though the Keweenaw didn't have long springs, it had magnificent summers and glorious autumns. And then in the winter, the Keweenaw came to life. Douglass State held Winter Carnival, complete with giant snow statues. The snowmobilers came. The ski hill opened. And she could still cycle because she had a fat bike.

She felt connected to the earth with the ever-changing seasons.

Danny exited the bathroom and closed the door behind him. "You never said who your new tenants are. Would I know 'em?"

Of course he would, and he'd find out soon enough. The town was too small for him and the Smith boys not to cross paths. She just didn't want to be the one to tell him.

"Why are you looking at me like that?" Danny sat in the chair across from her.

"It's the Smith boys. Patty and Ron's son-in-law and grandson."

"Aaah." He looked out the window, nodding his head slowly. "Yep. I've seen them in town."

Marcella didn't know much about the situation. Danny was a couple years older than she, but of course she knew about him and Kristine. Everyone in high school knew about Danny and Kristine. They were both super popular. He was a jock. She was a cheerleader. But when they graduated, Danny took off for downstate. Kristine married Drew a few months after. Marcella had all but forgotten about them until Drew showed up as a potential renter. She had never known about the kid, and she didn't draw a connection to Danny until Senja mentioned it.

"Danny, we need your help again." Beth called from the

bathroom.

Danny slipped in, and less than a minute later the door opened "All right, she's ready for you." He carried Louisa directly to the massage table, while Beth pushed the wheelchair out and sat on the bed.

"Thank you, Danny." Louisa lay on the table dressed in a sweat suit with her one leg straight while the other splayed. One arm dangled off the table.

Marcella adjusted Louisa's legs and arms. As she held her hands above Louisa's stomach, she felt a twinge in her own arm. "Should I start with your arm?"

"That's good." Louisa mumbled the words. "You always have a sense for these things."

Marcella put a couple drops of pine essential oil in her palm and then squirted massage oil on her hand. She vigorously rubbed her hands together, warming them with friction. She began kneading Louisa's forearm from the elbow down to the wrist, pulling on the muscles like squeezing paste out of a tube. Marcella closed her eyes. Let go, she thought. *Let go.* She whispered, "You can let go. I've got you." She felt Louisa's bound-up forearm muscles relax.

"Beth, how's my house doing?" Louisa asked.

"It's doing fine."

"Are you keeping the bird feeder full?"

"Nobody's there to watch them," Beth said.

"But my chickadees depend on me to feed them."

"I'll fill it up tonight," Danny said.

"I told Marcella she could stop by to pick peppermint from the garden."

"Oh good," Beth said. "And maybe she can tell me what's a weed and what's a plant."

Marcella opened her eyes briefly and smiled at Beth, who had moved to the end of the massage table and was rubbing her grandma's foot.

"You miss it, don't you?" Beth asked.

"Dreadfully." Louisa closed her eyes tightly.

"I thought you were happy here." Beth rotated the ball of

Louisa's foot around to loosen her ankle.

"I'm content."

"That's Grandma Lou-speak for not being happy here," Danny said. "You have a ramp to get into your house, and we said we'd help." He and Beth exchanged a glance.

"I try to be content in all things," Louisa said softly.

Marcella moved around the table and worked the muscles of Louisa's other arm, but she had lost the connection. It was hard to see Louisa soldiering through. She reminded her of her mom. Mom was so tired, in so much pain, yet she didn't complain. Sometimes Marcella had wished she would. It would've given her permission to express her own frustrations. It's hard to complain when someone's dying stoically. So she saved her rants for others. That's when one learns who's a friend and who's an acquaintance.

*Life's hard. Dying's hard.* The negative energy was affecting her massage. She needed to concentrate on feeling Louisa's pain. She closed her eyes.

She had learned to feel the pain of others when she massaged her mother's feet. Mom would be sick from chemo, and she'd recline back in her chair. As Marcella worked her feet, she could feel the pain in her own chest.

A knock came from the door.

"I'll get that." Danny jumped up from the chair and opened the door. "Hello, pastor. Come in."

"Am I interrupting?" A gray-haired man with a big smile paused in the doorway.

"No. No." Louisa struggled to lift her head to see him. "I'm glad you're here."

The man entered the room and sat on the bed where Beth had been sitting earlier. He was the pastor of Pinehurst Church. Marcella had grown up at Pinehurst, but back then there was another pastor.

"I came to pray with Lou." He extended his hand to Marcella. "Hi, I'm Chip Atkinson."

"I'm Marcella." She showed him her oily hand and quickly pulled it away. She looked down at her feet. The last thing she wanted to do was hear prayers for Louisa's healing. Claiming the promises of God. She had prayed those prayers for her mom. Her youth pastor encouraged her, saying, "Miracles happen. You just need to believe." Mom and Dad prayed. They believed, but Mom died anyway. Anxiety rose in her chest.

"Excuse me." She grabbed her purse and stepped into the bathroom, where she leaned against the wall. Breathe. She focused on breathing deeply for a few minutes. Positive energy in and negative energy out. She opened her purse and found her lavender oil. She placed a drop on each temple and closed her eyes, waiting until calm came over her.

As she came out of the bathroom, the pastor stood and placed a hand on Louisa's forehead. "May the Lord bless you and keep you. May he make his face shine upon you and give you peace."

Louisa's face broke into a smile and joy filled her eyes.

Marcella drew her breath in. "That's beautiful." The words tumbled from her mouth.

"It's from the Book of Numbers." He squeezed Louisa's shoulders. "It was a pleasure being with you." He waved on his way out.

# Chapter 5

"You can settle in here." Drew's boss, Janet, stepped into the cubicle across the hall from her office. "Here's your ID and password." She placed a Post-It on the keyboard.

Drew nodded and took a seat at his desk wrapped by three gray, fabric-covered walls. A considerable downgrade from Wausau Electronics, where his office had a door and a view of the Wisconsin River. But even with the cut in pay, he was doing what was best for AJ, because money can't buy family. Drew forced a smile and spun around. "Thanks for the opportunity."

"No, thank *you*. We really need the help." Janet handed him a binder labeled Douglass State New Employee Orientation. "Look through this until Senja arrives, and then we'll meet in my office."

Drew thumbed through a few pages of the binder. Dress code. Core hours. Campus map. Statement of diversity. Pretty standard stuff.

He logged on to the computer. After updating his password, he opened the internet browser and searched for *Douglass Quincy churches*. Pinehurst Church was at the top of the search results. He scanned for his in-laws' church, but it wasn't on the first page of results. On the family's occasional, and increasingly rare, visits to the Copper Country, they had attended church with Ron and Patty. It was ornate, having been built during the copper boom in the late 1800s, and it seemed like a fine church, but there weren't many kids. He needed to find a place where AJ would thrive, like the church they had attended in Wausau.

The Pinehurst site looked professional, although nothing fancy. There were a number of programs advertised on the right sidebar. Young mothers. Kids club. Trailblazers.

"I don't have time for a meeting." An indignant voice carried over the cubicle wall.

"And that's why we hired somebody, so you'd have time." Janet spoke in hushed tones.

"I'd have time if you didn't make me use this newfangled accounting system." The voice was laced with frustration.

"Senja, the accounting system's over four years old."

"You like everything new. You replace the old accounting system, now you're replacing the old lady with some young kid."

"He's sitting in the cubicle right next to us," Janet said, and the debate turned to whispers.

Drew reviewed the Pinehurst site to distract himself. He checked out the Trailblazers page. Hiking. Canoeing. Camping. For boys grades six to eight. It might be a good program for AJ in a year. He hadn't done many of those things as a kid, but he had grown to love the outdoors during his time in college.

"Drew," Janet said, and he spun around. "This is Senja Cote. Senja, Andrew Smith."

"Oh." There was knowing in her voice, and her frown turned to a look of sympathy and interest. "It's you. You couldn't be that young."

"I'm thirty-two, and I have nine years of experience working with both Oracle and SAP."

"Private sector?"

Drew nodded.

Senja folded her arms. "No experience with Banner?"

"The concepts are the same in any ERP system, and I worked with another Oracle-based system."

"And he can help us document procedures." Janet motioned for Drew to stand. "Let's continue this in my office."

"Do you have any experience with fund accounting?"

"I always have fun accounting." Drew smiled, attempting to break the ice.

Senja rolled her eyes, but her lips pulled up at the corners.

They crossed the hallway to Janet's office.

"Drew graduated with a degree in accounting from Douglass, and he's a CPA." Janet sat behind her desk, and Drew and Senja took the two seats across from her.

"I'm sure he's very capable, but you're asking me to train him on my job." Senja's voice showed signs of frustration again.

"We should all learn each other's jobs, Senja. You know we appreciate you, but you're nearing retirement."

"I'm not retiring anytime soon. My full retirement age isn't until I'm sixty-six and six months."

"Nobody's asking you to retire," Janet said.

"Maybe I should come back." Drew stood.

"No, sit down. Senja and I can discuss this later." Janet handed each of them a piece of paper. "Here are the month-end close procedures."

Drew reviewed the document. They were not so much procedures as a list.

"Senja, I'd like you to train Drew on each of these. And Drew, I'd like you to document the steps."

"I've been documenting the process," Senja said.

"We're going on our fifth year with the system," Janet said. "Drew has experience with this."

Senja scoffed.

"You can start today. Work with him at his desk. Show him around the system." Janet stood, indicating the meeting was over.

Senja slumped back in her chair. She looked defeated. Janet had said they needed help, but she hadn't explained why. Now it was making sense.

Drew excused himself and went back to his office. He reviewed the list. Senja was worried he was taking her job, but he didn't want it. He had long since moved on to more meaningful work in Wausau. This job was definitely a step back. A cubicle. Lower pay. Entry-level accounting. Sometimes one has to take a step back to move forward, he tried to convince himself. He wasn't sure if there was a forward for him at Douglass State, but he was less concerned about his career than he was about AJ.

"Can we start over?" Senja stood in his cubicle with a sheepish smile. "I'm Senja."

"Hi, Senja. I'm Drew." He extended his hand, and she shook it. "I'll get your chair for you." Drew circled around to the other side of the wall and rolled Senja's chair back to his office.

"Are you thinking about going to Pinehurst?" Senja nodded to the computer screen. "It's a lovely church, and we'd love to have you."

"I don't know. It was the first site I pulled up." He positioned Senja's chair behind her. "They have that Trailblazers boys' club, but it doesn't start until sixth grade. My son's in fifth."

She sat. "AJ, right?"

Drew nodded. *How did she know his son's name? Small-town living.* He smiled. "We had a father-son group at our church in Wausau. I'd like to find something like that here."

"They're not sticklers for rules, so I'm sure Danny would be fine with him taking part in activities this year."

"Then maybe we'll try it." Drew took his seat. "Maybe I could help with the group."

"You don't think it'll be awkward at all?"

"What would be awkward?"

"Well, if you..." Senja's pale complexion turned pink. "I don't know what I was thinking. Of course it wouldn't be awkward. Let's get right to it. You obviously figured out how to log on to the computer. I'll show you how to get into Banner." Senja looked positively flustered.

"What's wrong?"

She avoided eye-contact. "I wasn't thinking. This has not been a good day. My dearest friend's sick. That's why I was late this morning. I'm being replaced by newer systems and younger accountants."

Understanding dawned. She didn't want to worship with the guy who was taking over her job. He shook his head. Small-town living. If it was the best church for AJ, then that's where they'd attend.

"I can understand that it's hard on you. I hope you can keep all of your accounting responsibilities. I'm sure Janet can find other things for me to do. But I'm happy to train on them and help you whenever you need a hand." Drew leaned forward to make the point clear. "I hope we can work well together, Senja, and I don't think it'll be an issue at all to worship with you, if I do end up attending Pinehurst."

Senja let out a breath, and her shoulders relaxed. She brushed gray hairs from her face. "Of course it wouldn't be awkward to worship together." She smiled.

# Chapter 6

"*T*hanks, man." Drew slapped his father-in-law's shoulder.

"No problem. Glad to help." Ron sat on the couch, surrounded by boxes in the living room.

"It didn't seem like that much stuff when I had a crew of folks from church loading." Drew stretched his back and plopped down on the other end of the couch.

"I would've rounded up help, but my friends aren't as spry as they used to be," Ron said.

Patty popped her head in. "Drew, do you want the silverware to the left or right of the sink?"

"Whatever you think is fine. Thanks." He was glad to let her set up the kitchen.

"I thought Danny was going to come help." Patty frowned. "Do you remember meeting him at Kristine's funeral?"

"Yeah. I'm even Facebook friends with him. He friended me after the funeral." Drew leaned forward, stretching his back.

"Didn't you ask him to help today?" Patty asked Ron.

"Nah, we had AJ." Ron got off the couch and walked toward the kitchen, pausing in front of a bedroom. "How are you doing in there, buddy?"

"Good." AJ's voice came from the room.

Ron disappeared into the kitchen. As Patty followed him, she asked again, "Did you ask Danny if he could help?"

Ron's reply was mumbled.

Drew lay on the hardwood floor. He put his right foot over his left knee, twisting and stretching his back. A couple pops, but the pain persisted. He put his left foot over his right knee and did the same.

"What are you doing?" Ron chuckled as he reentered the room.

"My back's killing me. I'm not as spry as I used to be, either." Drew got to his knees and back on the couch.

Ron handed him a Sprecher Root Beer. "You don't have any of this sans root?"

"No, man. I haven't drunk for…" Drew thought for a moment. AJ was still pretty young, sleeping through the commotion. "…six years." He twisted the cap off the bottle.

"That's good. You're better off without it." Ron took a swig. "AJ's better without it." His eyes darkened. "Maybe if I hadn't…"

"It's not your fault."

Ron closed his eyes tight and pinched the top of his nose. He shook his head. "I tell myself that."

The men sat in silence.

"I think I pulled something." Drew leaned forward again, reaching around with one hand to rub his lower back. "Do you know where I can get a good massage?"

"Marcella's a great masseuse. She's got magic in those fingers of hers."

"Marcella? My landlord?"

"The very same. That's how I know her."

"She's Danny's massage therapist, too," Patty yelled from the kitchen.

"I have a standing appointment with her at Shear Delight every other Wednesday. I'll call to let them know you'll take my appointment tomorrow. Can you get off work at ten?"

"I think so. I don't have much to do yet other than read policy manuals. But it might be a little weird."

"Why would it be weird?" Ron cocked his head.

Now this is weird, Drew thought. He had massages before, but not by women he'd been attracted to. He had to hand it to the fifty-something-year-old, happily married man. His cluelessness showed his integrity. Pain coursed through his back. "You're right. It shouldn't be weird. I'll take the appointment."

"She'll get you all fixed up. She has an uncanny sense to find pain. You don't even need to tell her what hurts. She's gifted. In the meantime, put heat on it."

"Heat?"

"Or a cold pack." Ron shrugged his shoulders. "Just alternate between the two."

"You have no idea, do you?"

"Not really." He laughed.

"Okay, guys." Patty came into the living room. "The kitchen's unpacked, but you have no food."

The four walked from Drew and AJ's new flat up the hill to a neighborhood with relatively newer homes where Ron and Patty lived. Another few blocks would take AJ to the elementary school.

"I'm so disappointed that Danny didn't show up. I wanted him to meet AJ." Patty fell in step with Drew as Ron and AJ lagged behind.

"He already met AJ at the funeral," Drew said.

"I mean I want him to get to know AJ. And AJ should know him."

"Okay?"

"Patty!" Ron caught up to the two. "I need to talk to you."

Drew dropped back with AJ, who was playing with a stick he had found along the way. Ron bustled Patty forward and spoke in hushed tones for the remainder of the walk.

The Hiltunens lived in the house they bought when they were first married. It was where they had raised their children, Kristine being the middle child. Three girls. Three very different outcomes. The oldest girl married young and followed her husband to North Carolina where they had five kids. Ron and Patty didn't get to see them often. The youngest became an

RN and got a job as a traveling nurse. They were both well-behaved kids, but Kristine was the rebel.

Drew wasn't one to judge. He liked to party, too, but he could turn it off. He could take it or leave it, and he left it when he noticed how Kristine's drinking affected her parenting. AJ avoided her when she was hung over or drunk. You could tell it worried him, and Drew wanted to be a more stable presence in his life. A better role model.

He wondered if he should've left it alone, but her drinking seemed to be getting worse and worse. He had just come home from work, and they picked up the argument from that morning when she was too drunk to get out of bed. He said something like "I don't want you around AJ when you're drinking," and she accused him of kicking her out of the house. He couldn't remember exactly what he said, but he sure didn't mean for her to leave permanently. She headed up north to spend time with her parents, and she was sober when she left. He would've taken the keys if she tried leaving while she was drunk, but he couldn't control what she did once she was gone. It had been an argument like any other argument.

It was January 7 of the year prior, 6:12 p.m., when he got a call from the Houghton County sheriff. Kristine had survived the accident, and Drew and AJ left immediately. But by the time they got to Quincy, she had been transported to Marquette. So they drove to Marquette, but by then she had been airlifted to Ann Arbor. She died the next day.

"I have frozen chicken nuggets I can heat up in the oven for AJ," Patty said after they entered the house. "Would you guys like some of those? I also have leftover pasty casserole."

"I'll have pasty casserole." Drew lay on the living room floor.

"Me, too." Ron plopped into his recliner and kicked the footrest up.

AJ wandered to the corner of the living room where Patty had assembled a shrine of sorts to Kristine. Her eight-by-ten graduation photo hung on the wall. Candles sat atop a small round table along with a few trinkets, such as her class ring.

Her senior yearbook and photo albums were stacked on a lower shelf. AJ tended to go there whenever he first entered the house.

"Your back's still giving you trouble?" Ron asked.

Drew groaned an affirmative response.

"Marcella will take care of you tomorrow," Ron said. "Should I get you a heating pack?"

"Maybe a cold pack." Drew reached a hand under his lower back. "I think it's inflamed."

"Patty?" Ron called to the other room. "Could you bring an ice pack for Drew? And a beer for me?"

Drew laughed. "Is that how you get things?" He got to his knees. "Don't worry about it, Patty. I'll get it myself."

Drew went to the kitchen, found a gel pack in the freezer, and returned to the living room.

"Hey, Dad." AJ was looking at a page of a photo album. "I found me in this old class picture."

"Huh?" Drew looked at the photo in the album AJ held out toward him. He squinted. "Where?"

"Right there." AJ pointed to the back row. "Grandpa, come here. This boy looks like me. He even has the gap in his teeth."

"Are you a time traveler?" Ron released the footrest, and the La-Z-Boy sprung back into an upright position. He grabbed the album from AJ and placed it on the shelf. "Come on. Let's go help Grandma with dinner."

# Chapter 7

$A$s predicted, Drew's duties were still limited to reading employee handbooks as the month had not yet ended. The following week would be crazy, no doubt. The life of an accountant. So he set out on foot for his massage downtown, which was a dozen blocks from the Douglass State campus. He needed it. His back was still sore from moving, and he also needed to get rid of his tension headache.

He walked past a few churches and several Greek houses, with occasional glimpses of the canal between buildings and trees. A wooded neighborhood rose up on his left as the highway became ever more a street and followed the gentle arc of the base of the hill. He passed the miner statue that greeted visitors entering downtown Douglass, where the road diverged into three terraced streets. He followed the flow of traffic onto Avery Avenue, the main street. Douglass had an old-world charm with stylized lampposts and a brick-paver street. Basalt rock peeked out between buildings, as if the foundation for each had been chiseled into the side of the hill. Steep side streets rose up to second-floor entrances halfway up the block. A few of the buildings showed nineteenth century roots, and nothing seemed much newer than mid-twentieth century.

Decently maintained. A mix of businesses. Restaurants. A bank. Financial services. A tattoo parlor. And past a gift shop, Shear Delight.

He checked in with the receptionist and took a seat next to a plant near the window in the waiting area. He looked out at folks passing by on the sidewalk. After only a week in town, he already recognized a few faces. He had second thoughts about getting a massage from his landlord. It just seemed weird. Wausau was not a particularly large city, but it was populous enough to maintain anonymity.

"Hey, neighbor." Marcella smiled and pulled her head to the side, motioning for him.

He stood and followed. "Are you okay with this?"

"What's that?" She tossed her hair over her shoulder and glanced back at him. She led him past the salon chairs where one middle-aged woman sat with clumps of tinfoil clipped to her hair.

"Are you okay with giving me a massage?" He mumbled the words.

"Of course." She walked a few steps backward. "Are you feeling okay?" She looked concerned.

"Yes." His cheeks were probably red again. It happened at the most inopportune times, usually when he was trying to hide embarrassment. A casualty of being Irish, he supposed. He didn't really know, but it would explain his freckled, rosy complexion and red hair. His parents only knew that his birth mom had been a teenage girl. His bio-dad was not listed on the birth certificate. "I guess I'm a little overheated." He did feel flushed from the brisk walk, enough for that to be an excuse.

"I suppose it doesn't help that it's not air-conditioned in here." Marcella stopped short of the door at the back of the salon. "You can go on in, undress, and get under the sheet. I'll give you a minute."

Drew stepped in, and she closed the door behind him. A fluorescent light in a drop ceiling cast diffused light through silk scarves tucked into the tiles. A small lamp sat on a table along with a lit candle and an assortment of essential oils.

He took off his shirt and pants. He wished he'd brought gym shorts. He'd be under a sheet anyhow, but still…

He lay face down on the massage table and pulled the sheet up to his tailbone.

Marcella knocked. "Ready for me?"

"Yeah. Come in." Drew stared at the floor through the open headrest.

Marcella entered and closed the door.

He studied a pattern on the floor rug until the lights dimmed with the sound of a switch.

She put her hand on his shoulder. The light touch of a finger or two glided down his back, along his hip, and down his leg. He felt a chill run up his spine. She pulled the sheet up on his feet and grabbed his ankles, lifting both slightly, and then each alternately, a couple inches up and down. "We'll start on your lower back if that's okay?"

"That's good." He remembered what Ron had said about Marcella being able to sense pain.

Drew heard the distinctive squeak of a pump bottle and then the sound of her rubbing her hands together. She placed her hands on his lower back and slowly rubbed in oil.

The massage felt good. He missed the physical touch that was a part of marriage, even as rocky as his marriage had been. Was it too soon to consider dating? Would Marcella be interested? Just because he felt this magnetic pull toward her didn't mean she felt anything. Probably not the best move to become her client. Being her tenant would be awkward enough if things didn't work out. But man, she was beautiful, and she smelled good. He needed a distraction. A conversation. "So, are you from the area?"

"Born and raised."

It was working. He wasn't thinking so much of her hands on his body, but of her soft voice. The casualness of her reply. "Have you ever thought of leaving?"

"I've thought of it, but not too seriously. I do like to travel. I went down to Cancun last winter to soak in the sun."

He imagined her lying on a beach. The conversation wasn't

helping matters.

"So why did you move up to the UP?" Marcella asked.

"For AJ." Drew was glad to turn the topic to his son. "I thought he'd be better off near family. It was either the Detroit area or here. Ron and Patty are much younger than my parents, and the schools are better up here, so it seemed like the right choice. But now I'm second guessing my decision." Drew let out a sigh. The job was a huge step down, and for some reason, Patty was fixated on AJ getting to know Kristine's ex-boyfriend.

Marcella slid a thumb deep into the muscles along each side of the spine. "How's he coping?"

"As well as could be expected. He doesn't talk about it much, which worries me." Drew hadn't seen AJ break down in tears. He handled it all rather stoically. No sobbing. "He's had some respect issues since then, but it's hard to know if it's the grief or just his age. I've been a bit concerned because he hasn't been interested in having friends come over and play since his mother died. I read that kids who lose mothers at a young age have a hard time forming friendships and trusting relationships."

Marcella worked the muscles, moving further from the spine. She hit a sore spot on the left side, and Drew groaned.

"That hurts there?" she asked.

"Yeah."

"You have some inflammation."

As she continued to work the muscles, he breathed deeply through his nostrils. She had strong thumbs for a rather light woman. Or maybe it was her elbow. Actually, he was sure it was her elbow as he felt her hair brush his back.

"So anyhow, AJ's in a much better place here with his grandparents close by." He needed to get his mind off her and back onto his kid. "AJ used to come home to his mother, but I can't get off work to be home when he gets off school. Now he can go to his grandparents' house, except when Patty has meetings."

"I'd be happy to watch him when Patty's not available, on

any day that I'm home. I'll give you my schedule and my cell number."

"You would do that?"

"Of course. I like to think of my tenants as friends." She continued to work his back. It felt like she was rolling her whole forearm over the muscles from bottom to top. He occasionally felt her hair dance off his shoulders at the beginning of each sweep.

"That feels great." His back relaxed, and even his tension headache began to dissipate.

Marcella moved on to his calves. "Sometimes lower back pain is due to tight leg and glute muscles."

*Oh boy.*

She worked his legs hard and discreetly pressed into his glutes through the sheet. She was a professional.

He turned the conversation back to his son. "AJ's apprehensive about starting a new school, but I'm sure he'll do fine. I just hope he makes friends. Now I need to find a good church. I was looking at Pinehurst Community Church on the internet. Have you heard of it?"

"Mm-hm."

Drew could sense a shift in the mood of the room, and a change in her massage. She nearly drilled her elbow into his glute.

"Ow! That hurts a little."

"I'm sorry. I lost my focus." She massaged more lightly. "It's funny how the muscular guys are the most sensitive. There are more nerve endings in muscle than fat." She eased off a bit and continued to work his legs and glutes. She massaged his calves and feet, and then rubbed down his arms.

Drew's breathing became more rhythmic, and he began to drift off. But then he became aware of the stillness in the room, and he wondered if Marcella had left. He opened his eyes and saw bare feet on the rug in front of him.

She was standing there, but not touching him. The rug below him had a new wet spot where he supposed he had drooled. Embarrassing. He licked his lips. "Maybe I should get

going. I don't want to take too long a lunch on my third day
of work."

"Let me finish my energy work. It'll help your headache."

"How did you know I had a headache?"

"I could feel your pain between my temples as soon as I
started working on you," she said in a near whisper. "You can
let go."

His headache was already gone.

That evening, Drew made AJ macaroni and cheese and hot
dogs. They weren't just any hot dogs. They were natural casing
wieners from a local meatpacking company that all the locals
raved about. But he wasn't kidding himself, he was no chef.

"I'm going to go bike," AJ said.

"First, throw away your paper plate. And stay off the highway." Drew could hardly believe his own ears. In Wausau, he
was cautious about his ten-year-old leaving his own block, but
Quincy was a safe place for kids to wander. "When you get
back, I'll be in the basement doing laundry and working out."
His back had felt better after the massage, but it had started
to tighten up again, and sometimes the chest press gave him
needed relief.

AJ bolted out the back door.

Drew tossed his own plate in the garbage, and he washed
two pots, a mixing spoon, and two forks in the sink. He remembered with fondness the mess that Kristine would make
when she cooked. The main entrée, a couple side dishes, regular plates and glasses. She'd cook, and he'd clean. That was the
arrangement.

After he cleaned up the kitchen, he gathered laundry out
of his and AJ's rooms and the bathroom. He slipped out of his
work clothes, adding them to the basket, and put on shorts
and a T-shirt. He went down to the basement and filled the
washer with a mix of colors and whites. He knew he was supposed to separate them, but he just washed it all on cold. They

didn't have enough laundry between the two of them anyhow.

With the machine going, he crossed to the other corner of the basement where he had set up his incline bench. Bras were hanging from each side of the barbell, and silky blouses on hangers dangled from the middle. He chuckled. He did say she could use his weight set.

He wanted to start with chest presses, but what would he do with the bras and shirts? There wasn't really anyplace in the basement to hang them.

He pulled twenty-five-pound dumbbells from the rack against the wall. He positioned himself in front of a mirror he had leaned against the rock wall, checking his posture, and curled each arm alternately. He exchanged the two twenty-five-pound weights for a fifteen-pound dumbbell and leaned over the bench, resting the palm of one hand on it, as he worked his triceps by pulling the weight up behind him.

Since he hadn't worked out for a few days, he could work on his lower body, too. He put a couple forty-five-pound plates on his leg curl machine, sat on the bench, and worked his quads with leg extensions.

A clicking of feet descended the stairs. Marcella landed in the basement, dressed in biking shorts and a jersey, like a Tour de France rider.

"Hello, neighbor," Drew said.

Marcella jumped. "Oh, you *are* here. You're lifting weights."

"I'm doing what I can do considering my equipment's a bit tied up."

"I know. I'm sorry. I met AJ down the street on his bike, and he said that you were home doing laundry." She rushed over to the incline bench, the hard toes of her biking shoes clicking on the cement, and grabbed the bras. She wadded them in a hand and hid them behind her back.

Drew laughed. "I did say you could use it."

Marcella's cheeks grew red. "I know, but I..." She grabbed the blouses from the hangers. "I put these on there this morning, when you were at work, and I forgot about them until AJ said you were here."

"Seriously, it's not a big deal." Drew pulled a plate from his leg curl machine and put it back on the floor next to the dumbbell rack. "I was married for eight years. There were things hanging from every hook and rod in the bathroom."

"It won't happen again."

"I don't mind if it happens again." Drew took off another plate. "I like living with a woman," he said without thinking. Then he could feel the warmth of his cheeks. "Not that we're living together, but you know what I mean."

"I do." Marcella moved toward the stairs.

"Hey, should I make you a clothesline down here?"

"How's that?"

"I have rappelling rope upstairs. I'll string up a line from the floor joist braces." Drew glanced up to the wooden cross sections that formed X's between the boards of the basement ceiling.

Marcella smiled. "Sure."

"Hold on a second, then you can tell me exactly where you want it." Drew ran upstairs and dug the rope out of his climbing bag.

When he returned to the basement, she had her clothes neatly folded and set on the dryer, with silky shirts on the top and bottom of the pile.

"How about over here," Marcella said, pointing to an area alongside the laundry tub.

Drew strung up the rope, leaving loops dangling down from every other joist. In his Wausau house, he'd first put up one long run, but it sagged too far in the middle where the clothes bunched up and touched the floor.

"Are you a climber?" Marcella asked.

"A little bit. I mostly went to an indoor climbing gym in Wausau. Douglass has a climbing wall, too, and there are some great rock faces around here, but I'd need to find a climbing buddy."

"I'd love to try it. Would you teach me?"

"Sure." Drew cut the rope, and coiled up the remainder. "You should be all set."

"And, you know, I kind of like living with a guy." Marcella blushed after she said it. "I'm going to go back out and see if AJ's still biking. I'll show him how to get to the trail."

Drew transferred the remaining plates from the leg curl machine to the barbell and added a couple more. He'd take it light, because he didn't have a spotter. As he pushed the barbell off and lowered it to his chest, his back popped. It was instant relief. His back felt better.

And he sensed relief for his life in general.

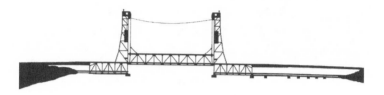

# Chapter 8

*M*arcella set her massage chair on the floor and reached back to close the door to Louisa's farmhouse. "Should I set my chair up in the living room near Louisa?"

"That would be perfect." Senja pressed her back against the wall to let Marcella pass. "Keep her company while we prep snacks and tea."

Marcella caught a glimpse down the hall of the women in the kitchen as she lugged the chair into the other room. "Hi, Louisa."

Louisa mouthed a hello and then sat with a contented smile, undoubtedly pleased to be back in her house for Aimee's bridal shower.

Senja followed her into the living room. "Marcella, you'll never believe who the new guy is at work." Senja didn't wait for an answer. "Drew Smith!" She pushed a few kitchen chairs away from the wall, giving Marcella room to set up the massage chair behind them.

"It's a small town." Marcella unfolded the massage chair in front of an open window that offered a gentle cross breeze on the early September afternoon.

"I better get back to help my sisters. Everybody else should

be arriving shortly." Senja passed through the living room to
the kitchen on the other side.

"I'm glad you could come, dear," Louisa said softly. "These
ladies are going to be in for a treat."

"Should I start with you?" Marcella came around the
wheelchair and placed her hands on Louisa's shoulders.

"Thank you. How are you, my dear?"

It was the way she said it—so empathetically, as if she
genuinely cared—that often resulted in Marcella saying a little more than the obligatory "I'm fine." She massaged lightly.
"My dad and Kandy are moving. He got a job in Madison, so
they'll be selling all the rental properties and the lake house.
I'm feeling a bit anxious about what the future holds, and I'll
miss going home." She paused. Here she was talking about the
future to a woman with a terminal disease. "I'm sure it'll all
work out. It's just a house."

"Oh, dear. But it's the house you grew up in. I know how
I feel about *this* house. So many good memories with Sam—
along with the tough ones."

"Yeah." Marcella felt a catch in her throat. "Even though
I don't get there often, I like knowing I *can* go there. I still go
every fall to pick apples from the same tree where Mom and I
got them to make applesauce. I'll miss that."

"I didn't know your dad was looking for another position."

"I didn't, either." Marcella said the words sadly. She and
Dad weren't as connected as a father and daughter should be.
"I'm not sure when he'll sell the duplex I live in. Drew signed
a one-year lease for the lower unit, but I don't have any kind
of rental agreement with my dad, so I hope he'll give me time."

"Sounds like a visit with your dad might be in order,"
Louisa said. "I happen to know that Kandy will be out of town
this weekend. She planned a crafting retreat for the church
ladies."

Marcella patted Louisa's shoulder. "Thanks. That does
sound like a good time for a visit with my dad." She kneaded Louisa's tight shoulder muscles. "Can you look straight
ahead?"

"I guess I can't. My head wants to turn left now." Louisa dropped her head with her nose pointing to the left armrest of the power wheelchair.

"Did you hear that?" Louisa cocked her head even further to the side, looking at the outside wall.

"Hear what?"

"That scratching in the wall," Louisa said in hushed tones, softer than what her weak voice typically produced.

All Marcella could hear was the clink of dishes and a murmur of conversation from the kitchen.

Louisa lifted her head, still cocked to one side. "I heard it before the ladies arrived, and I can still hear it if I listen carefully."

The door opened.

"Hello, ladies," Aimee yelled as she entered, and the women in the kitchen quickly met her in the hallway with hugs.

Louisa looked back to the extent she could to get Marcella's attention. "You know Senja, of course. That's Aimee's aunt Lorna and mother Sophia."

"Come in here, Mom. Let me take a look at you." Aimee backed into the living room. She looked her mother up and down.

Sophia lifted her arms and turned a slow 360. "I've lost a few more pounds since you were up for the Fourth."

"More than a few pounds. Are you still doing Zumba?" Aimee asked.

Lorna laughed. "Oh, no. We haven't done that since last year. She's still on a Paleo diet though, and we're in a cardio drumming class."

"Good for you." Aimee then turned her attention to Louisa, bending and giving her a hug.

"Hello, dear," Louisa said.

"It's good to see you." Aimee's eyes moistened. "You've lost weight, too."

"I'm fine," Louisa said stoically.

Aimee straightened and hugged Marcella. "Thanks for coming."

"My pleasure."

Over the next fifteen minutes, the door opened and closed several more times as more women arrived, each kicking off another round of hugs and greetings.

"Should we get started?" Senja's voice rose above the clamor, and she clapped her hands.

"We can't get started without Beth," Aimee said, "my matron of honor."

"I'm sure she's tied up in traffic," Louisa said, and a few of the women turned to her, their faces showing regret that they couldn't hear what she'd said.

"She said Beth's tied up in traffic," Marcella repeated, and the ladies laughed, because Beth in fact lived next door. Marcella smiled. Her friend was often running late.

"We'll wait for her to arrive, so make yourselves comfortable." Senja motioned for them to sit in the living room. "We'll get started with tea and snacks shortly."

Aimee's aunts returned to the kitchen while the other women found seats.

The door opened again, and Aimee stood. "That must be Beth."

"Where's Aimee? Where's Aimee?" A gruff voice called out.

"That's Maribel Myers," Louisa said in Marcella's ear. "She's my neighbor."

Aimee crossed the room to greet the woman, who, dressed in polyester pants and a patterned shirt, held out a quilt.

"Here it is. I finally found it. It's a quilt for two." Maribel thrust it toward Aimee.

"Thank you." Aimee unfolded it a bit. "It's beautiful." She held it up so all could see the exquisite design with red, blue, and green gingham squares.

"I finally found it." Maribel said again, triumph in her voice. She shuffled in and sat in the first empty seat, without making eye contact with the others.

"I'm so glad you're here, that you were able to get out of your house." Aimee gave the elderly woman a one-armed hug.

"Of course I get out. How do you think I eat? I saw Senja at the grocery store last week and asked her about you and that carpenter. She said you were getting married." Maribel clapped her hands. "I guess I called that one right. Danny and Beth, too." She sat tall in her chair, chin up. "I've got a sense about these things."

Aimee laughed. "I'm glad you could come, Mrs. Myers."

The outside door opened again. "Sorry I'm late." Beth set a box at the door to the living room and stood with her arms stretched out. "I was cutting paper for our project and lost track of time."

Aimee met her hug. "Just don't be late for the wedding."

"I promise."

Maribel stood and addressed Beth. "Becky, when can you come help me organize my linens?"

Louisa offered an explanation to Marcella. "She knew Beth's mother, and she keeps calling Beth by her name."

"I'll try to stop by soon," Beth told her. Beth retrieved her box and brought it to a card table that sat in a corner. "I have a scrapbook for the recipes you all brought," she announced. "As you have time, you can stop by the card table with your recipe and decorate your page for Aimee's new recipe book."

"Marcella," Louisa looked concerned. "I have the recipes for my *nisu* and *riisipuuroa* in my purse. I had Senja write them out for me, but I'm not going to be able to paste them in the book. Could you give them to Beth?"

"Sure." Marcella retrieved the recipes from Louisa's purse and then dug in her own purse for the recipes she'd brought. She handed them to Beth. "Can you add these? I should start the chair massages." There were about a dozen women there. At ten minutes per massage, it would take a couple hours to get to everyone.

Beth looked down at the recipes and smiled. "You're giving Aimee Achara's Pad Krapow Gai recipe. Can I get it too? I love that dish."

"Sure. I'll text it to you."

"I miss her and Aat." Beth glanced at Marcella's second

recipe. "Your peppermint iced tea. I should learn to make that, too. Do you have time to help me with my grandma's garden? It's gotten out of control and I'm a bit overwhelmed."

"I'd be happy to. Text me some times that work for you, and I'll check my schedule." She loved gardening and wished she had more space for a larger one like Louisa's.

Senja clapped her hands to get the group's attention. "Let's get started. Marcella's here to give you ladies chair massages. Beth's heading up the recipe scrapbook, and we have tea and sweets in the kitchen. We'll eat and then have games and gifts. Let's pray first."

Senja bowed her head and the other women followed her lead. "Father, we ask that your blessing be upon Aimee. Help her feel loved by us. We pray that the planning goes well for the wedding. Guide us to the right location. And we thank you for this time today and the food you have blessed us with."

Before Senja could close with an *amen*, a loud scratching noise came from the wall. There was silence, and then Senja continued her prayer. "Help us figure out what to do about that squirrel."

"A squirrel," Maribel Myers intoned as she stood up. "You have a squirrel in the wall?" Maribel crouched with her ear to the wall. She tapped on it. "They're always quiet when they know you're listening. They know I'm listening. I'll get my gun."

The other women stared at her dumbfounded and then exchanged looks, uncertain as to what they should do.

"We'll ask Danny to take care of the squirrel," Louisa said softly, but Maribel didn't hear her.

Marcella crossed the room and placed her hand on Maribel's shoulder. "Louisa will have Danny take care of the squirrel."

"Danny? Danny's not here." Confusion crossed Maribel's face.

"Will you come have a massage?" Marcella said the words soothingly.

Maribel nodded, and Marcella guided the elderly woman

to the massage chair.

Beth passed by them, mouthing the words *thank you* to Marcella. "I'll text Danny and ask him to stop by later."

As Marcella massaged Maribel's shoulders, she wondered how she'd take care of the duplex without her dad around. What would she do if a squirrel got in her wall? She managed the lower unit insofar as she screened the renters and collected the rent checks—or pestered tenants until they paid. She hadn't even had to do that over the last four years, and her dad did all the maintenance.

Once the Puntasrimas' bathtub faucet got stuck in the on position. The tub was filling faster than it was draining, and Achara panicked. She knocked on Marcella's door at ten thirty in the evening. Marcella went to the basement and shut off the water valve to the whole house, and her dad was out the next morning to replace the faucet cartridge. He had picked up the part for fifty dollars at a local hardware store. It wasn't a big deal, but it would've been a $200 plumbing bill without him.

Marcella massaged Maribel's neck. It wasn't long before she heard deep snoring. She patted the woman's back and smiled. Crisis averted. Thank God—or the universe—that the gun situation had been resolved peacefully. And she also was grateful that Louisa had Danny to help her with the house. A house was a big project, yet somehow Louisa had managed all those years with a disabled husband and then as a widow.

Maribel slept through the visiting, games, and gift opening, so Marcella participated in the festivities rather than giving massages. When Maribel woke, the other guests were leaving. She didn't mention the squirrel, but calmly joined the group heading out.

Marcella wiped down the massage chair. "Aimee, do you want a massage?"

"I'd love one." Aimee plopped down in the chair. "This wedding planning business is stressful."

Marcella could feel the tension in Aimee's shoulders. She willed it away, but Aimee wasn't relaxing. "Breathe," Marcella said softly.

Aimee exhaled. "There's so much to do. We haven't nailed down a location for the wedding and it's just two months away. The big sticking point is Russ's family. They won't come to the wedding if it's at Pinehurst, and we can't have it at his family's church unless I join." She sighed. "I'm disappointed that Russ's mom and sisters didn't come to the shower today."

Marcella massaged more deeply. For a religion that claimed its greatest commandments were to love God and love one's neighbor, there certainly was a lot of infighting.

Aimee jumped. "Ouch, that's a tender spot."

"Sorry." Marcella massaged more gently, focusing on Aimee.

Beth, Aimee's mom, and her aunts joined them in the living room. Louisa had reclined back in her wheelchair and was resting, her eyes closed.

"Oh. I'm pooped." Sophia sat on the couch.

"Me, too." Senja took a seat on the other end. "I'm glad everyone was able to come."

"Even Maribel Myers," Senja said. "When I saw her at the grocery store I mentioned we were having a shower. I'm not sure how she found out when and where it was."

"Coming back from Chicago makes me realize how small this town is." Aimee laughed.

"Who's going to walk you down the aisle?" Sophia asked. "I bet Eddie would be happy to do it."

"Eddie?" Aimee asked, her voice incredulous.

"You remember Eddie. I told you about him the last time you were up. We had just started dating then, but I think he's going to stick around."

"Mom, I'm not going to have your boyfriend walk me down the aisle. I don't even know him."

Sophia considered that for a moment. "You can carry Dad's ashes. I'll put them in a little vial."

"Mom, stop, please."

"Mak could give you away," Lorna said as she joined her sisters on the couch.

Marcella felt Aimee's neck stiffen.

Aimee lifted her head. "Give me away? As if I'm someone's possession?" She shook her head. "I'll walk myself down the aisle."

After she had finished Aimee's massage, Marcella wiped down and put away her massage chair. As she said goodbye to the women, she realized Louisa and Beth had disappeared. She found them sitting at the kitchen table with peppermint tea. They were talking softly and watching the birds at the feeder. Louisa laughed at something Beth said and Marcella was struck by the joy on her face.

She gave each of them a hug. "It's good to see you smiling," she told Louisa.

"It's good to be home." Louisa's eyes twinkled.

Louisa seemed so happy to be back in her farmhouse. She wished there was a way for Louisa to return home, where she belonged.

# *Chapter 9*

"You're going to make delicious Pad Krapow Gai," Marcella told the basil as it fell into a bowl. Achara and Aat had made the dish for her and then taught her how to make it. This was the second year she had planted Thai basil. It held hints of licorice, cinnamon, and mint and had a stronger flavor and aroma than her sweet basil.

She held a leaf to her nose and breathed in the scent. She missed Achara. They'd had so much fun. She thought of her new neighbors. Maybe she'd invite them over for Thai food—or would Drew take that the wrong way? Although she'd admit she found him attractive, she was not interested in invading their family the way Kandy had hers when she was sixteen. Her heart went out to AJ. She knew his pain too well.

She inspected her romaine. They were still giving her a steady supply of leaves, but she'd need to harvest the entire plants soon before they bolted. She'd heard talk of frost, but the days were yet too warm for her to believe it would come that night.

The bok choy was resilient, and the carrots would get sweeter with each frost. She'd wait until October to harvest them. The cabbage was ready to make into sauerkraut, but she'd have to come back later with a larger container. Today, herbs were on her agenda. She wanted to harvest the lavender, peppermint, and basil. She'd make essential oil with much of the lavender. She'd dry the basil and peppermint to use for spices and tea.

She moved the bowl of basil to the bottom of the stack she was holding, and she clipped lavender into the top bowl. It took so much to make a bit of the precious oil, but it was worth it. "You're so calming," she told the lavender.

"Who are you talking to?"

Marcella looked up at her neighbor boy. "Hi, AJ. I'm harvesting herbs."

"Are you talking to them?" He looked at her incredulously.

She nodded. "I affirm them and thank them for sharing their leaves with me."

AJ looked at her somberly. He was a tender soul, like she had been at that age.

She smiled at him. "And the lavender and peppermint will be back next year." She plucked a basil leaf and held it out to him. "The basil won't survive our winters, so I'll have to plant it again."

He held it to his nose and then looked at it thoughtfully.

Marcella continued, "It's kind of like getting a haircut. It doesn't hurt them."

AJ smiled. "I know it doesn't hurt them, but you're talking to them—"

"Yeah?" She wondered what was troubling him.

"—and then you eat them?" He popped the leaf in his mouth and chewed.

She laughed. "So you think it's funny that I talk to things I eat?"

With a slight smile, he shrugged his shoulders, a polite way of saying she wasn't normal. She would admit to being a bit out there with her relationships with plants.

"Do you want help?" he asked.

"Sure. Do you like tea? You can cut peppermint leaves." She handed the scissors over along with an empty bowl. "You could thank the peppermint plant for the delicious tea we'll make." She grinned.

"Or can I pretend I'm a samurai warrior?" He was teasing her.

"Noooo!" She clutched her hand to her chest melodramatically.

He laughed.

"I'll go grab another pair of scissors." She went back into her house.

She set the bowls of basil and lavender on the table. She dug in her junk drawer and found scissors, and she pulled a plastic zipper bag out of a box. She looked out her kitchen window. AJ's mouth moved as he diligently clipped leaves. She wished she could read lips. Then Drew came into the yard, and AJ held out the bowl to show him. Drew's face crinkled into a smile as AJ talked.

She opened her container of dried peppermint leaves and scooped several servings into the bag. She grabbed another empty bowl and walked down the stairs and into the backyard.

"Hi, Marcella." Drew's eyes shone with amusement as she came near the garden.

"Hi."

"So you have my boy talking to plants." He smiled.

"He's a sweet kid."

"I hear you're going to have us for tea," Drew said.

"Oh." She had planned to just give AJ a baggie of dried peppermint leaves, but she could make tea for them, too.

"Can we do it now?" AJ looked at her hopefully.

"Did you finish your homework?" Drew asked him.

AJ nodded. "Yeah. I did it at school. It was just a math worksheet, and it was review."

"Okay, let's do it." She led the guys up to her apartment.

"I called somebody to deliver firewood, by the way," Drew said as they were ascending the stairs. "I got a referral from my father-in-law."

"Ah, who's that?"

"A guy named Mak."

"Mak Maki?" Marcella asked, slipping out of her shoes at the top of the landing.

"Yeah, that's it." Drew took his shoes off and told his son to do the same.

Marcella opened the back door. "He's a good guy. He plows for me—for all my dad's properties." She set her bowl, scissors, and dried tea leaves on the table. "He'll know where to stack it."

Drew surveyed her kitchen. "I like what you've done with the place. It feels homey."

"Thanks." She grabbed the bowl and scissors from AJ.

Drew poked his head through the door to the living room.

"Do you want to look around?" Marcella asked.

"Yeah."

They stepped into the other room, and Drew nodded his approval.

She had inherited some of her mother's antique pieces. An old oak desk was pushed against one wall. A rocking chair sat atop a hand-braided rug. Wooden stands held her aloe vera and spider plants.

"It's pretty much the same as downstairs," she said.

"But it's not," Drew said. "It's what you've done with it. It's cozy, inviting."

"But no fireplace." AJ pointed to the wall where theirs was located.

"Nope. That was the trade-off for not having to hear footsteps above me." She regretted saying it, because it had never been an issue for the Puntasrimas. "But I walk pretty softly, and I don't wear my shoes past the entryway, and you have the advantage of more privacy. Sometimes voices from upstairs carry..."

Drew was smiling at her.

"I should stop talking, right?"

"We'll need to have you downstairs to roast marshmallows after Mak delivers the firewood," Drew said. "Do you mind if I use your bathroom?"

"Go ahead," she answered reflexively. As he entered the

bathroom, she remembered what she had hanging from the shower rod. "Wait. Let me tidy up a bit."

He had already shut the door. She cringed, resolving to buy a laundry rack and dry her bras in her bedroom.

While Drew was in the bathroom, Marcella directed AJ to wash his hands and asked, "How was your first week of school?"

He shrugged. "It was okay." He turned to her with wet hands held out, and his face brightened. "We get to go to Mackinac Island at the end of the year."

"Oh, yes." She handed him a towel. "I was in the first class that did that trip. I think the Quincy Elementary fifth grade has done it every year since."

She filled her stainless steel tea kettle and placed it on the gas stove. She dug in a drawer for a tea infuser and spoon. "Fresh leaves make even better tea than dried." She handed the spoon to AJ. "The key is to crush the leaves so they release their essential oils while the tea's brewing. Use the spoon to crush the leaves against the sides of the bowl, and then pack them in this." She set the infuser on the table.

Drew stepped into the kitchen and took a seat. She looked at him sheepishly, but he didn't react. The guy had been married, was even still wearing his ring, and it was just underwear. So why was she embarrassed? It just seemed too personal, too family-ish, and she was really starting to like him. She frowned as she admitted that to herself.

"Are you okay?" Drew asked.

"I'm fine." She took a deep breath, relaxing.

"Why do you have rocks in your kitchen?" AJ asked, nodding to the corner.

"Because they're pretty, and it's fun to see how high I can stack them. My tallest tower so far is eleven rocks." The kettle whistled, and she turned off the stove. She dropped in the tea infuser to allow the leaves to steep. "Let's see if we can break my record."

Marcella gathered the Lake Superior rocks and set them on the table. These were rocks that didn't make the cut for her massages, but they were perfect for stacking.

"Let's each take turns," Marcella said. "If the tower collapses, then…" She searched for the words, because it would be easier to play with two people so that one would win and the other would lose.

"They're the grand loser," AJ said, "and the other two win."

"Okay," Drew said. "The youngest goes first."

AJ wisely selected the largest stone. They each took a turn, and then Marcella retrieved large mugs and poured tea for each of them.

"This is good," AJ said when he'd tasted it. He placed another rock on top of the pile.

Drew's phone dinged, and he looked at the text. "Grandpa's here to take you fishing."

"Oh, boy!" AJ stood, bumping the table, and the rocks fell. "That didn't count. Can we play this later?"

"Sure," Marcella said, and AJ raced out the door and down the stairs.

Drew didn't rise from the table.

"You're not going with them?" she asked.

Drew shook his head. "Nope." He leaned back in his chair, holding the tea mug with both hands. He had a patient gaze and a warm smile.

Drew wasn't in a hurry to get going. He was enjoying her company too much—her casual confidence, her wit, and her beauty. Her sundress, printed with bright red flowers, lay lightly over her thin frame. She was like no other woman he had dated. The last women he dated, before he hooked up with Kristine, were practically girls, and he was still a boy in his freshman and sophomore years of college.

But Marcella was mature and comfortable in her own skin. Talented in her garden, a creative eye for decorating her home, and athletic. And he knew she was strong, remembering how she worked his knotted muscles. Strong physically, but also tough mentally, it seemed, and good with AJ. He wondered how much of it was true, or if he was projecting his own desires onto such a beautiful person.

He forced himself to look away. He didn't want to be a creep. He looked down at his tea and took a sip. He glanced up at the kitchen cabinets, and then his eyes drifted back across the table to where she sat, her blonde hair lying over one shoulder. Her other shoulder was bare, except for the thin strap of her dress. She was looking at him contentedly as she cradled her tea.

It seemed the attraction was mutual. She had seemed embarrassed when he saw her laundry, and she yelled about tidying up the bathroom after he was already in it. It was as if she wanted to impress him. He hadn't really thought of dating before, but it wouldn't be so bad for AJ to have a woman in his life, somebody other than Patty.

Maybe it was time to consider dating again. He sipped his tea, working up his courage. He hadn't been out with another woman since Kristine's death. With his thumb, he twisted his wedding ring on the same hand. He loved marriage. Sure, they had their fights, but they also had passion. But now, a year and a half later, he was a thirty-two-year-old man with red blood pumping through his veins. He wondered how old Marcella was. Maybe mid-twenties.

Marcella laughed nervously. "You're looking kind of intense over there. What are you thinking about?"

Drew felt that red blood rush to his cheeks. "You look great," he said.

She looked momentarily puzzled. "Thanks."

Why had he said that? He had been out of this game for too long. He pressed onward, setting his mug on the table and leaning forward. "Would you want to go out sometime?" There. He had put himself out there.

Her eyes widened, and she looked down at her tea before meeting his gaze. "Drew, I like to think of my tenants as friends, but I don't think us dating is a good idea."

Disappointment washed over him. He had misread things.

"Well, then." He forced a smile.

"I'm sorry." Marcella's voice was smooth as silk. "It's just that…" She took a deep breath and then reached across the table and rested her hand on his arm.

He was acutely aware of her touch. Did she not feel the chemistry between them? Man. Mixed signals here.

"It's because of AJ."

He felt himself stiffen. Okay. That was a deal breaker. "Oh. I understand." He could hear the edge in his voice. He sat back in his chair, folding his arms. She had seemed to connect with AJ—had even offered to babysit—but many women didn't want to deal with kids from another marriage. Some didn't even want to have kids.

"It's not that." Marcella tossed her hair. "I like kids, and AJ's awesome."

It was as if she'd read his mind. His face must've been worth a thousand words.

"For one thing," she continued, "I don't think you're ready to date. You're still wearing your wedding ring, but I especially don't want to come between you and your son."

"I wasn't planning on inviting him on our date." He forced a laugh.

"Let me explain." She sighed. "My mom died, and my dad remarried the following year. It was really traumatic for me. I wouldn't do that to a kid. I'd love to be friends with you both, though." Sitting back, she smiled with sadness in her eyes.

He raised his mug. "To friendship then."

She leaned in, and they clinked cups.

It was the sweetest rejection he had ever received, and one that gave him hope. She was concerned about a ring. The ring could come off. He'd wait till later, of course. And her concern about AJ seemed more a matter of timing than principle.

"So…" He locked eyes with her as he searched for a subject. "What do you do for fun? I mean, besides biking and gardening."

"I play the guitar," she offered.

"Me, too!" he said and then thought to temper his voice

so he didn't seem too eager. "We'll have to play together some-time. I had just started playing on the worship team at my church in Wausau. I'd like to plug into a church up here and maybe play there, too."

"That's cool." She flipped her hair back onto her shoulder.

"Yeah, you know, faith has been a game-changer for me. I wasn't raised in a church. I think we went twice, a couple Christmases, but I never had interest in it until Kristine and I started having problems." He paused, as she looked uneasy. He probably shouldn't be talking about his deceased wife. "Anyhow, I was talking to a buddy at work over lunch, and he invited me to his church. Jesus changed my heart toward Kri—"

He caught himself. It was hard to extricate his thoughts and words from someone who'd been present for the bulk of his adult life. "He made me a better man. A better father. I couldn't do life well without God." He realized he was monop-olizing the conversation, and she looked disengaged at best.

"What about you? Did you grow up in a church? Are you a Christian?"

She looked down and stirred her tea, although it was luke-warm by now. She was silent for a moment. "The short of it is that I had a hard time with faith after my mom died. I'm not sure of my beliefs anymore." She lifted her chin. "But I am a fan of Jesus and his teachings."

"I'm sorry about your mom." She was so sweet in her obvi-ous attempt to make him feel comfortable about his faith, but it seemed the real issue was her mom, as her face flashed grief when she mentioned her passing. "When did she die?"

"Thirteen years ago."

"You must've been young."

"Fifteen."

"That's horrible."

"Thank you," she said, getting up from the table and re-filling her mug. "Do you want more?" She held the kettle up.

He nodded and set his mug on the table.

"It *was* horrible," she said as she poured tea, "and I have a hard time conceiving of a god who'd let her suffer the way she did." She finished the sentence in a way that brought finality to the topic.

He sipped his tea. "I'm looking forward to State hockey games this winter. That was one of my favorite things about attending Douglass, and I can't wait to take AJ. What about you? Are you a fan of the Bobcats?"

"Yeah." She spun around from the sink, where she had set the kettle. She walked back to her seat with the hem of her sundress dancing on her thighs with each step. She sat and crossed her legs. Her eyes sparkled. Everything about her showed signs of interest, except for the rejection.

# Chapter 10

*M*arcella didn't visit her dad often. She didn't enjoy being around Kandy, and even her dad had become somebody she didn't really know. She hadn't realized how disconnected she had become from him until he and Kandy shared the news of their relocation.

Marcella drove along the north side of the canal on her way to have dinner with her father. Teenagers played volleyball in the sand courts by Quincy Beach. It was a warm Friday evening for early September, in the low 70s—possibly the last beautiful weekend of summer. It would've been a perfect day to be on her bike, but she'd be getting back too late.

Past the gravel quarry the road neared the canal, but no matter how close it came to the shoreline, someone always found room to build a lake house. Parking spots off the road were above rooflines, and stairs led down to the back doors. Dad told stories about how he and Mom had thought about buying on the canal, but there were always trade-offs in life. They chose to build a log home on an interior lake.

She had so many fond memories of growing up on the lake. Canoeing. Campfires by the shore. Jumping in the lake after warming up in the sauna. Once her friends built a raft for her birthday. She thought they were ignoring her for a week, but then on the morning of her party her best friend and her boyfriend floated it from the other side of the lake with canoe paddles.

She turned down a gravel road. That was another thing that made biking there less than ideal, although she preferred it to the pothole-ridden paved country roads, which were almost impassable, especially after the frost lifted in the spring. There were better ways of getting a lymphatic massage.

She pulled into her dad's driveway, where Kandy's red sedan was parked in front of the garage. Ugh. She wanted to have dinner with just her father, and he even verified that Kandy was going to the women's retreat. She stopped near the end of the driveway. Did she really want to go in? She'd go home, think of an excuse, and call her dad with regrets.

As she put her SUV in reverse, the door opened and her dad stepped out on the porch. He waved. That's that. She'd have to put on her big girl pants. She put the vehicle back in drive and parked near the front steps.

"Hi, Dad."

He gave her a big hug, wrapping his arms around her and squeezing. He kissed her on the forehead. She always loved that.

"Hi, Marcella," Kandy said, standing in front of her electric pressure cooker. She flipped a lever, and steam shot out from the top. "I made stew, and there's a loaf of bread in the oven for dinner."

"Yum." Marcella would try to be positive.

Kandy kissed Marcella's dad. "You can eat leftover stew this weekend, and there are frozen pasties in the freezer."

"Thank you," he said.

Hope rose within Marcella. Was she leaving?

"Why don't you at least stay for dinner?" Dad asked Kandy.

Kandy picked up her phone and hit the home button. "I don't have time." She grabbed her car keys. "I'll have dinner with the ladies when I get there tonight."

Marcella felt a huge sense of relief. "Do you need help

carrying anything to your car?"

Dad grabbed a tub of crafting supplies, and Marcella rolled Kandy's suitcase out to the car. Kandy stood with her door open and keys in hand while Dad gave her a hug and kissed her on the lips. "I'll be okay," he said. "Don't worry."

Giving them privacy, Marcella slipped off to the nearest old gnarled apple tree in the small orchard. She hugged the trunk as best she could as the lowest branches were chest high. She drew from its strength. She inspected the fruit, plucking an apple from the tree. It was still too sour. Those apples were best late in September.

After Kandy left, the two dished stew into Mikasa bowls. Kandy had registered for the set of heavy ceramic dishes when she married Dad, and Marcella had inherited her mom's Corelle ware. They settled in at the kitchen table, the same table from her childhood that matched the log home motif.

Marcella closed her eyes as her dad said grace. While he pulled the freshly baked bread from the warm oven, she savored the flavors of the stew—carrots, celery, onions, and garlic melded together with the beef. She had to admit that Kandy was an incredible cook. And what she did with the home was quite remarkable, too. Cloth placemats. A centerpiece of artificial flowers and dried naturals.

Marcella's issue was more that it no longer felt like home. Some elements were unchanged, such as the dining room table, the upright piano her mom used to play, and the native rock stonework around the fireplace. But the braided rag rugs had been replaced with oriental wool carpets. New living room furniture. Modern table lamps.

Some of it didn't match the character of the log home with its field stone fireplace. That was fine, but it just didn't feel like her home anymore. It was as if Kandy picked and chose what she wanted to keep and what she wanted to replace, with no more sentimentality than sorting through an estate sale.

Marcella felt a sense of loss.

"It'll be hard to leave this house." Her dad's voice broke into her thoughts. "We have good memories here."

"Yeah." Marcella looked down at the table. "I was thinking the same thing." Tears welled up in her eyes.

"I know, Marce-mallow," he said, using the pet name he'd given her as a child.

Dad sliced off the *kantapää* and offered it to her. She buttered it and took a bite. She had to hand it to Kandy on that one, too. She could bake. She almost resented how Kandy did things as well as her mother.

"We'll be renting in Madison until the houses sell," Dad said. "That'll give us time to get the lay of the land and figure out where we want to live." He paused. "I'll be back and forth on weekends while we get things packed up. The house might not sell until spring."

"I'll bet it'll sell quickly—a lake house fifteen minutes from Douglass State."

"Maybe. It's kind of a swampy lake."

"It is *not*." She wasn't sure why she felt defensive. She looked out the window at Bear Lake. So many memories. It did get mucky toward the end of summer.

"So when are you going to put the rentals on the market?"

"I've already signed all the papers with the real estate agent. He'll get them listed next week."

"So what about me?" She felt a pain in her gut. Where would she live? At this time of year, most of the decent apartments had already been rented.

He considered this. "Chances are it won't sell until next summer. I guess it's a great location, but with the price, anybody interested probably works for Douglass State, and they've probably already settled into housing before the semester began."

"But what if it does sell right away?"

"Then you'll rent from the new owners." His words were not providing much comfort.

"Do you seriously think they'll accept for rent what I pay you?" She pushed the rest of her stew aside. "And they might want to live there themselves. Remember, I don't have a lease."

"If they don't want to rent to you, you'll have a month to

find something. You could always move into one of the Smelter Street apartments. There's usually a vacancy or two there."

That was for good reason. The building in Douglass was bare bones. Students rented the small apartments.

"Okay." Marcella felt a pain in her gut. When she brought up the lease, she was hoping he'd offer to sign one with her, but she could understand how that would limit the house's value. She had a pretty sweet deal. Cheap rent in exchange for managing the other unit, but he still did all the maintenance. She screened the tenants, but that was only several hours of work every couple years because they seldom turned over, due to her diligent screening, she supposed. Nonetheless, she couldn't imagine how any new owner would see the value in what she did.

"Are *you* interested in buying it?" he asked.

"Ha!" she said. It was as if he had no idea what she did for work and how little money she made. She didn't have many career options coming out of high school. Her academics suffered while she was caring for Mom. Her dad had to go off to work, but Marcella couldn't bear to leave her mother in misery. Before she realized it, she had missed so much school that she was in over her head. She managed to graduate but was ill-prepared for college.

"The other thing to consider is what you might want from the house. Kandy wants something with more modern flair, so we'll buy new furniture."

"Kandy wants something more modern, but what do you want?"

"I want her to be happy."

"But this was your dream house. A log home with these big timbers." Marcella stared up at the ceiling.

"It *was* my dream house. Now I have new dreams."

"It's like you completely changed."

"I suppose I have, Marce," he said matter of factly, as if there was no issue. He turned to look at the clock on the wall behind him. "The sauna should be hot, if you want to take a steam before you head out."

Marcella walked out to the small log building near the lake. After undressing in the dressing room, she entered the steam room and sat on the high bench. She ladled water onto the hot rocks and waited. The steam rolled down the wall and enveloped her head and then the rest of her body, except for her feet. She pulled her legs up on the bench and leaned against the wall. She threw another scoop of water on the stove and her ears began to sting. She enjoyed the burning sensation, even though it hurt a little bit. After a few steams, she took a break in the dressing room. After cooling down, she went back for more. This was another thing she'd miss about her childhood home.

# Chapter 11

When her mother first got sick, Marcella didn't consider the fact that she might die. With the chemotherapy, Mom didn't have energy to start her plants indoors or get the garden in soon enough to grow tomatoes and herbs, but other than that, life didn't change drastically. Marcella didn't worry, because Mom wasn't worried. The survival rate for breast cancer was very high. The pastor of Pinehurst brought up her name for prayer, and the church organized meal deliveries during the worst of the treatment. And then she seemed to beat it, and life went on as normal.

Now, Marcella sat on her living room floor with her guitar, fingerpicking the beginning of Kansas's "Dust in the Wind," her thumb and pinky laying down the relentless rhythm while her index and middle fingers plucked out the melody. The song gave her solace after her mother died. A beautifully sad song. Singing the first line, she closed her eyes for a moment.

When the cancer returned, there were renewed prayers from the pulpit, claiming the promises of God. Her mom's name went back into the monthly prayer insert in the bulletin. Marcella would share updates with her small group at youth group, and they'd pray for her along with other girls' upcoming tests or boyfriend problems. There was hope.

Mr. Rogers, one of the deacons, had told Marcella not to worry. He had a sense that her mom would pull through. "Just have faith God will heal her," he said confidently. He spoke of his own battle with thyroid cancer. "God gives us troubles so we can have a testimony," he said. "You don't have a testimony without a test." Marcella wasn't too worried then, either. Her mom had beat cancer before. Lots of people beat it. God wouldn't let her mother die.

Life changed when the cancer came back seemingly in every place at once. In her lungs, pancreas, and elsewhere. Marcella knew it was serious when the elders showed up at the house and prayed over Mom, anointing her with oil. But their optimistic prayers turned to fatalism. Resignation to God's will. "God, you number our days," one of them said.

Marcella wasn't sure that was true, so she looked it up in the Bible. It was there, or something to that effect. But it made her wonder. Did God have it all planned out that her mother would only live so long? After that, Marcella became sensitive to what people were saying in attempts to comfort her. *It's all part of God's plan. God has your mom right where he wants her. All things work for good for those who love him. Everything happens for a reason.* But Marcella hated God's plan. God had her mom in a horrible place. There was nothing good about cancer. And whatever the reason for it happening, it wasn't worth it.

Her voice cracked as she sang the "Dust in the Wind" refrain.

She continued picking the same pattern over and over again with her right hand as her left hand changed chords. It was the first song she learned to fingerpick, using Travis-style fingering. It sounded more complicated than it was.

She'd sit with Mom for hours and eventually run out of things to say. So she'd strum away on her guitar, singing contemporary worship songs. One day Mom requested the Kansas song, either with confidence in Marcella's ability or ignorance that fingerpicking was in an entirely different league from strumming chords. It would be like assuming a cashier could do calculus because she counts change all day. But Marcella worked at it and found solace in having something to think about other than cancer.

After Mom died, that same deacon who'd said her mom wasn't going to die told Marcella, "God has healed her at last." It seemed like a cop out. Had God ignored their prayers? Did he care? Did he even exist?

And then there was Kandy. She volunteered at Pinehurst, working with the youth, leading the girls' small group. She was all right. Marcella didn't think much of her one way or the other, but then she started dating her dad. Less than a year after Mom died, they were engaged. It was too much for Marcella when Kandy told her, "You need to trust that this is God's good plan. I've been praying for a godly husband for years, and your dad and I would never have ended up together if your mom hadn't died."

That was the end of Marcella attending youth group, and she found excuses to stay home from church. When she was seventeen, she was allowed to legally move out of the house. Her dad, with Kandy's encouragement, agreed to let her live in the upper duplex he owned. And once she was out of the house, she pretty much quit church altogether.

The faith that had been so carefully knitted together during her early childhood with vacation Bible schools, Sunday school, and bedtime prayers unraveled when there were no answers. Cancer was evil. Was God a giver of evil? Why wouldn't he intervene? She couldn't make sense of it. She couldn't put her faith back into anything definitive, though she still sometimes longed for a spiritual connection.

On holidays, she sometimes slipped in the back of one of the old, ornate churches on Copper Island. She was particularly fond of St. Anne's, named for the patron saint of miners. The church was built in the late 1800s, its stained glass windows, oak wainscoting, and ornate carvings reflecting the wealth of the copper boom. When she couldn't find comfort in her own thoughts and reasoning, she could transcend herself through her senses. The aesthetic beauty. The fragrance of the incense.

The majesty of the pipe organ and the choir. The familiar words of Scripture recited in a calm voice.

Any faith she had left seemed to be communal, like being a part of the broader human family, but she struggled with a personal faith in the God who ignored prayers. It seemed talking to her oak tree was just as effective. If God was all-loving and all-powerful, he would've let her mother live, or at least not suffer the way she did. The last months of Mom's life had been a living hell. If that was God's will, then he was cruel, but that didn't make sense either.

Marcella moved on to the instrumental bridge of the song as her thoughts shifted to the lake house. She was grieving the loss of her childhood home. The sauna. The orchard. And of course the lake, as swampy as it might be.

But she was glad to be rid of Kandy. She was not a bad person, and Marcella hated her feeling of antipathy toward her. But Marcella had a hard time shaking the resentment she felt. Kandy came between her and her dad at a time when she most needed him. And Kandy had tried too hard to forge a relationship with her, planning girls' nights out, renting sappy movies like *While You Were Sleeping*, or even worse, *Sleepless in Seattle*. A movie about a boy who had also lost his mother to cancer and wanted his father to find a new wife. Subtle she was not.

Kandy didn't bother to find out what Marcella liked. She and her mom watched movies like *The Sound of Music* or *Les Misérables*. Not that she would've wanted to watch those with Kandy, either. Those were things she had shared with Mom.

Kandy tried to assume an intimacy she hadn't earned or been given. "Let me pray for you," she'd often said during the horrible year after she married Dad. She'd put her hand on Marcella's shoulder and pray that God would bond the two of them together. So awkward. But nothing was more awkward than when she said, "You can call me Mom."

Sorry. That wasn't going to happen.

Marcella began the final verse about nothing lasting forever but the earth and sky.

She hoped that wasn't true. She hoped there was more. Her

mom believed there was more, and she died in peace. Maybe that was all the faith one needed, just enough to die in peace.

Tears rose in Marcella's eyes. She looked up and said, "Did you like that, Mom?"

From down in his apartment, Drew could hear her singing. Her voice was hauntingly beautiful. He had enjoyed their non-date, having tea in her kitchen, and was pleased they had become friends, not that he was overly happy about the just-friends part. He stretched out on the couch.

AJ hadn't made it back yet. Ron had called to say Patty started the sauna, and AJ wanted to warm up. Drew was fine with that. AJ seemed to soak in the heat and steam, while Drew felt flushed and uncomfortable after a few minutes. He supposed AJ had inherited enough of the Finnish blood from Kristine to make it enjoyable for him.

AJ likely wouldn't be back for an hour. What to do with his free time? It had been so long since he had the luxury of time to himself he wasn't sure what to do. A thought crossed his mind, and he smiled. He grabbed his guitar and headed up the back stairs. He'd see if Marcella wanted to have the jam session they'd talked about.

By the time he reached her back door, the music had stopped. He thought he heard weeping. He put his ear to the door. She was right about sounds traveling through the building. He knocked and then waited a minute.

"Drew!" She looked surprised.

He felt sheepish. He should have texted or called. "I heard you playing and thought I'd see if you wanted company. I got a call from Patty that Ron and AJ are heading to the sauna."

"You're not going?"

"I'm sure they'd be fine with me joining them, but I'm not a fan of sitting in a small room, getting hot and sweaty."

"I don't know if I've ever met anyone who didn't like a sauna." She said the words with a challenge, teasingly.

"You're Finnish?" The Finns of Copper Island, like Kristine's family, took their ancestry seriously.

"Half. My dad's Finnish. My mom was a mix of everything. What are your roots?"

He shrugged. "I was adopted, so I don't know." He realized he was still standing in the hallway. "So do you want to play a little guitar?"

"Why don't you come in?"

He eagerly stepped inside her apartment again, struck with the coziness of it. "Maybe you can give me decorating tips." He wanted to turn the downstairs unit into a home for AJ.

She smiled that perfect smile again and led the way to the living room.

"Are you okay?" he asked.

"Sure. Why do you ask?"

"I thought I heard you crying."

"Yeah, I cry every now and then." She motioned for him to sit on the couch. "Sometimes it feels good."

Drew sat leaning forward with his guitar on his knee. "Did I hear you playing 'Dust in the Wind?'"

"Yeah, do you know it?"

Drew regretted asking about the song after hearing the excitement in her voice. "I'm not that advanced. I just play chords. Mostly worship tunes."

"I don't know any current worship songs." She grabbed her guitar and sat on the floor in front of him. "What else do you know?"

He was drawing a blank. "Do you know 'The Duck Song?'" he asked with a laugh.

"About the duck who walked to a lemonade stand?"

"Yeah." It was a kids' song for the YouTube generation. He used to sing it for AJ.

"Go ahead and start. I'll follow along."

They got through the song reasonably well. But more importantly, Marcella's mood lightened as they laughed together, and Drew was glad he'd cheered her up.

# Chapter 12

 $D$ rew stacked firewood next to the shed as Mak tossed the pieces from the back of his full-ton pickup truck faster than Drew could stack them. After removing half the face cord from the truck, the old man hopped down to the ground, belying his age.

"Marcella said you plow for her." Drew picked up another piece of wood.

"Yah, I make wood, move snow, and write." Mak put particular emphasis on that last word.

"Write?" Drew wasn't sure he'd heard that correctly. The man looked like a Super Yooper, the kind of guy who works with his hands and spends his free time fishing and hunting.

"That's right." Mak stacked two pieces of the split hardwood for every one of Drew's. "I gots a book comin' out in November."

"Self-published?" Anybody could be an author in these days of digital print-on-demand and online retailers.

"Nope," he said with obvious pride. "I got me a publisher."

"Ah-ha. Do you pay this publisher?" Drew supposed Mak didn't even know what self-publishing was. Drew had helped his mom navigate the myriad of options when she put together a book of family history.

"Oh, no." Mak paused from his work, leaving a few logs for Drew. "It's a small publisher. I ain't gettin' an advance or anything, but they'll do the editin', typesettin', and cover design." He jumped back into the bed of the truck.

Drew was impressed. He wasn't a writer, but as a business guy he was always interested in different markets and industries. He knew it wasn't easy to get a publisher, small or not.

Mak tossed more wood from the truck. "I just completed a big rewrite," he continued. "I had to put a bonnet on it." He laughed.

"Put a bonnet on it?"

"Yeah, I had to rewrite it as Amish fiction. That's what's selling."

"Amish fiction, as in women's romance?"

"Yep."

"You don't strike me as a man who'd like Amish fiction."

"I don't. I don't like romances, either. I like readin' crime novels, or used to. Can't read most of da stuff out there now that I know a thing or two about writin'." Mak stopped throwing wood and stood tall. "Writin's ruined readin'. I'm glad I didn't become a gynecologist." He guffawed and stared at Drew expectantly.

"That's funny. You've been thinking about that line for a while, haven't you?"

Mak tossed another log on the pile. "My first book was about hunters found dead in their stands, but da snow covered all da tracks. I sent it to dozens of agents and publishers, but there were no takers. Then I heard Western romances were sellin', especially Texas romances, so I wrote that."

Drew laughed. The Yoop was full of surprises. Here he was, having a conversation about marketing strategy with the man who was delivering his wood. "And you found a publisher, but they wanted it to be Amish?"

"Yep. Fortunately da Amish are everywhere. It's a Texas, Western, Amish romance."

"You certainly have the bases covered. Have you been to

Texas?"

"Nah. But who needs to travel when you have da Google." Mak threw the last few pieces out of the truck. "Writers write. You know that sayin', 'Write what you know?' It should be 'Know what you write.' With enough research, I can put in enough details to make anything sound believable." He sat on the tailgate watching Drew stack the wood. "My book, *The Child of Rumspringa*, is about a schoolteacher who falls in love with a man, but he has a past."

Drew stacked wood with his head down, but could feel the man looking at him. He took a break.

"He has a son from a prior relationship," Mak continued.

"Okay?"

"But that boy was raised by another man. How do you think that other man would feel if he found out the boy wasn't his?"

"How would I know?"

Mak slid off the tailgate. "Aaah, just wondering." He pitched in and helped Drew with the rest of the pile.

"This must be it." Drew pulled into a driveway flanked by tall red pines. "The GPS sent us way past here."

"Yeah, there's the sauna." AJ pointed to an outbuilding with smoke billowing from the chimney.

Boys in swimsuits queued at a diving board over a stock pond, jumping in, crawling out, and getting back in line. Trailblazers was meeting at the Herrala homestead on a crisp fall evening. There was an old stucco farmhouse with a new wheelchair ramp. A newer garage. An old garage with a greenhouse attached to the back. A garden surrounded by six-foot fencing. And other outbuildings. Farther out in the field, halfway to a broken-down barn, a pile of wood was ready to be set ablaze. The wood didn't look like campfire logs so much as brush and branches.

Drew parked next to a couple other cars and the church

van. AJ crawled out from the truck's rear jumper seat and stood near Drew's side, as if his excitement had turned to apprehension. Danny waved to them and approached with a big, gap-toothed grin. Drew was glad to see his welcoming look, after Danny's initial hesitation about having them attend. At Pinehurst the prior Sunday, Drew had asked him about AJ attending Trailblazers even though he was only in fifth grade. Danny hemmed and hawed, but then his wife said, "Of course he can come."

Danny reached out his hand. "I'm glad you could make it." Drew shook his hand. "This is quite a place."

"Yeah, hey." Danny then addressed AJ. "Are you excited?"

"Yeah!" AJ stepped forward. "Is the sauna hot?"

"You bet. Are you ready to sauna-swim?" Danny asked. "Did you bring your suit?"

"I'm wearing it." AJ pulled up the hem of his shirt to show the waistband of his trunks sticking out from his jeans.

"Well, get going." Drew nudged his shoulder, and AJ took off. "I appreciate you letting AJ come to this. I'd be happy to stick around and help chaperone."

Danny grimaced, but said, "I won't lie. I could use more parental involvement." He surveyed the activities. A few boys tossing a football. Another boy throwing more sticks on the unlit bonfire. "Can you keep an eye on the sauna?"

"Sure."

"I'll be in to sauna in a bit. I'm expecting a few more kids, yet."

Drew grabbed his swim trunks out of the truck. After changing, he found AJ in the steam room talking and laughing on the top bench with a couple other boys. Drew climbed up on the bench next to them. The fire in the stove was roaring, and heat radiated from it like a blast furnace. The thermostat on the wall read 180 degrees, which was incredibly hot considering boys were running in and out for warm-ups and breathers.

As a chaperone, there wasn't much for Drew to do. The boys were well-behaved, and the only thing that concerned him was the excessive use of steam. But his objections fell on deaf ears, and even AJ teased him for not being able to take it after Drew moved to a lower bench on the sidewall.

Drew was never much for saunas, though he had learned to pronounce the word the Yooper way during his time at Douglass State. Locals reacted strongly when someone mispronounced the Finnish word. Drew took an occasional sauna at the health club, but the Wausau saunas were not like the Yooper saunas. Yooper saunas put out a type of heat that made him feel like his brain was going to boil. He had saunaed a couple times with his father-in-law Ron, who had what he called a fake sauna in his basement. By *fake* Ron meant it had an electric stove rather than wood, but he still got that room up to 170 degrees. Drew usually passed on the sauna, but AJ always jumped at the chance to sauna with grandpa.

The door to the steam room opened once again, and Danny stepped in. "Make room for me," he said, motioning for the boys to slide over on the bench.

"Should I put on more steam?" AJ sat on the far side of the bench from Danny, with his hand already on the ladle in the bucket.

"You bet," Danny said.

AJ tossed water on the rocks, and steam instantly shot to the ceiling, leaving the rocks dry within a second.

"That one stung," AJ said, laughing.

"Hit me again," Danny said.

Before AJ could splash the stove again, the other boys cleared out. Drew wanted to clear out, too, but he found himself looking at Danny and AJ on the top bench. They were sitting there with matching gap-toothed grins on their faces. Danny's hair was shaved and showing the beginnings of a receding hairline, but it was clearly dark brown. Brown eyes.

The realization hit him, and a chill ran down his spine in spite of the heat. He was looking at father and son.

Drew felt nauseous. "I need a breather." He staggered through the dressing room and out the front of the sauna. He went around to the side and put a stiff arm against a birch tree to steady himself. Pieces of information flashed through his mind. Kristine getting pregnant on their first date. AJ's supposed early arrival, although he was a seven-and-a-half-pound baby. How he grew to not look like either of them. Finding out that Danny was Kristine's high school sweetheart. Patty's odd behavior, trying to push Danny into their lives. Danny seeming uncomfortable around them.

Drew pulled air deep into his lungs and exhaled. His queasiness gave way to numbness, and then he straightened. AJ had had his fun in the sauna. It was time to go.

Drew reentered the sauna, where other boys sat on the top bench, but AJ and Danny were gone. Drew checked around back—they were both coming out of the pond.

"Now get back in for a warm-up," Danny told AJ.

"Dad, try jumping in the pond after you're hot. It's awesome." AJ darted past Drew.

"We should be going," Drew called after him.

AJ didn't slow down a bit or look back.

"Already? Your kid's having a blast," Danny said, "and the sauna's only half the fun. You've got to stick around for the bonfire devotional." He turned to the pond to supervise the swimming.

Drew joined AJ on the top bench in the sauna. "Having fun, buddy?"

"Dad, this is so awesome. I've already made friends."

"Who's that?"

"I don't know their names." AJ grabbed the ladle handle. "Do you want more steam?"

Drew forced a smile. "Yeah, hit me."

The steam rose and rolled along the ceiling and down the wall. It stung as it hit his back, but he was glad for it. As uncomfortable as it was, it calmed him. AJ seemed happier than he had in the last year and a half. They'd stay for the bonfire. He'd get through the night, and then figure out what he should do.

Danny gathered the boys in a half ring on the upwind side of the fire.

"I think most of you already know that I'm a trooper with the Michigan State Police." Danny held up his badge that hung on a lanyard around his neck. Sometime while Drew and AJ were roasting marshmallows with the other boys, Danny had put on a State Police uniform. "What do you think a cop's most useful tools are?"

Hands shot up. "Your gun," one boy blurted out.

Danny laughed. "My duty weapon?" He tapped the grip of his sidearm. "I haven't used it, except for practice. Someday it may save my life, but on a regular basis it's not the most useful tool I have. Anything else?"

"Your uniform," an older boy said.

"How so?" Danny asked.

"So people know you're a cop."

He chuckled. "I hadn't thought of that. I suppose that is important. Anything else?"

The boys sat in expectant stillness.

"I have a lot of tools. I have my radio." He pulled it out of his belt and replaced it. He reached into a breast pocket. "I have a notepad and pen." He put the pen and pad away, and then pulled a flashlight from his belt. "But this is my most useful tool."

"Your flashlight," AJ yelled, and then recoiled a bit when the other boys looked at him.

"That's right. My flashlight. I use it all the time, especially up here in the Yoop. This is a 1200-lumen LED flashlight. Do you want to see how bright it is?"

A murmur of yeses came from the boys.

"I'll turn it on."

He had the boys captivated. He pointed it out to the field and clicked. *Click. Click.* Nothing happened. He looked back at the boys. "What do you think happened?"

"Your batteries are dead," a boy said.

"Maybe." He tossed the flashlight to the boy. "Could you check? You unscrew the back."

The boy fiddled with it for a few seconds. "Ha. There are no batteries in it."

"That's right. There are no batteries. We're kind of like flashlights without batteries until we find Jesus. And with Jesus, we can shine with his light." He reached into his pocket and handed batteries to the boy. "Put these in."

Drew wondered how his life, how his marriage, would've been different if he'd been raised to know God, to plug into the divine power. At least he knew God now and could teach his son.

The boy dropped batteries in, then clicked the button. No light. "Your batteries aren't charged."

"You don't charge this kind of battery," Danny said.

Drew almost felt bad for him. It would've been a great object lesson if the batteries had worked.

"But I guarantee they're new." Danny took the flashlight and unscrewed the back. "Let's see what's going on here." He emptied the batteries in the palm of his hand and put them back in his pocket. "There's something else in here. He tapped the bottom of the flashlight against his hand. He held up a wadded piece of paper towel. "There was junk in it. Garbage."

Drew looked down at AJ, who sat leaning forward, eyes fixated on Danny.

As he pulled each battery out of his pocket and dropped it in the flashlight, he continued. "I know most of you have already surrendered your life to Jesus. You have the Holy Spirit living in you. But for you to experience the power of the Holy Spirit, for you to be a light of Christ in this world, you've got to get the junk out. I know what it's like to be a teenage boy, and I'm going to leave it at this—if you've got something in your life that's keeping you from being the man God wants you to be, then knock it off, and you can find Christ to be the most important tool on your belt."

He turned the flashlight on, illuminating the ground at his feet. He pointed it away from the fire, and the spotlight lit the trees on the other side of the field. Danny finished by reading a verse from 1 John and praying.

"That was so cool," AJ told Drew when they were in the truck on their way home. "I want to be a cop."

"Not an accountant?" Drew gave a nervous laugh.

"What's that?" AJ sounded as if he'd never heard the word.

"That's what I do. We make sure companies and organizations are spending their money wisely."

"Well…" AJ looked down. He was such a sensitive kid, and he probably perceived that Drew felt slighted.

"But as a cop you'd get to carry a gun."

AJ brightened. "Yeah, a duty weapon."

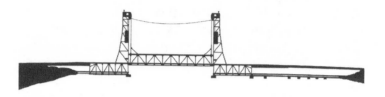

# Chapter 13

"Why are we here?" AJ asked as Drew pulled into Faith Church's parking lot.

"I thought we'd give it a try." Drew didn't think it wise to attend Pinehurst. AJ survived ten-and-a-half years without knowing Danny, and he could survive the rest of his life without him. The town might be too small to keep the rumors from circulating among adults, but there was no need to expose AJ to interactions that would cause other kids to ask questions.

"This church is boring." AJ lifted his foot and stomped it on the center console.

"You don't know that. We've only come here on Christmas and Easter."

"There's no other kids here." AJ sat in the rear seat with his arms folded and bottom lip out.

"Give it a chance." Drew put the truck in park and got out, holding the door open for AJ.

"Will Danny let me go to Trailblazers if we go to a different church?"

Drew didn't know what to say to that. "Hurry up."

AJ crawled out of the truck, and they went inside. They hadn't been in the church since Kristine's funeral, but it looked the same. It probably looked the same as it had for the last century. Dark woodwork. Stained-glass windows. Stained-glass chandeliers. The carpeting had been updated and there was a box with earphones for the elderly with hearing problems—that was definitely new.

Drew caught himself. He didn't need to be so negative. He had no issue with the appearance of the church. It was beautiful. His only concern was the fit of the church for him and his boy. AJ was right. There were few kids.

"Surprise. Surprise." Ron approached them eagerly. "How's my boy?" he asked AJ as he thumped him on the shoulder.

"Great. I had so much fun last night, Grandpa. They had a sauna, and we jumped in the pond, and we had a bonfire and roasted marshmallows."

Ron glanced at Drew inquisitively.

"Trailblazers."

"Ah."

Patty approached. "This is unexpected."

"We thought we'd give it a try," Drew said. "Is there a children's church or Sunday school for AJ?"

"Oh, yes," Patty said. "But that's before the service. AJ can sit with us."

"AJ, " a woman said with surprise in her voice. She bent at the knees slightly to meet his eyes. "It's good to see you here."

"Hi, Mrs. Davis," AJ said.

The woman straightened and extended her hand to Drew. "You must be AJ's father."

"Drew Smith." He shook her hand. "It's a pleasure to meet you, Mrs. Davis."

"Actually, it's Miss Davis." Color flooded her cheeks. "You can call me Brooke." She wore a blue midi dress that showed the contours of her legs, hips, and waist. Long, brown hair from the top and sides of her head was pulled back with a clip. "I teach fifth grade at Quincy Elementary."

"You're one of AJ's teachers?"

"Nope. I'm not that lucky." She smiled at AJ.

The service was fine, at least by Drew's standards. A

guitarist led them in worship with a mix of contemporary music and hymns. Piano accompaniment. An older man on bongos. A couple women, including Brooke, singing into a common microphone. On Drew's previous visits there were only hymns, but he supposed the Christmas and Easter crowd expected more traditional services. The preaching was pretty good, too.

AJ was bored, however. He doodled on the bulletin and squirmed in the pew. Drew looked around and could see maybe one or two other kids close to AJ's age. Even if they attended Sunday school, it would be a small class.

After the service, Patty pulled Drew aside. "I'm happy you came, but I have to say I'm surprised."

"Why's that?"

"We come here because our friends are here. We raised the girls in this church, and thirty years ago there were a lot of young families. I just thought Pinehurst would work better for AJ."

Drew shrugged and looked away. "This is a good church, too."

"You're avoiding Danny. Aren't you?"

Drew didn't know what to say to that. Of course that was the reason, not that it was any of her business.

"You know, he has a right to know his son."

"What's wrong with you?" Drew knew he sounded harsh, but he couldn't bite back the words. "You've been trying to push him into our lives ever since Kristine died."

Patty's face reddened. "She wouldn't be dead if you hadn't kicked her out of the house."

"I didn't kick her out of the house," Drew snapped back. He'd had no idea she blamed him for his wife's death, or even that she knew of their fight on the day of the accident. Kristine must've called her in the car, and of course Patty would've taken her side. "Kristine might've said that, but it's not true. She left in a huff and never came back." He turned his back to Patty as he fought back tears. "I didn't even get to say goodbye to her. I didn't make her drink and drive."

"I didn't, either. I knew she had a problem with alcohol, but I loved her unconditionally."

He faced her, shoulders square. "I loved her too much to let her ruin her life and AJ's."

Patty huffed, then yelled over to Ron, "Come on, Ron. Let's go." She marched out of the sanctuary.

Ron and AJ came alongside Drew.

"Is it okay if we take AJ with us?" Ron asked, "I'd like to take him fishing this afternoon."

"Please, Dad?" AJ grabbed Drew's arm.

"I'll bring him home before dinner," Ron offered.

Drew nodded dumbly. He needed time to clear his head.

Although food was the farthest thing from his mind, his stomach growled, signaling that his body needed to eat. So he stopped at the Copper Country Co-op and grabbed a sandwich from the deli. He drove down the canal road toward the state park, taking bites as he drove.

At the park, he followed a trail into the woods. He kicked at the wood-chip covered path and then broke into a jog. He ran up and down hills, catching snippets of Lake Superior in his peripheral vision when the path veered near the bluff overlooking the lake. He stopped to catch his breath and leaned against a tree. The bark felt rough against his arm. He looked around. There was no one in sight.

He wrapped his arms around the tree and squeezed it. Marcella was right. It was grounding to hug a tree. He wasn't sure how long he stood there hugging the tree before he tilted his face toward the sky, peering through branches and leaves to where the sun shone down into the woods. *God, what do I do now?* He sat, his back against the trunk. A red squirrel scampered by. Birds chirped overhead. He closed his eyes.

How had he missed the obvious for so long? For ten years. Even though AJ didn't look much like either him or Kristine, it had never crossed his mind to question it. After all, Drew had been adopted and had no idea what his own biological parents looked like. He rubbed his forehead. Maybe it *was* all a coincidence. Maybe one of his birth parents had brown hair and a gap-toothed smile, and it just skipped a generation. He didn't know how recessive genes worked. *Nah.* He wasn't going to try to fool himself.

He had so many questions, but the only person who could answer them was gone. Why had Kristine picked him rather than Danny if she had slept with both of them? Why had she never told him? What would he have done if she had? There wasn't much sense in being mad at her. She was gone, and if things had been different, if Danny had known he was a father, then—

Drew couldn't imagine his life without AJ. He'd always be his dad, he told himself. No matter what. Fatherhood was so much more than biology. He knew that, being adopted himself. But even though he loved his parents, a part of him sometimes wondered about his bio father and mother. It was a closed adoption, so he'd never know.

He could never bring himself to admit to anyone else, especially not his parents, that he was curious about his roots. Other kids talked about their ethnic background. For some reason, it was a big deal in the Copper Country. Everyone wanted to know if you were Finnish or French or something else. "Smith. English, right?" they'd ask.

He'd nod. His parents were mostly English, but he didn't know what his roots were. Sometimes he'd say he was Irish. He had no idea if it was true, but it fit with the red hair. Maybe someday he'd do one of those DNA tests and find out his ethnicity. He drew in his breath. DNA. They could test AJ and Danny and get conclusive proof. But would that be wise?

He rubbed his forehead. AJ was bound to find out about Danny. He remembered when he first learned he was adopted. He was young, and his parents had never attempted to hide the truth, but it was still weird. He asked his parents why they hadn't told him sooner. They said they'd talked about it, but he was probably too young to remember. And besides, it wasn't important on a day-to-day basis. It didn't define who they were, who he was, or their relationship. It only came up when he was at a doctor's appointment and the nurse asked about his birth-family's health history. That was awkward.

He got up and retraced his steps, walking back to his truck. As he climbed in a thought crossed his mind. Patty had said Danny had a *right* to know his son. He'd thought she was talking about morality, as in, what was the right thing to do, but now he wondered about the law. Did Danny have a legal right to be involved in AJ's life? What would that look like? Visitation rights? Did he have custody rights? Drew felt like he'd been hit in the gut. He robotically put the truck in drive and somehow made it back to the duplex.

Drew relaxed as he pulled into the driveway and saw Marcella working in her garden. Somehow just seeing her took his anxiety level down a notch. He had to find his equilibrium so he could figure out what to do—so he could go to work the next day.

"Hi, neighbor." He walked over to the garden plot.

"Hi." She looked up, studying his face with concern. "Are you okay?"

"Do you have time for peppermint tea?" He had to talk to someone or he might go crazy.

Her smile calmed him. "Okay."

They settled in at her kitchen table with hot tea, and he told her how he'd missed the obvious. But he had no regrets because he couldn't imagine life without AJ. He'd do anything for him, even if that meant being around Danny, as uncomfortable as that was for Drew. He told her how AJ idolized Danny. What ten-year-old boy wouldn't think police work was more exciting than accounting. Heck, sometimes even he wondered why he had gone into his chosen profession. But how would this work out? Did Danny have rights to AJ? He was tempted to pack up and head to the other side of the country.

Once he finished baring his soul, he waited to hear what she had to say. There was something about her that made him think she'd have wisdom to offer—maybe because she'd lost her mother as a teenager, she had a depth about her.

"Take deep breaths," she finally said. "They're therapeutic." She rose from the table. "I'll get lavender oil."

He closed his eyes as he inhaled and exhaled slowly and deeply. Then he felt her gentle touch on his temples and he breathed in the scent of lavender.

"There," she whispered. "That's better."

"Thanks." He looked at her, mesmerized.

She sat back down and took a sip of tea.

"I should probably talk to a lawyer." He lifted his mug to his lips. Somehow, after discussing the issue with her, life seemed more manageable. "Thanks for the advice."

Marcella smiled, showing those perfect teeth.

Drew could have slapped himself. He was being inconsiderate, talking only about himself. He'd been married long enough to know better. "So how was your day?"

"I'm dealing with stress, too, but nothing like yours." She shrugged. "I'm sure my situation will work out."

That night, after AJ went to bed, Drew opened his laptop and Googled *Family Lawyer Douglass MI*.

A lawyer named Matthew J. Stott was at the top of the list. He was the only lawyer with Google reviews, and they were positive, so he clicked the guy's website and skimmed the information. He specialized in family law—and also OWIs, criminal defense, estate planning, and civil litigation. *Free initial consultation.* Drew took a deep breath. He'd call in the morning.

# Chapter 14

*D*rew returned to his desk after the third meeting of the morning. He was getting dragged into more and more projects, so had increasingly less downtime. He'd have to begin blocking time on his calendar, like he had at Wausau Electronics.

He grabbed a candy bar from his son's fundraising box on his desk, unwrapped it, and took a bite. It was the first box of several AJ would need to sell to be able to go on the year-end field trip to Mackinac Island. They didn't have a large network of friends yet in the area, so he brought the box to work. His coworkers had purchased a few. He had eaten more.

A light on his office phone flashed, signaling he had voice messages. The first was from a colleague asking if he wanted to grab lunch. He had planned to work through lunch, but it was important for his career to network, especially at a university, which was much more political than the corporate life he had left. The second message was Janet asking if he could make a four o'clock meeting with the department chair. It shouldn't be an issue. AJ was going to his grandparents' after school.

He woke up his computer and accepted the meeting invitation in the calendar. As he reached for his cell phone to call Patty and give her a heads-up, he saw there was a missed call from her. He listened to her voice message.

"Drew, so sorry I can't watch AJ this afternoon. I have a meeting that's come up. Ron's busy, too. Sorry again."

Drew pushed the air out of his lungs and took a deep breath. The single parenting business was hard. He'd have to admit that it had been much easier since he left Wausau, but it was still hard. He could probably get out of his late meeting by calling the department chair secretary right away. He likely wasn't critical to the meeting anyhow. Janet was probably pulling him in so he could get up to speed on whatever the project was.

On the other hand, maybe it was something he should attend. A good opportunity to show the value he brought to the organization. Besides, to get home in time for AJ he'd have to cancel his three o'clock meeting, too.

When he'd arranged AJ's after-school time with Patty, he gave her an out if she was ever tied up, but this was the first time she wasn't available. He hoped their confrontation at church wasn't the reason. He didn't think whatever hostility she had toward him would keep her from wanting to spend time with her grandkid. He liked that AJ didn't have to go to after-school care and could be with family like he had been when Kristine was alive. And it had worked most days.

*Marcella.* He'd take her up on her offer to help. He called her right away.

After exchanging pleasantries he got to the point. "Patty and Ron aren't available to watch AJ after school. I was wondering if he could hang out with you for a couple hours if you'll be around."

"What time does he get home?"

"A little after three thirty."

"That should work, but let me check my schedule to make sure they haven't scheduled anything else after my two o'clock."

Drew held for a minute, assuming she was using her phone to check her calendar.

"Okay. I'll meet him when he gets home."

"Thank you so much," he said. "I'll call the school to let

him know he should walk home. Could you feed him a snack? He can get a bit moody after school, especially if he's hungry. It's hard to tell because moody is kind of his baseline lately. And could you see if he has any homework?"

"No problem."

After finishing up with her last client of the day, Marcella hurriedly cleaned up and headed home. She drove up to the duplex as AJ turned on their block. She parked in the driveway and walked down the sidewalk to meet him.

"How was school?" She fell in step with him.

AJ shrugged.

"Your dad said I get to hang out with you today." He nodded.

"Should we pick carrots for a snack?" she asked. "We had a frost two nights ago, so now they're really sweet."

A hint of a smile crossed his face.

They made their way to the garden. She showed him how to pull the carrot near its base, first wiggling it, so the top wouldn't come off. They each pulled a few. "Let's go wash them up." Marcella led the way up to her apartment. She rinsed off the carrots and cut them into round coins. When she turned around with the plate, AJ was still standing there with his backpack on.

"Stay a while." She laughed, motioning to the table. "Should I make tea?"

That got a real smile out of him.

While they ate carrots and drank tea, AJ grew a little more talkative, telling Marcella about a game he and other kids had played at recess. She didn't understand the details, but gathered it was based on a video game. When they were done, he cleared his plate and mug.

"Time for homework?" Marcella asked.

AJ nodded. "I have to do my homework before I can play games on my iPad." He looked at her glumly.

"It can't be that bad," Marcella said. "What do you need to do?"

He opened his backpack and removed a folder, plopping it on the table. "I have to write an essay about a family tradition."

Marcella felt the energy drain out of the room.

"We don't have family traditions."

"There must be things that you do every year."

"Not anymore."

Ugh. Marcella felt his pain. All those awkward moments that keep on happening, reminding you that your parent is gone forever. "That's a tough one." She didn't want to push the issue. "Would you like more tea?"

AJ shrugged.

Marcella refilled their cups. "You can write about something you like to do."

"Everything I liked to do is in Wausau, like the waterpark." He looked down at the table. "What should I write about? I need to turn in the rough draft tomorrow."

"Hmm." Marcella thought for a moment. "What do you and your dad do for fun?"

He shrugged. "Nothing. He works and helps me with my homework."

This is probably what his father saw as moodiness. She recognized it as angst. She knew it too well.

"I'm sorry that you had to move from Wausau. I'm sorry your mom died."

AJ looked up and cocked his head a bit, as if he didn't know what to make of her.

"My mom died when I was fifteen." Marcella searched his eyes for signs of life. "But I didn't have to move. That must be hard on you."

AJ sipped his tea. "Thanks."

"Can you write about going fishing with your grandpa?"

AJ's face brightened. "I can write about sauna with my grandpa."

"There you go. Your mom probably saunaed in the very same sauna when she was a kid."

"Yeah, that's definitely a family tradition. At least on my mom's side. My dad can never take the heat. He turns beet red, which looks really funny with his hair." He laughed.

# Chapter 15

*M*arcella's calves burned as she climbed Quincy Hill, pedal after pedal, on her way to work on Louisa's garden with Beth. She didn't make the trek often on bike as it wasn't a relaxing ride, but today she needed to push her body physically to displace her stress. She shifted to a bigger gear and stood to utilize more of her hamstrings until they began to fatigue, and then she shifted to a lower gear and sat, engaging her glutes, and pedaled at a higher cadence to maintain her speed.

Halfway up the hill, as she passed the Keweenaw Waterway Scenic Turnout, her eyes followed the sparkling blue canal to where the lake widened and turned south. In the distance, the Huron Mountains rose up on the far side of Keweenaw Bay. Glints of yellow dotted the trees on the Douglass hillside. It would be a few more weeks till peak color, probably around the time of Aimee and Russ's wedding. She drew fresh air deep into her lungs. The sun warmed her face. Warm days in September were something to savor, as it wouldn't be long before cold weather pervaded.

A semi rumbled past her, bringing her mind back into focus, aware of the traffic. The engine strained as the driver struggled to pick up speed, and black smoke rolled over the top of the trailer. She rode through the sooty air until the truck crested the hill. She still couldn't believe her dad was moving. It was as if he'd become an entirely different person since he married Kandy.

She wasn't sure if that was true. Maybe it was just that she was an adult now, seeing him for who he was. But he had always seemed content living in the UP, and the log house was his dream home.

She crested the hill, shifted to a higher gear, and picked up speed on the slight decline. She heard another truck and glanced over her shoulder. A car was also coming, maintaining the left lane. The truck, pulling a semitrailer, wasn't going to move over. She swerved to avoid being clipped and rode right into road debris.

*Turkey.* She glared at the truck as it disappeared into the distance.

She got off her bike and inspected her tires. A glass shard. *Ugh!* She despised litter. She took deep breaths, willing the negativity away, as she dug in a side pocket of her bike tote. She unfolded her Leatherman to the needle-nose pliers and removed the glass from the tire. Fortunately, the glass hadn't been deeply embedded, and the tire didn't appear to be damaged.

Marcella took several deep breaths and climbed back on her bike. As she pedaled, she pulled her water bottle off the cage on the downtube and took a sip. A mile down the highway, she turned onto a quiet, county road.

Trees crowded the shoulder. She took in the paper birch trees, interspersed with strong oaks and maples, white cedar, and trees she used to call pseudo-birch before learning they were *popple*. She spotted an apple tree by the roadside. It was funny how she could look at the foliage of a tree, not noticing a single apple, and then suddenly see them all. There were more apple trees. She stopped by the snowmobile trail—or rather the ATV trail when it wasn't winter—pulling her bike off the road. The lower apples had already been picked, maybe by passing four-wheeler riders, but most likely by deer. She ducked under a branch to get to the base of the tree, climbed up, and picked an apple.

It was a small apple with a freckled light red complexion, like a Pink Lady. It had a small scab on it, probably from the relatively dry summer, but it was definitely organic. Back when the tree first took root, pesticides hadn't even been invented, and the tree had long since been left to the wild. With its location next to the old railroad-track-turned-recreation trail, she imagined the genesis of the tree was a casual toss of an apple core from a train engineer carrying copper ore off the Keweenaw.

She took a bite. Delicious. Crispy with an ever-so-slight tart bite. She liked them that way, before they got too sweet and soft.

Any apples not picked by passersby would not go to waste. The deer and bear would gobble up every last one after they fell to the ground. She picked a couple more and tucked them between her tight riding jersey and shirt.

After finishing her snack, she climbed back on her bike and lazily pedaled down the road, allowing momentum to carry her to Beth and Danny's little, blue house. She swapped her bike shoes with sandals from her tote and grabbed her water bottle.

Beth opened the door, still dressed in her work attire—black dress pants paired with a light blue top. "I'm glad this worked out today. It's glorious out there, isn't it?"

"It is." Marcella held up the apples. "I brought you and Danny a treat from down the road."

"Oh, yum. Come on in and make yourself at home, and put those on the kitchen counter while I change into my grubbies." Beth disappeared into the bedroom.

Marcella put the apples on the counter next to a short stack of books. Dr. Gerald Benley's book, *Your Intimate God*, sat on top. She picked it up. Beneath it was *What to Expect When You're Expecting*.

Marcella held back a laugh. That would explain the glow Louisa saw in Beth.

She examined the back of Dr. Benley's book. The heading above the blurb read *Connecting with the God Who Loves You*, and Marcella finished the sentence with her own words under her breath, "but let your mom die anyway."

"What was that?" Beth asked as she stepped into the dining room.

Marcella quickly returned the book to the pile. "Oh, nothing."

"Did you read Dr. Benley's new book?" Beth nodded to the stack. "It's fantastic."

"Hmmm." Marcella crossed to the sink to refill her water bottle. She'd had enough of Christian self-help to last a lifetime, but she didn't want to squash Beth's naïve enthusiasm.

Marcella unscrewed the cap and turned on the tap. As the bottle filled, she looked out the window into the field, where tall grass danced in the breeze. A doe darted across the field and then stood still by the tree line.

Beth came alongside Marcella with an empty glass.

Marcella motioned to the deer, which had been joined by another. "Beautiful. Aren't they?"

"Yeah." Beth took in the scene as she filled her glass. "I love watching them, but I hate hitting them."

Marcella laughed. "Yeah, that's one advantage to biking."

Beth took a big drink. "Okay, let's go."

They walked across the field on a mowed path that led to Louisa's house.

"I appreciate your help," Beth said. "Aimee and Russ decided to have the wedding here. It's a nice neutral location so maybe Russ's parents will come, and it would be the easiest for Grandma. I don't want her to be disappointed seeing her property overgrown."

Marcella surveyed the garden, a bit overwhelmed by the overgrowth.

"I know it's a jungle out here." Beth threw up her hands. "Danny and I haven't had much time to spend on it. We've been spending most evenings with Grandma, and I haven't had the energy because..." Beth's voice trailed off, and she looked down at the ground.

"Are you okay?" Marcella asked her friend.

"Not really. I feel bad for Grandma. It's not working out for her to be at High Cliff. She needs more care, but a nursing home won't give the kind of care she needs, either. She can't scratch itches or move her arm if she's uncomfortable." Beth looked up with tears in her eyes. "She can't press a button or make a call to get help. She needs somebody with her 24/7. I'm trying to be there as much as I can, but it's a lot with my new job, and—" Beth sobbed, "I'm pregnant."

In spite of the topic, Marcella couldn't stop the smile from breaking out across her face. "That's wonderful. Congratulations." She moved forward to hug her friend.

"Thanks. Please don't tell anyone. It's early and I want to make sure everything's okay." Beth wiped her tears on the hem of her T-shirt sleeve. "I have all these crazy hormones wreaking havoc on my emotions."

Marcella laid a hand on her friend's shoulder. "Deep breaths," she said softly, as she gently massaged.

Beth laughed, releasing tension in her shoulders. "Thanks. Now what should we do about the garden?"

Marcella looked around.

"It's that bad, isn't it?" Beth asked. "I can tell by your face."

"There's a lot of weeds, but I'm not sure pulling them will make much difference at this point. The growing season's pretty much done. Those look like bean vines crawling up the deer fencing, but there aren't many on there."

"The deer help themselves to the beans and peas on the outside, and I've been over here to pick them on the inside, but I mostly eat them off the vine." Beth chuckled.

"That's when they're best." Marcella picked one of the few remaining beans and popped it in her mouth. "We could thin the carrots. If it stays warm for a while, we might get growth out of them over the next month. And you can leave those in even after the snow flies. They'll be sweeter then."

Marcella pulled handfuls of carrots up and laid them in a neat pile. Out of the corner of her eye, she saw Beth casually tossing the carrots aside.

"You can still use these," Marcella said. "They're too small to peel, but you can wash them well and use them in stir fry."

After thinning the carrots, Marcella stood and assessed another part of the garden. "The lettuce is small and stalky, and crowded by weeds, but the peppermint's holding its own. In fact, half the weeds are peppermint. We need to thin that out before it overtakes the garden. It should really be planted in garden boxes." Marcella picked a leaf, and then crushed and rubbed it between her fingers. She smelled it and popped it in her mouth. "Yeah, it's good. Let's pick the peppermint so your grandma will have plenty of tea over the winter."

"Okay," Beth said. "I should have thought to bring a pail."

"Does Louisa have one in the greenhouse?"

They checked. Shovels, hoes, rakes—but no bucket. They made their way to the farmhouse.

In the kitchen, Beth dug in a cupboard and pulled out a stainless steel mixing bowl. "I think the scissors are in one of the drawers by the sink."

Marcella opened a drawer. Dishrags and towels. She tried the next one. The scissors were in there with other miscellaneous items. Everything was just as Louisa left it, ready for her to come home, if only she could. "Beth, what would it take for Louisa to move back here?"

Beth leaned against the counter. "She's spending a lot of money to be at High Cliff and then on top of that she pays for extra help. All they provide for the basic price are the meals and housing. It worked for a little while, but not now that she's needing more help." Beth shook her head. "I don't want to see her go in a nursing home. I don't think that would work well, either. If we could find the right people and build a team…"

Marcella looked out the window at the birdfeeder. Chickadees flitted from the feeder to the apple tree. She wanted that view for Louisa. "I'd like to be part of the team," she said.

Beth gave her a hug. "Thank you. I've been praying God would put it on the hearts of people."

Marcella shrugged off the comment. It was just how Beth talked.

Out in the garden, the two women clipped the peppermint in silence. Marcella pondered Beth's remark. She wished she still had the faith of her childhood, faith that there was a God who cared, who was involved, who intervened when bad things happened, who put things on the hearts of people. A monarch butterfly flitted past her head, and she paused to appreciate its beauty.

The butterfly settled on a milkweed plant, a plant she had previously considered a weed. Now Marcella realized it was sweet sustenance for the butterfly's long journey to Mexico. The warm September afforded a leisurely migration through the Upper Peninsula. It was that butterfly's first journey, yet it likely took the same route its ancestors had taken the year before. It fluttered away.

"*Adiós, mariposa*," Marcella said.

"*Hablas español?*" Beth asked.

Marcella laughed. "Just hello and goodbye, and a few pretty words."

"I'm from Los Angeles, so it's kind of a second language there." Beth put a handful of clippings in the bowl. "I worked with Spanish-speaking kids at the Family Resource Center, so I almost became fluent. But I never get to use it anymore. We have people at Douglass State representing just about every other language—Mandarin, Hindi, Farsi—but very few Spanish speakers."

A noise startled Marcella.

"What was that?" Beth asked, rising to her feet.

They walked to the greenhouse to investigate. A bird had flown into the glass and lay stunned on the ground. The two women bent over the tiny swallow, watching the lifeless creature.

"Do you think it's dead?" Beth asked, a catch in her throat.

Marcella picked up a twig from underneath a birch tree and gently prodded the small animal. "I think so."

Tears welled up in Beth's eyes. "I'm so emotional these

days—I can hardly stand to be around myself."

"This too shall pass." Marcella said, and then she went to the greenhouse and retrieved a shovel. She dug a hole right next to the poor animal. She knelt to the ground and picked up the bird. It twitched, and then flipped over to its feet. It looked left and right, back at Marcella, and quickly flew off.

The women laughed. Marcella fell back on her bottom and then lay on her back, looking up at the sky.

"That was a close call." Beth waved in the air. "*Adiós, dulce pajarito.*" Beth looked to the sky, clasping her hands. "God, thank you for protecting that little bird."

Marcella smiled, glad to see her hormonal friend happy, but she couldn't help but wonder why Beth didn't blame God when she thought the bird was dead. How was it that people gave God the credit for all that was right in the world, but didn't hold him responsible when things went terribly wrong?

# Chapter 16

"*I*'m here to see Mr. Stott," Drew told the middle-aged receptionist. "I'm Andrew Smith."

"Okay, help yourself to coffee and have a seat. I'll tell him you're here." She smiled demurely. As soon as Drew turned his back, she yelled, "Matt, Mr. Smith's here."

"All right. Tell him I'll be a minute."

"He'll be a minute," the woman said to Drew, as if he couldn't hear the lawyer.

Drew poured coffee into a paper travel cup and put a lid on it. Maybe caffeine would get rid of his tension headache. He sunk into an overstuffed black leather couch, which showed signs of decades of wear. He took a sip of the coffee. It was good. He glanced over at the coffee stand. A framed sign on the wall read *Proudly Serving Keweenaw's Best Local Micro Roast Coffee*. The office was not what he expected for an attorney. A bit dingy, with frayed carpet and modest furniture. Old metal file cabinets. There was no pretentiousness in the UP, except for the coffee.

Nonetheless, he was relieved to be there. The week had been difficult. He found it hard to concentrate. Senja had seemed smug when she found a mistake he'd made in a spreadsheet. It wasn't like him to make mistakes.

A few minutes later, Matthew Stott greeted him and shook his hand. The gray-haired man gave him half a smile. "We'll meet in my office."

Drew sat in a contoured plastic chair with a chrome frame opposite Stott, who sat behind a metal desk covered with stacks of file folders. A wall of shelves behind the attorney's desk held volume after volume of case law books and Michigan State statutes.

The lawyer leaned back in his chair and crossed his legs, holding a legal pad. "Mr. Smith, what can I do for you?"

Drew summarized the situation while the lawyer took notes. Stott didn't comment or ask questions until Drew had finished.

"What's this Danny's last name?" he asked.

"Johnson."

"Aah." The man nodded and made a note. "The State Trooper. Good guy."

Drew grimaced.

The man scratched his forehead. "So Danny wants custody of your son?"

"No, no." Drew shook his head. "I don't know. I doubt it. He hasn't said anything, but I think he suspects AJ's his son. I was just wondering if he'd have legal rights if we did a paternity test and he proved to be the father."

"Why would you do that?"

Drew shrugged. "I guess so we could know the truth."

The lawyer studied him. "It would seem this might be a situation where it would be best not to know the truth," he said slowly.

"Eventually the truth will come out, and AJ may want to know his biological roots. I was adopted, and I've always wanted to." Drew leaned forward, holding his coffee in both hands. "But I want to protect AJ—and myself."

Stott frowned as he looked over the notepad. "I've been doing this for thirty years and I haven't come across this one yet." He looked up at Drew. "You know, I'm not an expert in family law."

"But your website says you specialize—"

"Yeah, yeah." Stott flapped his hand. "We need to dabble in a little bit of everything to get enough business to survive." The attorney tapped his pen on his legal pad and looked up at the ceiling in thought. "You were married when AJ was born, right?"

"Correct."

"And your name's on the birth certificate, right?"

"That's also correct." Drew liked where this was going.

"Traditionally, in Michigan, the husband at conception or birth is presumed to be the father, and no one else would have standing."

Drew leaned back in the chair and exhaled. He sipped his coffee. "That's music to my ears."

"But…" Stott leaned forward in his chair and put the legal pad on the desk. He flipped to a clean sheet of paper.

"But what?" Drew struggled to get air back into his lungs.

"Michigan passed new legislation a few years ago that gives putative fathers an opportunity to petition that."

"Putative?"

"Or assumed, alleged, whatever. The baby daddy can get custody, but there's a time limit." He closed his notepad. "I can't remember what that is and whether it's from the birth of the child or from when the guy finds out about the child. I'd have to look into that." He opened the side drawer of his desk and removed a manila folder. He pulled a sheet from the folder and set it in front of Drew. "Here's a list of my fees."

Drew looked at the paper and gulped. A thousand-dollar retainer and two-hundred dollars per hour thereafter, plus expenses. "I'll have to think about it."

He walked out of the office into blinding sunlight and immediately his head throbbed. Maybe he was going overboard by talking to a lawyer. Who's to say it would ever come to that? But at least the free consultation revealed there were laws on the matter. It might be best if Danny didn't know he was the father, but Drew wanted to know the truth. Until he knew for sure, he'd assume the worst. He didn't want this hanging over his head, always waiting for the other shoe to drop.

He found it hard to drive back to work with a raging headache, so he pulled into Shop-Mart's parking lot.

As he searched for the pain reliever aisle, a box caught his eye. *Ancestry Genetic Testing Kit.* He'd been thinking about doing that to find out his roots. It was right next to another product, *At Home Paternity Test.* He glanced around to make sure no one was watching him before picking up the box. Living in a small town was definitely losing its charm. He read the back of the box. *Know before they grow.* It was a little late for that.

The test looked simple enough. Swab the inside of the mouth. Send the samples back to the lab, and they'd analyze it for a hundred bucks and send the results. His mind worked. Ideally, he could get a sample from Danny, too, just to confirm. But how would he do that? He imagined himself at Trailblazers, swiping a soda can after Danny had taken a drink. Would it be a large enough sample?

He held the box close to him to obscure what he was buying. After finding ibuprofen, he made his way to the checkout counter. His headache dissipated as the clerk rang up the purchase.

As Marcella rode her bike into her driveway, unclipping her toes from the pedals, she heard gravel crunching under rolling tires behind her.

Drew parked his truck and got out. "Danny sees you for massages, right?" he asked, a Shop-Mart bag dangling from one hand and his briefcase in the other.

Marcella took off her helmet. "I don't discuss my clients."

"Patty said that you're his massage therapist," Drew said. "Could you collect a sample of his spit?"

"What?" Marcella stared at him. "Why would you want his spit?"

"I got a DNA test." Drew held up the bag. "If he's not the

dad, then I don't have anything to worry about." He pulled the test kit out of the bag, flipped it over, and handed it to her. "It looks pretty simple."

She took the box and read the directions on the back. "You want me to ask him if I can swab his cheek for you?" Was he nuts?

"No, just get him relaxed so he falls asleep on the massage table. He's bound to drool. It's hard not to with your face in that headrest. And then put a bowl under his face."

"Drew, I'm not going to collect saliva samples from my clients." She walked her bike around the house.

"So he *is* your client." He looked momentarily gleeful, and then sadness returned to his face. Stress, maybe.

"How about we have peppermint tea? It's soothing."

"Sure, but first let me leave a note for AJ on the door." Drew squatted, setting his briefcase on the ground. He shoved the shopping bag in it and pulled out a Post-it pad and pen.

While he scribbled a note for AJ, she put her bike in the shed.

They went up to her apartment, and Marcella put water to boil on the stove.

"Why don't you give yourself the test?" Marcella asked, as she pulled a mason jar from the cupboard.

"I've been thinking about the timing, and I think there's a good chance I didn't father AJ."

"Mmhmm."

"But even if I proved that I'm not his biological father, it still wouldn't prove Danny is."

"Mmhmm." Marcella stuffed a tea infuser with dried leaves. She lifted the lid of her stainless steel teakettle and dropped in the ball.

Drew continued, "And if he's not the father, then I don't have any reason to keep AJ away from him."

Marcella joined him at the table, crossing her legs. She reached around the back of her head and removed the scrunchy from her ponytail. She pulled her hair around and rested in on her shoulder.

Drew was staring.

"What?"

He shook his head. "How do you end up looking so amazing after a hard bike ride?"

Marcella smiled. He looked pretty good himself in a crisp, blue button-up shirt with khaki pants.

"I'm sorry." Drew looked flustered as his cheeks reddened.

"No, I'm sorry. I should've said thank you."

Drew's shoulders dropped back, and he let out his breath. "What is it about you that makes me want to open up?"

"I have a lot of practice listening with my job," Marcella said.

"Yes, you're listening. You haven't said much about what I should do."

"I try not to give too much advice."

"But I'm asking for your advice." Drew leaned forward. "As a friend."

The kettle whistled, and Marcella got up and turned off the burner. She didn't like giving relationship advice. It was against her ethos. She glanced back at Drew before pulling cups out of the cupboard. She imagined how lonely it was for him after losing his wife. Some guys don't have many friends anyhow, and living in a new town, well, it would be hard to start over. She poured their tea and set the cups on the table.

Marcella sat and sipped her tea. "It doesn't seem ethical to test Danny without his permission. Do you have the test kit in your briefcase?"

"Yeah." Drew pulled it out.

"Let's take a look at it."

Drew opened the package and pulled out the contents.

Marcella reviewed the instructions. "Yeah, you need permission from everyone being tested, except you can sign for AJ because you're his father."

"I hope."

"Drew, you're his father no matter what. No court will ever take that away from you."

"There's a new law."

"I don't know about that." Marcella set the instructions back on the table. "But I seriously doubt any court will ever take AJ from you."

"Maybe Danny could get visitation?" Drew was getting worked up again.

"Okay, you need to relax." Marcella came around and stood behind his chair. She placed two fingers on each of his temples and gently massaged. She could feel his tension, and she willed it to enter her body.

His body didn't want to hold on to the worry, and he relaxed fairly quickly. "Thank you."

She snapped her fingers, releasing the negative energy. She took her seat again and sipped her tea.

"We've spent so much time talking about me. I want to know more about you." Drew's blue-green eyes pierced her defenses. "You said you're dealing with some issues. Did they work themselves out?"

He remembered. She had made the comment in passing, wanting to be honest but not forthcoming.

"My dad's moving out of state, and he's going to be selling the rental properties."

"Seriously?" Drew's jaw dropped.

"Yeah. It was a shock."

"You've been here for quite a while, right?"

Marcella nodded.

"Have you thought of buying it from him?"

She laughed. "With all the money rolling in from massages? There's a massage school in town, and folks from all over the UP come here to be trained and many stay. In this area, we probably have one massage therapist for every ten people."

"Ouch. You're exaggerating, of course, but you're saying the supply curve's pushed pretty far to the right."

Marcella laughed. "I don't know what that means, but okay. You business guys are so poetical."

He sipped his tea.

"Why don't *you* buy it?" Marcella asked.

"I'm not sure I'm up for being a landlord."

"With me as a tenant?"

"That would certainly sweeten the deal, but I'd really like to get a place with a bigger yard for AJ. We were at a house in the country for the Trailblazers sauna and bonfire. Those boys had a great time running around and swimming in the pond."

"Oh, that was at my dear friend Louisa's house." Marcella sipped her tea. She, too, would love country living. She longed to have space for a larger garden. She smiled at Drew and he met her gaze. She was enjoying their talk. It had been a long time since she'd opened up like that.

Drew crossed his legs and interlaced his fingers, placing his hands on his knee. He was still wearing his wedding ring.

The exterior door opened, and AJ stepped in. "Hey, are you having tea without me?"

Drew practically jumped out of his chair. He quickly gathered the contents of the DNA test kit and shoved it in his briefcase.

"A DNA test?" AJ asked. "Are you going do that ancestry thing?"

"Yeah, I'm going to do that," Drew said, his face beet red.

# Chapter 17

*M*arcella hit the calendar app on her phone and checked her appointments. Two massages in the morning and three in the afternoon. Four was normally her max, as she wanted to be fully present and give each client her best, but her nine o'clock was Dorothy Brisbois, who had few aches and pains and virtually no drama. The rest of Marcella's day would make up for that. Her ten o'clock was Danny Johnson. Danny had the normal aches and pains from being an active thirty-year-old, and he had a lot on his mind—excitement and anxiety. In the afternoon, she had a pregnant mother and then a young boy with autism. After the first two afternoon massages, she'd have enough time to bike home to get her SUV, and then she'd drive to see Louisa. That massage would definitely wipe her out.

It wasn't the physical exhaustion from the massages, but rather the emotional energy she put into them. Louisa... well, Louisa's muscles were spastic. She had no control over most of them, but her brain kept sending bad signals, causing tightness and cramping. And as stoic as she acted, Marcella knew Louisa's living situation at High Cliff was eating at her.

Marcella put fresh linens and a change of clothes in her bike tote. She grabbed her helmet and headed out her back door and down the stairs.

"Hey, neighbor," Marcella called out to Drew. She neared the landing as he was coming out of his apartment.

"Oh, hi." He looked startled. "I hope you don't think I was waiting for you to leave."

"Why would I think that?" She smiled to ease the tension. "Maybe *I* was waiting for *you* to leave."

Drew laughed.

"Actually," Marcella continued, "don't you usually leave earlier to take AJ to school?"

"Yeah, I came back to take care of a little business." He held up an express envelope. "I'm running ancestry tests on me and AJ."

"Oh good, so I don't need to collect Danny's drool?" she asked jokingly, trying to keep things light.

He shook his head as his cheeks turned red, but he did smile briefly before looking serious. "I don't know what's going to happen when AJ's test comes back different than mine." A look of panic flashed across his face. "I mean, *if*. I'm trying to stay positive. *If* the tests come back different, I might not tell him I took one, too. I have six to eight weeks to think about it." Drew looked down at his feet. "Is that wrong?"

Marcella put her hand on his shoulder. "What's right is that you want to protect him."

"Thanks, friend."

By the time she pulled her bike out of the shed, he was already gone. She wished she could have given him one last wave. Maybe she'd run into him later that night. The thought made her smile.

She put an ear bud in one ear, keeping the other free to listen for traffic, and tuned her portable radio to the local AM station. She clipped her left toes to the pedal and swung her right leg over the seat. After finding a break in the morning traffic on US-41, she got up to speed and maintained a steady distance behind the car in front of her until it stopped at the end of the queue for a red light.

Riding close to the curb, she flew by Drew's truck. Before

she got to the intersection, the light turned green, and she rode with the traffic through Quincy. She smiled at the thought of her economical and equally fast commute, not to mention being better for the environment and good for her health. She picked up even more speed as the road dipped, but then lost momentum as it rose back up. She glanced over her shoulder, and Drew was a few car lengths back but gaining on her. The road dipped down again, and she picked up as much speed as she could to carry her up the next hill.

She maintained her lead, but as she crested the hill she could see the lift bridge was partially elevated. That meant traffic was on the lower deck, and the road surface was a metal grate. She had crossed it before, but didn't like the feeling of it grabbing her tires and didn't want to risk falling. She'd have to walk her bike across on the sidewalk. She pumped the pedals hard, pulling away from Drew. On the fixed section of the bridge, she stopped short of the first tower, dismounted, and hopped over the guardrail.

Drew tapped his horn as he passed, and she waved.

Marcella hoisted her bike over the rail and onto the sidewalk. With the race lost, she turned her focus to the talk on the radio as she walked. She slipped her other earbud in. The current temperature was 42, and they expected a high for the day of 58. She wasn't feeling the cold due to the adrenaline from the ride, plus the rising sun on her face. The sun wasn't high enough in the sky yet to warm her skin, but it did much for her soul.

"Marjorie Peterson of Douglass, age eighty-six, passed away September 2nd surrounded by her family." The radio announcer began reading the obituaries and Marcella listened intently as she began the over-under game. *Game* being a euphemism for where her mind went naturally after ten years of the habit.

"Plus forty-six," Marcella said to herself.

As the announcer read through others, some having died in their 70s and one in her 90s, she quickly did the math. Plus thirty-two. Plus fifty-four. Minus two. That was rare, for somebody to die in his 30s. It was a traffic accident, as she remembered the news from the week before.

Her mother's death shortly after her fortieth birthday made the math easy. Most of the obituaries were for people who had twice the life span of her mother.

"Alicia Jacobs of Quincy, age twenty-nine, passed away in childbirth at Copper Island Hospital on September 7th."

"Plus one," Marcella said to herself, realizing she didn't say *minus eleven*. The woman was only a year older than Marcella. One didn't expect women to die during childbirth these days. She didn't know Alicia, but couldn't help wondering about her. She was twenty-nine, so she could have had other children. How was her husband coping? Did the baby survive?

It brought tears to her eyes. It seemed so random. So arbitrary.

At the end of the bridge, she jumped back on her bike. She ducked off to the right and looped around, underneath the end of the bridge she'd just crossed, and rode through town on the lower street. She chained her bike to a rack behind the building she worked in and walked up the side street to Avery Avenue.

In Shear Delight, Marcella freshened up and changed into black scrubs. She pulled fresh linens from her tote and stacked them on the lower shelf of her console table. She pulled the top sheet off the stack, stretched it over the massage table, and put a clean cover on the headrest. She switched on the hot plate to heat a small pot of water. She pulled her water bottle from her tote and added water to the pot, fully submerging half dozen Lake Superior stones.

She searched on her phone for relaxing harp music and played it over the Bluetooth speaker. She unrolled her exercise mat, turned on a space heater and a lamp, and shut off the overhead light.

She sat on the mat cross-legged and took a deep breath, stretching one arm to the ceiling with her other arm behind her head and holding her elbow. She repeated the movement on the other side. She rolled to her knees and held her body up with her hands on the mat. She looked up to the ceiling, and then pushed her body back, placing her forehead on the mat. She rolled forward, keeping her chest close to the mat, until she lay on her stomach. She pushed herself to her knees and repeated the motion.

After completing her morning stretches and a series of deep breaths, she turned on the overhead light, rolled up the mat, and went to greet Dorothy.

When she was halfway through the salon, the door chimed, and Dorothy entered in a bright pink maxi coat with her Yorkie under her arm.

"Should I take your coat?" Marcella asked.

"Thank you." Dorothy handed Fritzi to Marcella, and then slipped out of the long jacket.

Marcella traded the dog for the coat. "This is beautiful. I haven't seen you in it before."

"I got it in Chicago. It was made in Italy."

Marcella hung the coat on the rack and led Dorothy back to her room. "When did you go to Chicago?"

"At the end of August. I love shopping the Magnificent Mile during the back-to-school rush. So much excitement." Dorothy followed Marcella.

"You and Max went?"

"Oh, no. He doesn't enjoy that sort of thing. I drove myself."

"And how old are you? Sixty-nine?" Marcella teased, as she stopped short of the open door.

Dorothy laughed. "Eighty-four years old." She stepped into the room.

Marcella closed the door behind her and gave Dorothy a few minutes.

Eighty-four years old, Marcella thought. Healthy. Still married. Her children had done well in life. Several grandchildren. The perfect life.

When she returned, Dorothy was lying on the table face down, and Fritzi was curled up on the rug. Marcella switched off the overhead light.

She turned off the hot plate and, using tongs, removed the

Lake Superior stones from the boiling water and placed them on a towel. She tested the temperature of the stones on the back of her hand and dipped each in a small bowl of room temperature water. As she waited for the rocks to cool, she placed the bowl of water next to Fritzi. He lapped it up. A thirsty dog.

On her smart phone, she turned off the harp music and went to the white noise app. She selected seashore sounds.

Marcella hovered her hands above Dorothy's shoulders, trying to sense where to start. She wasn't getting anything. She moved her hands down above her back. Nothing. Her legs. Feet. She moved up to her head. Marcella couldn't feel any pain that Dorothy might be having.

"Is anything bothering you today?" Marcella tried the old-school approach.

"Oh, no. I'm here to relax. To be treated like a queen."

Marcella took two palm-sized stones and tested each by holding them against the inside of her wrist. She pulled the sheet down and gently massaged Dorothy's back with the stones.

"It's heavenly," Dorothy murmured.

After massaging her back, Marcella placed the stones between Dorothy's shoulder blades. She placed other stones along her spine and covered her back with the sheet. Marcella massaged her feet with jojoba oil mixed with a drop of lemon oil. It wasn't long before Dorothy fell asleep. Even Fritzi lay on his side, feet twitching as if dreaming.

When her fifty minutes expired, Marcella whispered in her ear, "That's it."

Dorothy yawned and stretched, and upon hearing his mistress wake, Fritzi did the same. Marcella went to the front of the salon and waited.

Dorothy joined her up front, with the dog under one arm and holding cash in the other hand.

As Marcella took the dog, handing Dorothy her coat, she asked, "Now that Chicago's out of the way, what's your next big adventure?"

"Like every year, Max and I will head down to Fort Myers

and spend the winter on the boat." Dorothy put on her coat.

Marcella was happy for her. She was a delightful woman and deserved everything she had. Marcella wished everyone could be so fortunate. "A charmed life."

Dorothy laughed. "If you don't look too hard." She buttoned up her coat and looked at Marcella thoughtfully as she took Fritzi back. "You're right though. I've had less catastrophes and more opportunities than many. But you're just seeing a snapshot of my life. You don't get to be eighty years old without having hard times. Max and I were dirt poor, then wealthy, then lost it all before we got to where we are now. I lost a child. I fought cancer—twice. My body's doing all right, now, but I come here because I love the company. I'm lonely and bored. Max is a stick in the mud, and all he wants to do is spend time on his boats and golf, either here or in Florida. And all of my friends have died." She paused and studied Marcella's face. "Oh, don't you cry."

A tear escaped Marcella's eye as she said that, and Marcella wiped it from her cheek.

"Give me a hug." Dorothy shuffled toward her.

Marcella hugged her, and Fritzi licked Marcella's cheek.

Dorothy left, and Marcella readied the room for Danny.

After he arrived and got situated, she began work on his back—his usual problem area. He had chronic tightness on the right side of his spine, and although she managed to release it in most sessions, it would return the following month.

He'd benefit from more frequent massage. She'd suggested it once, but didn't want to push. He was a busy guy and massage was expensive.

"None of the smelly stuff," he'd told her the first time he came in. "I just want a deep therapeutic massage."

She complied, amused. He wouldn't benefit from essential oil therapy anyway if his mind was blocking it. That was okay. She was happy to work with her clients' preferences.

Some clients liked to sleep. Some ended up releasing emotions with tears as their bodies released tension. And others talked through the entire session. To each his own, she thought with a smile. Danny was a talker.

"So Beth told me she spilled the beans," Danny said as she ran her elbow along one side of his spine.

Marcella wasn't going to mention it unless he did. "I'm so happy for you guys. Congratulations!" Her friends would be great parents.

She listened to Danny ramble about how he was looking forward to having a son or daughter and all the things they'd do. Sledding. Ice Skating. Building sand castles. "It's amazing how I love that little person so much and I haven't even met him or her," he concluded.

Marcella smiled ruefully. She wasn't so sure she wanted that dream for herself. Hard to bring children into the world, knowing that you can't protect them from the pain of life.

"So, how's your tenant working out?" Danny changed the topic of conversation as she began work on his neck. His neck held more tension than usual, and he grimaced under her moderate pressure. She lightened up.

"Great," she said. She couldn't help smiling. She looked forward to her chance meetings with Drew and with AJ.

"He's a great kid, isn't he?" Danny asked, not waiting for a reply. "They came to Trailblazers the other week."

She felt his neck relax, and she increased her pressure slightly, willing the muscles to let go even further. "You can let go," she whispered softly.

"You probably know—I don't know if Beth's told you—but I think people have pretty much figured it out—at least there's talk." Danny's back rose as he inhaled deeply, and then he exhaled. "AJ looks like I did at that age and with the timing of when Kristine and I were together, it's likely he could be my biological son. When you said 'let go,' it made me think of how I've been learning that lately. I guess it's something we all need to learn, sooner or later."

"Mm-hmm." Marcella massaged his shoulders.

He was on a roll, sermonizing. "I had to learn it when I let go of Beth. I thought it was likely I'd never see her again, but she came back from California. When I first met AJ at his mom's funeral and realized he could very well be my biological son, I didn't know what to do—but I had to let go of trying to figure it out—and in time, well, here he is back on Copper Island. I'm jazzed I'm getting the chance to get to know him. And now we have this new baby..." He grew silent.

Marcella smiled.

"Please don't tell anybody," he continued. "It's still early. Anyhow, I can't wait to meet this little guy or gal, and it makes me wish I could have seen those early years of AJ's life, too."

Marcella moved down to his feet and gently rubbed in jojoba oil.

After some time, his breathing became deeper, and she wondered if he was asleep. She looked over at the bowl she had left on the rug as a thought crossed her mind.

"Nah," she said to herself. She'd never violate his trust, but even if she did slide that bowl under his headrest, his DNA results would probably come back as part Yorkie.

# Chapter 18

*A*s Marcella pulled into the High Cliff parking lot, Beth and Danny got out of his Jeep. Marcella took the spot next to them and popped her hatch. She got out and hugged Beth, whispering in her ear, "How are you feeling?"

"Good."

Marcella opened the hatch.

"Let me get that for you," Danny said.

Marcella stepped aside, and he pulled the massage table from the vehicle and slung the strap of the carrying case over his shoulder.

Marcella grabbed her bag of oils and closed the hatch. "Have you made progress in putting a team together?" she asked Beth, as the three made their way into the building.

"There's you and me. Senja said she can continue helping with dinner and stay through early evening. Lorna can help during the day, because she doesn't work a regular job. Danny and Mak can keep her company, scratch itches—stuff like that—but I don't think Grandma would want them to help with her personal care. And Danny's shift is constantly changing, so it's hard to schedule him for anything."

Danny hit the accessible button to open the door, stepping

aside to let the women go in first.

"It's hard to find people." Beth sighed.

In the dining room, Louisa's usual table was empty.

"Have you seen Louisa Herrala yet this evening?" Danny asked Margaret, who sat at a neighboring table.

"I would hope she's in her room." She turned up her nose.

"Thank you," Beth said.

She was so sweet, Marcella thought. Saying thank you to the obviously hostile woman.

Danny walked toward the elevator. "Let's go meet her there. If she hasn't eaten yet, at least we can drop off the table in her room."

In the apartment, the three found Senja helping Louisa eat meatloaf.

"Hello," Senja greeted them curtly. "Shall I tell them the latest development?" she asked Louisa.

Louisa nodded.

"High Cliff has a new policy." Senja's voice had an edge to it. "The powers-that-be have decided residents unable to feed themselves need to eat in their rooms."

"What?" Marcella, Beth, and Danny said in near unison.

Beth huffed. "Unbelievable."

"Is that even legal?" Marcella asked. "What about the Americans with Disabilities Act?"

They all looked to Danny.

He shrugged. "I don't know the law. I just enforce it."

Louisa chuckled.

"Seriously," Danny continued, "we covered the ADA in the academy, but it was more about how to treat people. How to look for signs of a disability when we pull someone over. And rules for service dogs in public places. But this might be a question for a lawyer."

"I'll ask Aimee," Beth said, pulling out her phone.

"No, no, no." Louisa shook her head.

Senja sniffed. "I can't believe that Margaret."

Beth punched at her phone, texting.

Senja continued, "Why can't she mind her own business?"

"All right, my dears," Louisa said softly.

"I'm going to go talk to somebody in the office." Danny moved toward the door.

Senja continued to murmur something. Beth was focused on her phone, texting with two thumbs.

Louisa looked agitated.

"Hold on, everybody," Marcella said. "Louisa's trying to say something."

The room became still. Now that she had the floor, Louisa inhaled and exhaled slowly. "There are battles I don't want to fight." Her voice faded near the end of the sentence.

"It's not acceptable that they're forcing you to eat in your room." Beth's voice cracked, and tears filled her eyes.

Senja held up Louisa's tea.

Louisa sipped through a straw. "Delicious. I haven't had a decent cup of tea since the bridal shower."

Beth burst into tears.

Danny put an arm around her shoulders. "She'll be okay. It'll pass in a minute."

Louisa chuckled again. "Still no news to tell me?"

"Oh, Grandma." Beth laughed through her tears. "I have something to tell you, but I wanted it to be…" She wiped her eyes. "…happier."

"Now's the best time to tell me. I need good news today."

"I'm pregnant," Beth said. She hugged her grandma, who looked delighted.

"Congratulations," Senja said.

"I'm so happy for you two." Marcella did her best to look surprised.

Beth's phone rang. "It's Aimee," she announced. "Hello?" Beth explained the dining room situation to Aimee, who worked as a paralegal in a Chicago law firm.

Louisa seemed to grow irritated, trying to say something, but nobody was listening. Marcella leaned in close.

"I don't want to fight the battle," Louisa said.

"Hey, guys," Marcella raised her voice. "Beth, could you put Aimee on speakerphone?"

Beth pushed the speaker option and set the phone on the

armrest of Louisa's wheelchair.

"Hi, everybody," Aimee said. "I can check if there's been any cases like this in the past. I can't give advice, but it wouldn't hurt for me to do research in my free time."

"I don't want to fight the battle." Louisa's voice had already weakened considerably from the earlier strain.

"She said she doesn't want to fight the battle," Marcella said forcefully.

"It's the principle of the matter, Grandma." Beth shook her head. "It's just not right."

Louisa drew in a breath. "It's not working out for me to be here anymore."

The others strained to listen, leaning in close.

"I used to be able to call for help with a cordless phone on my lap by hitting redial, but I can't press the button anymore. I have to have aides check on me every hour. I'm afraid it's time for me to go into a nursing home."

"Has it come to that already?" Senja set Louisa's dinner tray on the end table.

"It's probably past that point," Louisa said.

"I'm concerned about you going into a nursing home," Beth said, "because I've been reading that they're not fully equipped to help with such individualized care."

"They have people making the rounds," Danny said, "but you should have somebody in the room with you, especially when you're vented."

"I'm not getting a ventilator," Louisa said. "For goodness sake, I'm seventy-six years old."

Beth began to cry again.

Louisa added, "I don't want to delay going home."

"Oh, good," Marcella said. "Beth has been putting a care team together."

"I'm talking about heaven." Louisa slurred the words. "I don't want to delay going home to heaven."

Beth knelt in front of her grandma. "In the meantime, we can at least get you back to the farmhouse."

Louisa shook her head. "It's too much to ask of people."

"So you don't want me to check on ADA discrimination in

senior living homes?" Aimee asked.

"I guess not," Beth said in resignation.

"Aimee?" Louisa said.

Beth moved the phone close to Louisa's mouth. "Grandma wants to talk to you, Aimee."

"I'm here."

"Is everything set for the wedding next weekend?" Louisa asked softly and with a heavy tongue. It was just like her to change the topic.

"I'm sorry," Aimee said. "I didn't get that."

Marcella could understand Aimee's confusion, as she wasn't able to see Louisa's lips move. "She asked if everything was set for the wedding next weekend."

"Yes, and thanks for letting us use your property and house. Hopefully, Russ's parents will come with the wedding being there. They're still not talking to him."

"Aimee," Senja said, "maybe we should let you go. We need to talk to Louisa more about her living and caregiving arrangements."

"Ah," Aimee said. "That's what you're talking about. I wasn't quite following."

"We were talking about that, and I'm pregnant," Beth said with a smile.

Aimee squealed. "Yay! Congratulations!"

After ending the call with Aimee, Beth brought up the caregiving arrangements again. She had volunteers to cover the evenings, but she needed to work to fill the days and nights. Louisa made the point again that it was too much to ask of people, and then she shut down.

"Okay, I came to give her a massage." Marcella was concerned that the energy in the room would affect the massage. She unzipped the bag and set up the massage table.

After Danny transferred Louisa to the massage table, Beth rose from her chair. "I'm going to call Aimee back." She motioned for Danny to go with her.

"And let's see if someone's in the office." Senja followed them out the door.

# Chapter 19

"*T*hanks, that was fantastic." Drew cleared his plate from the table.

"You're welcome," Marcella said.

"AJ, you and I are on cleanup duty, since Marcella cooked for us."

AJ groaned.

Drew continued, "I was a little nervous when you said you were making Thai food—Thai Gai...?"

"Thai Gai *Yang*." Marcella sipped tea.

"Yeah. I was worried AJ wouldn't like it, but he finished his whole plate. It was a perfect blend of Asian and western cuisine." Drew grabbed Marcella's plate from the table. "Come on, AJ, give me a hand."

AJ stood with his shoulders slumped and begrudgingly carried his own plate to the sink. "Can I go now?"

"No. We're going to clean up."

"Thanks for hosting," Marcella said. "It made cooking the chicken more social, since the grill's right outside your door. I'm serious when I said you can use it. Just buy an occasional tank of propane if you use it a lot."

"I should."

"We never grill anymore," AJ said glumly as he collected the glasses from the table.

"Why not?" Marcella asked.

Drew raised an eyebrow, hoping she'd get the hint it was a not a topic to be discussed. The truth was they hadn't grilled since Kristine died. Drew had enough on his hands as a single parent. He didn't have much time to put into meal prep. Marcella's question went unanswered, and she didn't press the matter. Drew filled the sink with water and squirted dish soap into it.

AJ brought the last of the dishes to the counter. "Can I go now?"

"Sure." Drew began to scrub and rinse the dishes.

"Is he okay?" Marcella asked, after AJ had left the room.

"That's his normal." Drew didn't expect AJ to bounce back quickly from losing his mother, but neither did he expect his personality to change so much. He used to be a pretty chipper kid, but now there was a constant cloud of sadness hanging over him, except for a few glints of sunshine when he went to Trailblazers or fishing with his grandpa.

"We should play a board game tonight," Marcella suggested.

"Scrabble?" It was a good game for two.

"I'm thinking more of a board game that we'd all enjoy, including AJ."

"How about Settlers of Catan?" he suggested, pleased she was trying to draw AJ out of his shell.

"Perfect. Where is it?" Marcella stood.

"Go ask AJ to find it, and I'll finish up the dishes." Maybe AJ would be receptive to the idea if it came from her.

Drew quickly washed the rest of the dishes and wiped the table while Marcella went to get the game.

She returned to the kitchen. "He said he doesn't want to play. He's sitting in his dark room on his iPad."

"Parenting fail." Drew threw up his hands.

Her face was thoughtful. "Do you have any marshmallows?"

"No."

"I have an idea. Get a fire going in your fireplace, and I'll run down to the co-op. I'll bet he'll come out of his room."

While Marcella ran her errand, Drew hauled in several pieces of firewood. He dug his ax out of a rubber storage tub in the basement and split another log into kindling. With some pieces of cardboard torn from his moving boxes, he started a fire.

Marcella returned with a paper shopping bag and a couple stainless steel roasting sticks. "AJ," she called into his room from the doorway, "do you want to make s'mores?"

"Yeah." AJ came out of his room.

"Brilliant," Drew said.

Marcella sat on the floor and pulled the contents out of the bag.

"Root beer!" AJ exclaimed.

"Real, brewed root beer." Drew opened a bottle.

"AJ," Marcella said, "while we wait for the fire to settle a bit, why don't you go get Settlers of Catan?"

"Okay. Can I have a root beer, too?"

"It'll be waiting for you when you get back." Drew opened another bottle and AJ dug through the front closet.

By the time they got the game set up, the flames had died down, and Drew and AJ roasted the first marshmallows. Drew lowered his stick with his roasted marshmallow over the graham cracker and chocolate in Marcella's hand. She used another graham cracker to pull it off and make the sandwich.

"Are you ready for mine?" AJ pulled his flaming marshmallow from the fireplace and blew on it.

Marcella handed the s'more to Drew. "One second." She pulled another graham cracker from the box and broke off another piece of chocolate.

"This is fun," AJ said. He took a bite of his s'more.

"My turn to roast a marshmallow." Marcella took the stick from AJ. "One of my favorite memories as a kid was roasting marshmallows in our fireplace."

AJ seemed happy, especially after winning Settlers. He'd reached Drew's level of strategy since they'd last played, the

Christmas before his mother's death. The days are long, but the years are short, Drew thought. Things had been rocky lately, but tonight was a win. And that was due to Marcella. She was good for both of them.

# Chapter 20

*M*arcella craned her head to glance at Louisa, who sat with a contented smile in her wheelchair strapped into the transport van. They were on their way to her farmhouse for Aimee and Russ's wedding. It was the happiest Marcella had seen Louisa since she'd moved from High Cliff to the nursing home in Quincy. Marcella was relieved she was in a facility where she had access to more care, but it still wasn't home.

Bright yellows, oranges, and reds painted the contours of the Keweenaw Waterway Valley. A bank of thick white clouds lined the horizon to the south, and with a blue sky overhead and warm temperatures, the color tour was in full swing during the first week of October. People came from all over the Midwest to see the changing leaves. Cars and RVs filled the parking lot of the Quincy Mine where folks toured the shaft house, steam hoist, and the seventh level of an underground mine. Across the street, people queued at the order window of the fish market's outdoor café. Smoke billowed from a black-ened cabinet, carrying the aroma of smoked Lake Superior trout and whitefish. The forecast of rain was wrong, thankfully.

Louisa struggled to keep her head up as the driver braked and turned onto the county road. Her head bobbed when he crossed the concrete road section that connected the off-road vehicle trail where Marcella had picked apples. And Louisa's whole body listed to the side as he turned into her driveway. Through all that, her smile remained and even brightened after they passed the garage and her house came in view.

Marcella saw Drew's truck. "My tenant's here," she said loud enough for Louisa to hear over the engine.

Louisa mumbled something.

The driver parked near the porch, where Russ and Danny had built a ramp as a surprise for her the prior year when she returned from California. She only lived in the house a couple weeks before moving to High Cliff, but at least she could get into the house to visit.

Danny and Mak pulled metal poles from a construction trailer lettered with the words *Saarinen Contracting*, the business Russ left behind when he moved to Chicago for work and to be near Aimee. They carried them to the backyard where an event tent lay unfolded behind the house. Out in the yard, a few dozen chairs were set up with an aisle between them leading to a birch bough trellis. If Russ's family came, they'd easily fill all of the chairs. He had something like a dozen siblings, and some of them were married with kids. It looked as if Aimee and Russ didn't have much hope for them showing up. Marcella sighed. It was sad when divisions between church denominations prevented families from coming together.

Marcella stepped out of the van and waited for the driver to help Louisa out. He came around, opened the side door, and pressed a button to fold down the ramp. He jumped back into the van, released the wheelchair restraints, rolled Louisa onto the ramp, and pressed another button to lower her to the ground.

Marcella squatted down alongside the wheelchair and pushed a lever to reengage its transmission. "Drew's here. Do you know why?" she asked, feeling strangely excited. She would've asked him to come as a plus one if she hadn't been needed to care for Louisa. But he might have taken it wrong, as encouragement to pursue her. Marcella remained in a crouched position, placing her hand on Louisa's arm to listen to her response.

"I didn't know he was coming, but I imagine Senja asked him. She was in a tizzy over finding enough brawn to set up the tents." Louisa's speech was slightly slurred, but it was easy enough to understand her as it was early in the day and she hadn't yet fatigued her tongue.

"Shall I drive you into the house or do you want to go to the backyard where they're setting up the tent?"

"My house," Louisa said. "The yard will be bumpy, so I'll just do that drive once. Besides, I'm cold." It had to have been at least seventy degrees, but she lacked the muscle mass to maintain her temperature. Such a brutal disease.

Marcella walked alongside Louisa, using the wheelchair joystick to drive her to the ramp. Though she was thin, she couldn't squeeze in next to her, so she reduced the speed and walked backward in front of the wheelchair. It was slow going, and her brain hurt trying to figure which way to turn the joystick.

"Marcella?"

She turned around. "Drew! I thought that was your truck. What are you doing here?"

"Senja asked me to help set up the tent. I guess it's her niece's wedding."

"Is AJ here, too?"

"He's with his grandparents." Drew glanced back at Danny, who was carrying another load of poles. "Good thing," he said under his breath. "How about you?"

"Aimee's my friend, and I'm here with my friend." She motioned to Louisa. "Louisa, this is my tenant, Drew Smith."

Drew held out his hand.

Louisa smiled, glancing down at her limp arms. "I can't shake," she said softly.

Recoiling his hand, he looked sheepish.

"This is her home," Marcella said.

"Really?" Drew glanced around with obvious admiration. "I love this place."

"Yes," Louisa tilted her face up, positively beaming as she surveyed the yard. "I do, too. There's no place I'd rather be."

Marcella looked across the grounds, seeing the place through Louisa's eyes. The weathered sauna by the pond, built by her late husband. The field of tall grasses blowing in the wind, framing an old broken-down barn. She turned back to Drew. "Could you help me wheel Louisa in the house? I think it would be easier if I pull out the transmission and have you push her in."

Inside the farmhouse, Drew pulled up a kitchen chair next to Louisa's wheelchair. He took an interest in her, asking about her life at the farmhouse. The conversation moved to ALS, and Louisa even opened up a bit about her struggles with the disease. Her biggest complaint was that she was bored. She had long since lost the ability to turn pages in a book. Her son bought her an e-reader, but now even that was proving impractical. She'd never enjoyed watching television, never even owned a television, but that was all she could do now that her roommate had the thing on all day. The nursing home provided social activities, but she was ill-equipped to take part in games, and her voice wasn't strong enough to be heard by other residents, many of whom had poor hearing.

Marcella was touched by Drew's patience as he leaned in to listen to Louisa's soft voice and repeated back what he thought he heard. He asked questions and seemed genuinely interested. Marcella was a bit embarrassed she didn't know a lot of what her friend was telling Drew, but Louisa typically didn't open up about herself, and it seemed their conversations always went back to Marcella.

Danny entered the kitchen. "Hey, there you are," he said, looking at Drew. "Hey, Grandma Lou." Danny gave her a peck on the cheek, and then addressed Drew again. "We have all the poles in place. Thanks for helping," he said in jest. "Now we're ready to raise the tent, and we need your help."

"I'll talk to you later." Drew rose, lifting his hand in a wave to Louisa and then to Marcella before leaving with Danny.

"He's a good man, Marcella," Louisa said in a tone that

implied more.

"Yes, he is, but we're just friends."

"At some time, dear, you'll need to open up to someone. You shouldn't stay closed off for the rest of your life."

Marcella sat in the chair Drew had vacated. He was a nice guy. She enjoyed his company, not to mention that there was a spark between them. But there were issues. Primarily there was AJ. She wouldn't do to a kid what Kandy had done to her. And then there was his faith. If she were to be with a guy, she'd want him to have Christian values, but she didn't know where she stood on issues of faith anymore. She was glad God had helped him turn his life around. Changed his heart, he'd said. She sighed. She wasn't sure she wanted to be with anyone anyway.

Drew held a pole in place, lifting a corner of the tent, as Danny cranked a ratchet mechanism to pull it taut. Drew tried to ignore the awkwardness he felt by focusing on the project at hand. Mak and Russ worked together to raise another corner.

"Did you and AJ have fun at Trailblazers?" Danny asked, a bit too chipper.

"Sure." Drew shrugged. His only concern was that AJ had enjoyed it too much.

"I haven't seen you guys in church since then."

"We go to Faith."

"With Ron and Patty?"

"Yeah." He and Patty had come to an unspoken truce. They were civil, though the conversation didn't go beyond making arrangements for AJ.

"That makes sense," Danny said. "You guys are always welcome to come to Trailblazers."

"I'll keep that in mind. We're pretty busy." Drew walked under the partially-erected tent, lifting the fabric over his head until he reached the next pole. He lifted the pole and rested it on his shoulder.

Danny seated the base of the pole in its bracket on the ground. He helped Drew lift the pole above their heads, and Drew held it there while Danny ratcheted the slack out of the strap. Watching Danny work, he couldn't keep his mind off the paternity question. Danny even had similar facial expressions to AJ's.

"Johnson." Drew might not have another opportunity to ask him. "What kind of name is that? English?"

Danny laughed. "I'm a hundred-percent Norwegian."

"A hundred percent? Johnson sounds more English or Scottish." Drew would only care if the ancestry results showed that AJ's ethnicity didn't align with his, which he assumed would be Irish, or at least the British Isles.

"My parents are from Minnesota. The Norwegians of Minnesota are like the Finns up here. They're everywhere. My mom was a Nelson."

"That sounds English, too."

Danny laughed. "Okay. I'm English. Are we good?"

"Hey, Drew," Mak called. "Where's that boy of yours?" He looked at Drew expectantly, his hand resting on the pole he'd just ratcheted into place.

"He's not here." Drew changed the subject. "How's the book coming?"

Mak groaned in disgust. "My publisher's drivin' me nuts. She sent back da manuscript with a bunch of edits, and I just can't accept them. It's bad enough she wants me to get rid of every speech tag and replace 'em with random action beats like quirkin' eyebrows. Who quirks their eyebrows? But she also wants to turn up da heat. I won't do it. That stuff's indecent for Amish fiction."

"We got one more on our side," Russ called, lifting a pole. "Let's stay focused."

Drew worked with Danny to lift the last pole on their side of the tent.

# Chapter 21

*M*arcella glanced at the clock. "Thirty minutes to show time. Should we go out now?"

"I need a blanket," Louisa said. "There's an afghan in the living room."

Marcella found the hand-crocheted blanket over the back of the couch. She returned to the kitchen and laid it over Louisa's legs and chest, tucking it between her shoulders and the backrest of the wheelchair. She rolled her out of the house and backward down the ramp.

Walking beside her and using the joystick, Marcella drove Louisa across the yard and past the shed where the bride waited. Aimee had coordinated with Russ so he wouldn't see her in her dress. He stayed in the tent in the backyard while she snuck out of the house.

A birch trellis was set up at the end of the aisle. People moved around the outside of the seating area rather than passing through the trellis. Each folding chair had a burnt orange satin ribbon tied to the back. They faced the back of the property, where a field of golden grass swayed in the wind, surrounded by yellow-leaved *popple*. Two large speaker cabinets were set on either side of the ceremony area with a microphone between them. Behind one of the speakers a man sat at a table with a laptop computer and mixing board, playing classical music at a volume that allowed conversation.

The chairs were not yet full. Aimee's mother and brother sat with another man—probably Sophia's boyfriend—in the front row, along with Aimee's uncle Mak and aunt Lorna. Senja was no doubt directing the wedding party. On the other side, a few people Marcella didn't recognize sat in the second and third rows.

A gust of wind picked up the afghan and blew it in Louisa's face. Marcella pulled it down and tucked it between her legs and the wheelchair's thigh pads. She parked Louisa on the outside end of the second row of chairs behind Aimee's family. As Marcella took a seat, she noticed Sophia held a green and gold urn in her lap. Aimee's dad's ashes, she surmised.

"I'd like to go welcome them," Louisa said, nodding to the unfamiliar faces on the other side of the aisle.

Marcella wheeled Louisa over to the group, all of whom sat stiffly looking straight ahead, not even chatting amongst themselves. Louisa put them at ease with a warm smile and a greeting. They couldn't hear her, so Marcella relayed her words. They were some of Russ's sisters and brothers, along with their spouses.

Russ came up the aisle with Pastor Atkinson.

He reached over the first row of chairs and extended his hand to the men. The women came around and hugged him.

"Thanks for coming," he said. "Are Mom and Dad coming?"

The women exchanged glances.

One of the men shrugged.

Russ sighed. "I'm glad you came."

"We wouldn't miss it," one of his sisters said.

Marcella left them to work out their family conflict in private, driving Louisa back to her spot. The chairs were beginning to fill up, particularly on their side. Aimee had told people they weren't doing his-and-her-sides, but people are creatures of habit.

Drew crossed in front of Marcella and took the seat next

to her. He'd cleaned up nicely and was wearing a sport jacket. Russ and the pastor took their positions. Marcella checked her phone. It was time for the wedding to start. Russ lifted his head, and his eyes brightened. Marcella turned to see if Aimee was coming, but it was a full-size Ford van pulling into the driveway.

Senja came out from the shed and motioned, signaling to begin the ceremony.

"Hold on." Russ held up a hand.

A slender man and a matronly, gray-haired woman got out of the van. She held the man's arm and scurried across the lawn in her ankle-length skirt as the man took long steps.

Russ wiped a tear from his eye.

The man led the woman toward the trellis, but she pulled him to the side. They came around and sat in the front row. The couple must be his parents. Marcella was glad they'd decided to attend. It was important to have family with you on such a momentous occasion. If she ever got married, her mom wouldn't be a part of the special day, Marcella thought sadly. She glanced at Drew and then quickly looked away. She wondered for a moment if she should open herself to the possibility of something more than friendship with him.

Russ nodded to the DJ to play the processional song.

Danny escorted Beth up the aisle in her form-fitting chocolate brown dress. Marcella suspected it was a bit tighter than Beth had planned, but she looked great. The pregnancy helped fill out her otherwise thin frame.

"Should I drive you around to the front so you can see Aimee walk up?" Marcella whispered in Louisa's ear.

Louisa shook her head slightly.

Danny and Beth took their places, and the wedding march began to play. Sophia stood and the other attendees followed her lead. Aimee made her slow march, holding a bouquet of orange Gerbera daisies.

Pastor Atkinson said a few nice words about marriage. It was more than friendship. More than an exchange of promises. It was a covenant. Not a contract, but a commitment to give one's life to the other.

As the pastor finished his remarks, Marcella felt Drew's gaze. She turned to him, and he smiled at her.

Aimee and Russ exchanged vows and rings. They lit a unity candle while a song played. A puffy cloud rolled in front of the sun, and Marcella felt a chill. She checked Louisa's blanket. She sat back and rubbed her forearms, warming them with friction. Drew took off his jacket and offered it to her. She put it on and then leaned into him for additional warmth as he laid his arm over her shoulder. He was a good friend.

"And it's my pleasure to be the first to introduce Russ and Aimee Saarinen," the pastor said, concluding the ceremony. He invited everybody to join the newlyweds in the tent for a reception.

After filling two plates in the buffet line, Marcella set them down in front of Louisa at a table. "I'll get us drinks," she said.

Louisa dropped her face and grimaced. She lifted her head again, exhaling, and then said, "*Voi, paska.*" It wasn't like Louisa to curse, not even in Finnish.

"What's wrong?" Marcella leaned in so she could understand Louisa's soft, slurred speech.

"I need to *paska*. Sit on the toilet." Tears formed on her lower eyelids. "I'd hoped to be able to make it through the day without being such a burden. I should go back to Ridgeview."

"Can't you just go here?" Marcella rested a hand on Louisa's shoulder. "I'll help."

"No. No." Louisa shook her head. "My wheelchair won't fit in the bathroom. Could you call the transport driver?" A look of panic crossed her face and she clenched her jaw and breathed deeply. "I'm sorry, dear. I am going to need your help. I don't think I'll make it back to Ridgeview."

"I don't mind." Marcella said softly. "I helped my mom." She bent to release the transmission.

She snagged Drew from where he waited in the buffet line,

and he pushed the wheelchair across the bumpy lawn.

Louisa was right. The wheelchair wouldn't fit in the bathroom. "Good thing he's been lifting weights. This is easy for him." Marcella tried to lighten the mood as Drew lifted Louisa from the wheelchair.

The pair worked together and helped Louisa. They tried to preserve her privacy, but with the circumstances there wasn't much that could be done.

"This is the humiliating part of the disease—not being able to take care of basic needs. And such an unpleasant task. I'm sorry," Louisa said as Drew carried her back to her chair.

"Let's call it love." He positioned her in the wheelchair. "God's love."

Marcella's heart swelled at his words. She wasn't sure how or if God figured into it all, but if she were to someday consider a relationship, she'd want it to be with a guy like Drew.

"You're a bit cold." He tucked the afghan back around Louisa. "I'll go get your plates and bring them in here."

Marcella had chosen foods she hoped would be easy for Louisa to swallow—*riisipuuroa,* pasta salad. She lifted a spoonful of the rice dish to Louisa's mouth.

"It's nice to be here," Louisa said after swallowing a bite. "I'm thankful I have the chance to set foot in my house again." She looked down at her feet, resting on the footrests of the chair, and chuckled. "Or set my wheels in it anyway."

# Chapter 22

$D$rew pulled into the parking lot of the Copper Country Co-op. "Ready, Freddy?"

AJ rolled his eyes, but Drew had a sense that his son enjoyed the shtick. They got out of the truck and headed for the deli.

Drew surveyed the various items in the glass case. "Meatloaf?" he asked AJ.

The turkey meatloaf made with wild rice seemed like a real meal—the kind his mother made when he was a kid. The kind of meal Kristine had made. He and AJ ate too many meals of mac and cheese. Too many hot dogs and frozen pizzas.

AJ shrugged. Drew took that as agreement and ordered two pieces.

"Can we get those?" AJ pointed to the dessert case.

"Brownies? I don't know."

"They're organic," AJ said. "Marcella said that's healthy."

"Okay. Why not?"

AJ selected two large brownies and dropped them in a bag.

"Let's get some tater tots and fresh green beans." Drew led the way first to the frozen foods section. He felt good about this balanced meal. Marcella would be proud. He found himself smiling at that thought. Maybe, if she were around, he'd invite her to join them. He circled back to the deli to order another piece of meatloaf for her. He could always take it for his lunch if she wasn't home.

In the produce section, Drew held open a plastic bag as AJ scooped green beans into it.

"How are you? How are you?" An elderly woman approached them, focusing her gaze on AJ.

AJ looked to his dad for direction on how to respond.

"We're well," Drew said, tying the bag shut. "How are you?" He'd never met the lady, but this was Copper Island. Friendly folks everywhere.

"Do you wanna come pick apples?"

AJ's eyes widened.

"Apples," she barked.

Drew put his hand on AJ's shoulder. "We can buy apples here. Thank you."

"I need my apples picked. You're good at shimmying up the tree. A dollar a bushel. I'll pay fifty cents a bushel."

"You want to hire him?"

The woman looked at Drew and cocked her head to the side. "Yes. Who are you?"

"I'm Drew Smith."

"Maribel Myers." She turned her focus back to AJ. "How 'bout it?"

"I kind of have a lot of homework."

"Maybe another time." Drew smiled politely. Putting himself between his son and the woman, he ushered AJ toward the checkout.

The woman flapped her hand. "All right, Danny, suit yourself."

Drew didn't acknowledge her, hoping his son hadn't heard. He couldn't handle that conversation.

When they were in the truck, AJ asked, "Why did that lady call me Danny, Dad?"

"Maybe she was calling me Danny. She seems like a very confused woman." Drew turned on the radio.

Between Mak, Patty, and now random strangers, this wasn't going anywhere good. AJ was a smart kid. As much as he loved the natural beauty and the small-town culture of the area, it was only a matter of time before things blew up.

He should look online for jobs near his parents. He dreaded the thought of relocating again. Another school change for AJ. But it was probably the right thing to do.

He pulled into the driveway and, seeing Marcella's vehicle, felt a sense of anticipation. Unless she was out on her bike, she was home.

He shot her a text. *Are you home? Do you want to come eat dinner with us?*

His phone dinged as he unloaded the groceries. *I'd love to. Should I come down and help you cook?*

He couldn't keep the smile from his face. *Sure. Five minutes.*

He poked his head in AJ's room. "AJ, let's pick up this place a little." He threw an empty laundry basket onto the middle of the floor. "Marcella's going to come have dinner with us."

"Cool." AJ set down his iPad.

"Pick up your clothes and put the dirty towels in the basket, then clean up the bathroom." Drew put coats and shoes into the closet and wiped crumbs off the table and counter. He warmed the meatloaf in the microwave and preheated the oven to cook the tater tots.

There was a knock at the door. He opened it. She looked beautiful as always, even in jeans and a T-shirt.

She raised a glass pan covered in tinfoil. "Dessert. I made an apple crisp earlier."

"Cool," he said, realizing he was repeating his son. Why had he become inarticulate in her presence? "That smells great. Come on in."

She set the dessert on the counter. "What can I help with?"

"You can help snap green beans. The meatloaf's already done." He probably should set realistic expectations. "I picked it up from the Co-op deli."

He put the tater tots on a sheet in the oven and joined her

at the counter to work on the green beans. "I'm trying to be a good rolemodel by eating my veggies." He wrinkled his nose.

"You're not a fan of green beans?"

He shrugged.

"Can I cook them for you?"

"Sure."

She breezed out of the kitchen and returned shortly holding a clump of fresh garlic and a bottle of soy sauce."

"AJ, come set the table," he called.

AJ set the table while he talked up a storm.

"How's school going?" Marcella asked.

"Great. I got an *A* on my science project." He enthusiastically described the project he'd done in which he tested how much weight it took to sink a block into sand, varying the moisture content.

"So what'd you learn?"

"Buildings that are in wet areas need a strong foundation or they'll sink. Grandpa said there used to be a building really close to the canal. It didn't have a strong enough foundation, so it sank a little bit each year and they had to tear it down."

Marcella sautéed the green beans with oil and garlic and sprinkled in some soy sauce. "The green beans are ready," she announced. "Where's the meatloaf?"

"In the microwave." When Drew grabbed the plate, he could already tell the meatloaf had cooled. He touched the edge of the piece. He probably should've waited to heat it up. "This is going to need another minute."

As they sat to eat, a calm descended over Drew. It was as if things were just the way they should be. He grabbed Marcella's and AJ's hands and asked a blessing on their meal. A thought struck him, distracting him from his prayer.

He said a quick amen and then asked Marcella, "What are you doing for Thanksgiving? Do you want to come downstate with us to my parents'?"

Her mouth dropped open, "Uh." She had that deer-caught-in-the-headlights look.

"We're friends," he said preemptively. "This is what friends do." He had read that people who lose a parent have a hard time trusting and forming connections. Maybe that was her hang-up. "If I had a single buddy whose father had just moved out of town, I'd ask him. But you're my buddy."

"My buddy, too," AJ said. He took a bite of the green beans. "These are good."

"I'm glad you like them." Marcella looked relieved, as if she was glad for the change in subject.

"Are you going to come with us for Thanksgiving?" AJ asked.

"I'll think about it." She looked down at her dinner plate before lifting her chin. "Thanks for the invitation."

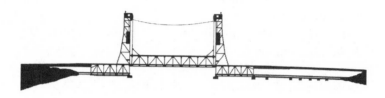

# Chapter 23

*M*arcella chopped the cabbage she'd use to make sauerkraut. Her phone beeped, and she put down the knife to check the text message. Her dad.

*Need you to go through the attic and see what you want. We have had a second showing and it sounds like an offer may be coming in on the lake house. Nothing on the duplex yet. I'm in Madison so call Kandy.*

She'd been putting it off long enough. She needed to arrange a time to go home. *Home.* That's how she still thought of it. She felt a fleeting sense of loss. She'd no longer be able to visit her childhood home.

She dialed Kandy's cell phone number.

Excitement rang in Kandy's voice when she greeted Marcella. "Did your dad tell you we found a condo to rent in downtown Madison while we look for our dream home?"

"Congratulations." No, her dad hadn't told her, but that was par for the course. Marcella made arrangements to stop by after dinner.

On her way out the door that evening, she grabbed a laundry basket. If Kandy hadn't made use of all the apples, she'd pick some and make sauce. Or perhaps she'd add apple to a batch of sauerkraut, with red cabbage and a hint of cloves. That would have a warm fall flavor. There was nothing more fun than jazzing up sauerkraut.

She savored the drive down the country road flanked by birch, cedar, and hemlock. Evening light filtered through the leaves. The sun was setting over the lake as she pulled up to the log house. In the dusk, she could see there were still apples on the tree—plenty for apple sauce. She retrieved her basket and picked the ones within reach, almost filling the basket. She looked at the tree, still full of apples near the top. She'd hate for them to end up as deer food on the ground. They'd reached perfection, crunchy sweetness with a tangy bite. She'd have to come back another time and use the apple picker to reach the high ones. The sauce she'd make with this one basket would carry her well into the winter, but with more she'd be able to share with her friends and neighbors. She thought of her young neighbor. AJ seemed so interested in gardening. Perhaps she'd teach him to make and can applesauce, like her mom taught her.

Marcella plastered a smile on her face and made her way to the house.

"Come in." Kandy grabbed her hand and pulled her in the door. "Let me show you pictures of the condo." She led Marcella to the kitchen island, where she pulled them up on the laptop. She flipped through pictures of the unit. Granite counters, stainless appliances, a gas fireplace in the living room, a balcony overlooking the lake.

"Nice," Marcella smiled politely. It did look like a lovely unit for a busy downtown area, and it was near the lake, though the lake was separated from the condo by two lanes of traffic. Not her cup of tea, and she was surprised her dad wanted to give up his quiet, woodsy location for such a busy area.

"God has been opening doors for us. We found this place as a sublease from one of your dad's coworkers. If we get a good price for the house and the rentals, we might buy a unit in the building, but I'm glad we'll get to see what it's like to live there before we buy. When you come to visit we can bike around the lake."

Marcella bit back a grimace. Kandy had said *when* rather than *if* she came to visit. She wanted to maintain a relationship with her dad, but with their move, it seemed like it would be harder to do that without embracing Kandy, and she wasn't sure how much of the perkiness she could stomach. She'd biked with Kandy once, and once was enough.

Kandy continued, "This unit has two bedrooms. If we buy, we'll want one with three bedrooms so there'll be a place for guests and an office. It's really luxurious. The condo even has a fitness center downstairs."

Marcella kept the smile on her face as she nodded. "Great."

Kandy didn't seem to realize that in selling the rentals to purchase a luxurious condo, they'd be putting Marcella out of her home. She'd made the apartment into a cozy nest for herself for the last decade. She hadn't had many choices when she was seventeen. It was either live with her dad and Kandy or in the upper flat her dad owned. She hadn't necessarily been planning on being there forever, but now she was being pushed out of her nest. It was time to figure out where she really wanted to be—to intentionally choose her life path.

Kandy led the way up to the attic where boxes were stacked along one wall. "Let's get started." Kandy pulled a box off a stack and set it on the middle of the floor. She opened it up and pulled out a doll. "Toys," she announced.

"Oh, my Cabbage Patch doll." Marcella reached for the doll. "Her name's Mindy." Marcella examined her once-beloved friend, who was now bedraggled. There was pen on the doll's face. As a young child, Marcella had tried to draw hearts on Mindy's cheeks and hadn't quite succeeded. Yarn hair, which had once been in ponytails, hung oddly, leaving bald gaps on the doll's head. "I didn't know my mom saved so much stuff. I thought it had gone to Goodwill."

"I never got around to sorting through what's up here." Kandy pulled another box down and opened it up. "A dress." She held the ivory dress in front of her and struck a pose.

Marcella grimaced and bit her tongue. She recognized

her mom's dress from wedding pictures. It seemed wrong for Kandy to treat it like a thrift store find. Some things were sacred. Of course, Kandy didn't know it was a wedding dress. The vintage dress had a simple A-line skirt with antique lace around the bottom hem.

Kandy held it out. "You should try it on. It's your style—kind of Bohemian."

Marcella took the dress, relieved she had possession of it. She fingered the lace. It was beautiful. *Maybe someday.* An image of Drew popped in her mind, but she blinked it away. She wouldn't even go there. "I'll put both of those boxes in a pile that I'll keep."

Kandy had moved on to the third box. "Oh, dishes. I put these up here when your dad and I got the set we registered for."

Marcella opened the dishes box to find her mom's vintage Franciscan dinnerware with a hand-painted apple pattern. "I'd love these." They were the plates her family had used on holidays and special occasions. She added the box to her keep pile. So much for minimalism. She'd have to rent a storage unit or turn her extra bedroom into a storage area. She hated to do that. It would interfere with the open flow of energy she liked to maintain in her home. She battled clutter so the small space would be welcoming and beautiful—a place to relax and recharge so she'd have plenty to give to her clients. She looked at the tall stack of boxes. Each item she took with her would need to find a spot. That would be difficult in her small flat, and she'd likely need to move soon anyhow. She put her old Cabbage Patch doll in the box with the wedding dress. She looked through the rest of the toys in the box. Nothing as special as her beloved doll, but she still felt a pang of regret as she moved the rest of the toys to a donate pile.

Kandy opened boxes. Marcella let go of some things easily. Old coats. A Crock-Pot—she already had one. Curtains. A bedspread. Tax papers from twenty years ago. These her dad could burn in the sauna stove. A box of books including her old Bibles. She opened her old *Teen Study Bible* and read the personalized dedication. *To Marcella on your 14th Birthday! Love, Mom and Dad.* She'd keep that box. Baby clothes. Her mom had saved her baby clothes? She sorted through them, recognizing some from photos. She selected a navy blue, polka-dotted dress she had worn as a toddler and added it to her keep pile. The rest she'd part with. Let someone else make use of them.

Kandy opened another box and pawed through it. "Papers and photos," she announced. Marcella set a box of *National Geographic* magazines in the trash pile. Her mom had kept such things to make collages and paper beads. She went to examine the box Kandy had opened. Kandy handed her a photo of Mom pushing her on a swing under the apple tree. Marcella wore the polka-dotted dress. She looked at the back of the photo. Her Mom's handwriting—*Marcella, age 2.* Tears rose to her eyes. She quickly flipped through the rest of the box. More photos. A certificate from Ridgeview Nursing Home commemorating Mom's five years of service.

Cards and letters addressed to her mom. She flipped through them, recognizing her dad's handwriting on a number of them. Love letters? Those belonged to her dad, but she hated the thought of him discarding them.

One card was addressed to her in her mom's handwriting. Wow. She flipped the envelope over and stared at the unbroken seal. Was it a birthday card she'd never opened? This she'd open in the privacy of her own home. She sat, unmoving, absorbing the love that still reached her from the other side. Memories of her childhood flitted through her mind. A lump rose in her throat.

"Are you okay?" Kandy's voice brought her back to the present.

"I'll take these boxes and go home," she told Kandy. "I'll have to come back another day."

At home, she washed the dust from a Franciscan Apple teacup while water warmed on the stove. She made a cup of tea and sat at the table with the letter.

Dear Marcella,

My greatest sorrow in dying is that I'm leaving when you're so young. I wish I could be there to watch you become an adult. Being your mother has been my greatest delight in life—watching you become who you are with your free spirit, your compassion, your depth, and tenderness. You have been pure grace to me, even when you were five and threw a tantrum for two hours after Dad shot a squirrel. Do you remember that? I thought they were cute too, even though they made a huge mess in the upstairs of the garage.

You took on so much as you cared for me through this illness—more than any teenager should have to deal with. I thank you for that and pray it wasn't too much for you, that you will heal, and that this loss doesn't crush your spirit. I pray you'll find peace and joy.

And someday when the right guy comes along—how I wish I could be there—take a chance on love and see where it leads.

With all my love,

Mom

Tears streamed down her face and she lay her head on the table. Sobs racked her body. It had been thirteen years. Although her mom was often in her thoughts, time had dulled the sense of pain. She hadn't cried this hard in years, though she always shed tears on the anniversary of Mom's passing.

She wasn't sure how long she sat there before a knock on her door jolted her to the present. She shuffled to the door and opened it halfway. "Hi, do you need something?" she asked her tenant.

Drew glanced away. "I was helping AJ get to bed and I heard you crying. I came up as soon as he fell asleep. I wanted to check and see if you were okay."

"Thanks." Marcella wiped her cheeks with her sleeve. "I'm fine." She opened the door the rest of the way.

He continued standing there.

"Do you want to come in?" She stepped aside.

"Sure. If we leave the doors open, I'll be able to hear if AJ wakes up."

Marcella rinsed a second cup from her mother's collection. She poured Drew a cup of tea. "Louisa says there's a reason God made tears." The words came unbidden. "I'm not sure who or what God is, or how or if God works, but today I got a letter from my mom and..." Marcella found herself smiling, remembering her mother's words. *A chance on love.* She looked down at the table and traced the wood grain with her finger and then looked up to meet his gaze. "I'd like to spend Thanksgiving with your family."

# *Chapter 24*

*D*rew exchanged a glance with Marcella. She laughed and shook her head as AJ droned on, "Thirty-six bottles of beer on the wall, thirty-six bottles of beer, take one down, pass it around, thirty-five bottles of beer on the wall."

Drew figured AJ had been trying to get a reaction when he started the song, but instead both Drew and Marcella joined in. Drew petered out after a dozen bottles, and Marcella lasted another dozen or so, but AJ was still going strong. Although it was getting annoying, at least AJ wasn't on his iPad, and Drew considered that a parenting victory. But rather than anything he'd done, it was more likely due to Marcella and the energy she brought to the ride. Instead of AJ immediately pulling out his iPad, they'd played the alphabet game and twenty questions for the first couple hours.

Since Marcella had agreed to come downstate when her emotions were running high, Drew thought at any point she might cancel. His heart sank one evening when she told him her dad and Kandy had invited her to Madison for Thanksgiving. But then she said she was glad to have a good excuse not to go.

Mom and Dad were enthused he was bringing a friend, always game for company. What he left out was that his friend happened to be a woman. He wasn't prepared for the inquisition, and he knew his parents would be gracious in front of Marcella. He sneaked a peek at her in the passenger seat. Her silky, blonde hair rested on one shoulder as she reclined back. She joined AJ in song for the countdown from ten bottles of beer, her voice rich and melodious.

"Whew," Marcella said when they'd finished. "We did it."

AJ reached a hand forward. "High five."

Marcella slapped his palm.

"Ninety-nine bottles of beer on the wall," AJ sang again.

"No!" Drew and Marcella yelled in unison.

AJ laughed.

Drew looked back at him in the rearview mirror. His son seemed happy, even upbeat, lately. A couple weeks prior, for the first time since his mother died, he had invited a friend over from school. Drew's pastor in Wausau had told him kids are resilient and AJ would be okay. He was starting to believe that was true, but he wasn't sure it would've happened without Marcella. She was good for him. She was good for both of them. She was a fellow traveler in grief, having lost her mom at a young age. She was just…

He glanced at her again, searching for the right word for his thoughts, wishing he could grab her hand. It was hard to describe his gratitude for her friendship. He shot her a smile, and her face lit up with one in return. She was sunshine.

Drew turned on the radio before AJ could suggest another game. He pressed seek until he came to a light rock station. AJ pulled out his iPad, but it wasn't long before his head drooped to one side. They'd woken early to get on the road, hoping to arrive before dinnertime.

"And he's out," Drew said softly. "Before we even reached the Mighty Mac. We'll have to wake him if he's still sleeping by then."

Marcella unbuckled and reached back to rescue his tablet so it wouldn't end up on the floor.

"So tell me about your parents," she said when she'd buckled back in.

"They're great," he said. "They're older. They adopted me when they were in their forties, so they're in their seventies now. My dad's seventy-eight." Hard to believe. They'd both really aged in the last decade, since AJ was born. "It's hard to see them get old," he added, and immediately wished he could take back the words. "I'm sorry. That was a stupid thing to say. I know I'm lucky to have the opportunity."

"It's okay," she said, sounding like she meant it. "How's their health?"

"My dad had a hip replacement last year and seemed to bounce back from that pretty quickly. My mom's doing well. They're both slowing down, but they still manage to head south every winter." That was another reason why he'd looked for a job near Patty and Ron, rather than near his parents.

Drew turned off the radio so he could focus on their conversation. They talked about their upbringings and adult lives. They were both only children. Neither had close connections to extended family. They both loved the outdoors. Marcella opened up more than she ever had, and Drew felt their connection deepen. The next hour and a half flew by.

As they passed through St. Ignace, Drew shook AJ's ankle. "Wake up, buddy. We're almost to the Mighty Mac."

Drew paid the four-dollar toll and continued onto the causeway. He looked back at his son.

AJ had his neck craned to his left. "There's Mackinac Island."

"I went there once with Granny and Pops when I was a kid." He'd been about AJ's age when they had vacationed on the island. It had been fun to explore, biking around.

"I brought my candy bars with me so I can sell some to Granny and Pops." AJ dug in his backpack and passed the fundraising box up front. "Do you want to buy one?"

"I'll buy ten," Marcella said.

"I've got a box on my desk at work." Drew thumped his gut. "I think I've bought more than my co-workers."

With the first support tower still in view, AJ squirmed in his seat. "Can I move over so I can look down?"

"Okay," Drew agreed.

Marcella glanced back. "Do it quickly so you can get buckled back in. The wind makes me nervous."

AJ scooted over and rebuckled.

"Five miles. I think this is the longest suspension bridge in the United States," Drew said, taking in the view of the waterway between Lakes Michigan and Huron.

"In the western hemisphere," AJ corrected. "We learned that in school."

When they neared the end of the bridge, water gave way to land on either side.

"Hey, Dad," AJ said. "Who lives here? Who lives below the bridge?"

"Don't say it."

"Trolls." He cackled.

"Did you learn that in school, too?"

AJ nodded.

"That's the problem with a Yooper education." Drew was delighted his son was happy, even at the expense of a downstate joke.

"I'm a real Yooper," AJ told Marcella. "I was born in Quincy."

"Me, too," she said, reaching back to give him a fist bump. He grinned.

Drew picked up speed as they continued down I-75.

"This is the song that never ends," AJ sang. "It goes on and on, my friends. Some people started singing it not knowing what it was. And they'll continue singing it forever just because—"

Drew and Marcella exchanged a look and then joined in. "—this is the song that never ends."

"So this was your home growing up?" Marcella asked as they pulled into the concrete semi-circle drive of the large, brick colonial located in a quiet cul-de-sac with large lawns and mature trees.

Drew shut off the truck. "Yup. They talk about downsizing, but I don't think it's going to happen. They have too much stuff."

"It's nice." Though she preferred natural beauty, there was something about the affluent neighborhood's neat landscaping and manicured lawns that appealed to her inner gardener.

"I'm going to the basement to play pool." AJ grabbed his backpack and climbed out.

"Hug your grandparents first."

AJ headed for the house.

Marcella slowly collected her purse and tote as Drew threw his computer bag over one shoulder and got out of the truck.

"I'll grab our bags." He circled around to the back of the truck and returned with his duffel and her small rolling suitcase. "Ready?" he asked.

"Okay." Her voice squeaked as she said it. Oh, why had she come? She was meeting his parents, and they weren't even dating.

He squeezed her shoulder. "Come on, my friend."

They were almost to the front door of the stately house when a slim, gray-haired woman in khaki pants and a wool sweater bustled out. "I'm Cynthia Smith," she said, extending a hand. "I'm so glad you could join us." Her eyes twinkled, and she wrapped her son in a hug. "And you did not tell us you were bringing a woman."

"You didn't know I was coming?" Marcella looked at Drew, aghast.

"Oh, we're delighted to have you." Cynthia said reassuringly, "And yes, Drew said he was bringing a friend, but he was very evasive as to who was accompanying him, and I don't pry." She looked at Drew with a raised eyebrow.

"Come with me, dear." She linked elbows with Marcella and led the way to the house with Drew following behind.

The foyer stretched to the second level of the home, its walls dotted with eclectic artwork. A crystal chandelier hung overhead, and a staircase led up to the open second floor framed by a wooden banister. Everything was carpeted with a light purple, plush pile, perhaps a little dated from the eighties, but obviously elegant and expensive in its day. Marcella slipped off her shoes and followed Drew's lead, hanging her coat on a brass antique coat rack.

Cynthia led the way into the kitchen. "Can I get you something to drink?" she asked. "A glass of wine? Lemonade? Cranberry juice?" Cynthia turned a knob on the stove.

"Lemonade would be great," Marcella said. "Can I help you with anything?"

Cynthia shook her head. "I have broccoli steaming, and the potatoes and ham are warming in the oven." She took glasses from the cupboard and filled them with ice from the dispenser on the refrigerator. She set the glasses on an elevated counter separating the kitchen and dining room. "Have a seat."

"Thanks, Mom, but we've been sitting all day." Drew twisted, stretching his back.

"I'm assuming you'd like lemonade, too?" she asked Drew.

He nodded, and she retrieved a pitcher of lemonade from the refrigerator.

Marcella sipped her beverage, looking around. Antique, hand-crank eggbeaters hung on one wall in the breakfast nook. On the other side of the nook and next to the living room there was a large glass cabinet, or maybe—

"How cool is that?" She moved closer to take a look. It was an old phone booth.

"That's my dad's," Drew came alongside her. "He's into antiques."

She peered in through the glass doors where an antique phone hung on the wall. The phone had three coin slots labeled *25, 10,* and *5.* Below that there were two bells and a strike arm between them. The handset hung off to the left of the number dial. "Does it work?"

Cynthia approached, a glass of wine in hand. "It was just a showpiece for many years. When Andrew left for college, Rick retired and had more time to tinker. He rewired it, so it works now."

"How fun!"

"Go ahead. Step in if you want," Cynthia encouraged her. "You can even call someone. You won't even need coins. Do you know how to use a rotary dial?"

"I should be able to figure it out." Marcella set her lemonade on the counter and stepped into the booth. A quirky surprise in a house she found a bit intimidating. She picked up the handset and heard a dial tone. So cool. She hesitated. Cynthia said she could call someone, but whom? She usually texted her friends. Come to think of it, she didn't know any friends' numbers by heart—only her dad's. He'd probably like to know she made it safely downstate. She dialed his number and took a seat on the wooden bench.

Dad sounded happy to hear from her. He listened to her enthusiastic description of the phone booth that had prompted her call. After a few minutes of chit-chat, she wished him a happy Thanksgiving, said good-bye, and hung up the phone.

"That's cool," she said, stepping out.

The mood in the room had drastically changed. Drew sat at the table, his laptop in front of him, his head resting in his hands. Cynthia sat next to him, her lips drawn tight as she stared at the computer screen.

"What's wrong?" Marcella asked, hanging back.

"I got the results," Drew said flatly. "I got an email from the ancestry testing company that my results were in, so I logged on and…" He sounded as if he were fighting back tears.

"You know what he's talking about?" Cynthia looked at Marcella questioningly.

She nodded and moved toward Drew. She laid a hand on his shoulder. "I'm sorry."

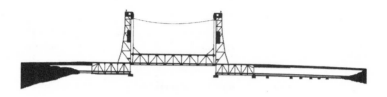

# Chapter 25

Drew couldn't believe it. Well, he could, but he didn't want to. He'd been hoping, praying, that the DNA test would assuage his fear. But it had confirmed what he already knew in his gut. There was no denying it. AJ was not his biological son.

He sat in silence with the two women who were the biggest supporters in his life at the moment. He glanced at his mom. She reached over and squeezed his arm. He cocked his head toward Marcella, who was gently massaging his shoulder. He felt a tightness in his chest.

Mom rotated the computer screen toward her. "So AJ's almost half Scandinavian, and the rest is Finnish except for 3% from the Iberian Peninsula." She frowned. "Where's the Iberian Peninsula?"

When no one replied, she tapped on the mouse. "Hmmm. Spain and Portugal."

"And I'm not any of those." Drew retrieved his computer and clicked on his results. "32% Ireland/Scotland/Wales, 21% Europe West, and 18% Great Britain."

Mom smiled. "Ireland. So that's where your red hair comes from. We have that in common. My great-grandmother was Irish." She frowned. "How accurate are these tests?"

Drew shrugged. "They say DNA doesn't lie, and AJ doesn't come up as one of my family matches." He clicked on the matches link. "Just a bunch of possible fourth to sixth cousins."

Drew's dad entered the room with AJ trailing behind. Drew snapped the computer shut. He stared at his son, seeing Danny with bits of Kristine.

"The apple doesn't fall far from the old block." Dad snorted a laugh, the way he always did when he found an opportunity to mix metaphors. "This grandson of mine beat me at pool." He looked at Marcella, doing a double take. "You're a woman."

Marcella laughed, releasing some of the tension in the room.

"Andrew didn't say his friend was a girlfriend."

"I'm a friend and a girl." Marcella extended her hand. "I'm Marcella."

"Glad you could make it." Dad gently clasped the fingers of her hand. "I'm delighted to make the acquaintance of my son's beautiful, mystery friend." He bowed. "I'm Rick." Addressing AJ, he asked, "This is the friend you were telling me about?"

AJ nodded.

"Junior was telling me about biking with his friend Marcella, but I imagined you were his age."

Marcella shrugged, smiling.

Dad came around Drew and placed both hands on his shoulders. "Glad to see you, son. You had to bring work home with you?"

His mom rose from the table. "We'll talk later." She headed to the kitchen, where she set food on the island along with thick ceramic plates, a basket of silverware, pitchers of lemonade and cranberry juice, and a bottle of wine.

Dad kept the conversation going, asking AJ questions about school and sharing stories about his latest finds at estate sales. Neither seemed to notice the somber mood of the others at dinner.

After dinner, Marcella challenged Rick and AJ to a game of pool in the basement. Drew had the feeling she'd suggested it to give him space to process.

AJ led the way. "I'm going to beat you again, Pops."

"Don't count your chickens before they cross the road." Dad chortled as he started down the basement steps. Marcella followed behind them.

Drew and his mom cleaned up the kitchen. When the food was put away and the dishwasher was running, they sat at the table and he again opened his laptop to the ancestry site.

"So you have family connections on the website." His mom sounded anxious. "I knew this day might come. You might find your birth mom and dad and a whole new family and—" His mom's voice caught. "This might sound silly, but I don't want you to forget all about us."

"That's not going to happen." Drew studied her face.

She looked as distraught as he felt, and he realized the parallel nature of their concerns. She was feeling that same sort of irrational, frantic desperation about him as he was about AJ.

"You'll always be my mom." He reached over and squeezed her shoulder. Maybe sometime he'd search for his birth parents, start combing through the fourth cousins on the DNA website and see if there was a path somewhere to his roots, but it might be better to leave well enough alone.

"You don't want to find your birth parents?"

"I don't know. My birth mom was a kid when she had me. Giving me up for adoption was the best thing for me." As he said this, he realized Kristine was basically a kid when she'd gotten pregnant, barely eighteen. Danny was a kid, too. "I'm not interested in looking for my birth family, not now anyway. We have enough drama in our lives at the moment."

Relief flooded his mom's face. "It's okay if you want to."

"Maybe someday. But right now, we need to focus on AJ."

She nodded slowly. "Do you know who his bio-father is?"

"Yeah."

Her brow wrinkled, and she drummed her fingers on the table. "He wouldn't have legal rights. Would he?" Her voice was anxious.

"I don't know. I had an initial meeting with a lawyer but didn't get beyond that. I'm not sure I want to know."

"I see." She nodded. "It may be best to leave well enough alone."

Marcella snuggled under the down comforter on the queen-sized bed in what they called Grandma's room. Apparently, Cynthia's mother had lived with them for several years when Drew was a boy. Probably what gave him such empathy in dealing with Louisa.

Though the pillow top bed was luxurious, she had trouble falling asleep. First on her mind was her concern for Drew. She had never seen him so off-kilter. No wonder. She tried to put herself in his shoes and shuddered. There were too many things that could go wrong in the world, too many ways to lose someone you loved. It was one reason she'd never have kids. How could people bear to bring innocent little children into such a pain-filled world?

She stretched out on the bed, looking up at the painting above the dresser. Rick had told her he was eighty percent certain it was a Renoir—a pond, flowers, greenery. He'd bought it at an auction. He was afraid to have it authenticated in case it was stolen. He didn't need the money, and he enjoyed the painting too much to risk it. After he told her about the possible Renoir, Cynthia said with a wink that they had a Monet in their room.

After tossing and turning, she got up and went downstairs to the kitchen to get a drink of water. As she passed by the living room, she saw that Drew was up, too, on the couch in front of a gas fireplace.

"Hi, my friend," she said, coming alongside him.

"Hey." He stared at the fire.

She hesitated. "Is it okay if I join you?"

He shrugged. Then he patted the cushion next to his. "Yeah. Sit down."

She sat next to him, not speaking.

"I'm sorry I'm being so..." His voice trailed off. He sighed and shifted on the cushion. Leaning back, he stretched his arm behind her across the top of the couch.

She studied his side profile. She hadn't seen this Drew—so somber, so brooding. "Would you rather I leave?"

He put his arm around her, squeezing her shoulder. "No. Thanks for being here. I'm just having a hard time with this."

After a few minutes of silence, he exhaled. "I'm mad at Kristine for not telling me. But what good does that do? She's dead. And what if she had told me? What would I have done? I don't know. I can't imagine my life without him."

"He's a great kid," Marcella said, staring into the fire.

"What are you guys doing?"

Drew was jolted awake, confused, disoriented. Marcella was leaning against his chest, and his arm was around her.

AJ stood in front of them, arms crossed. "You slept here? Together?"

Marcella pulled away from Drew. She rubbed her eyes and pulled her hair out of her face.

"I guess so," Drew said, looking at the clock on the mantle. It was six thirty. His son didn't sleep in, not even on vacation.

"What's going on?" AJ said the words accusingly.

His heart wrenched. *Here it comes.* He'd found out about the ancestry reports. He took a deep breath. He'd have to tell his son he was not his biological father.

"We were just talking and fell asleep," Marcella said. "Nothing's going on."

"So you're not dating?" AJ asked.

"No," Marcella said emphatically. "You don't need to worry about that." She rose, strode across the room, and headed upstairs.

AJ sat on the couch and turned on the TV. Drew felt a twinge of disappointment, along with a boatload of relief. Marcella wasn't softening on her position on dating. But it appeared the ancestry tests weren't on AJ's radar. He seemed more concerned about Drew's relationship with Marcella. He didn't need to hear the crazy news, not yet. Not today. Not on Thanksgiving.

His dad appeared a few minutes later, dressed in flannel pajama pants. "What do you say? Should we make waffles for breakfast?"

AJ was engrossed in a TV program.

"Sure, Dad." Drew turned off the fireplace and walked to the kitchen. He brewed coffee and poured a cup for himself and one for Dad.

"Mom told me what's going on." Dad spooned batter onto his cast iron, heart-shaped waffle press. "You had to know the truth. Now you want to protect AJ from it."

"That's pretty much it."

"That's rough. I'm sorry." He gently leveled the batter with the back of the spoon and closed the top. "I have no idea what you should do, but I have every confidence you'll figure it out," he offered. "You know what they say, 'When the going gets tough, the tough make orange juice.'"

Drew managed a smile. He knew the situation weighed heavily on his father, considering he didn't laugh at his own horrible mixed metaphor. "You mean lemonade."

"No. I mean orange juice. I'm serious. You should make orange juice. I'll make the waffles." He lifted the double-handled press from the stove top, twisted it around its pivot point, and lowered the opposite side onto the burner. "If I've learned anything in life, it's that grief needs action."

That afternoon, they sat in the formal dining room for Thanksgiving dinner. Everyone had pitched in to prepare the meal. Drew's mom made the stuffing and baked the turkey, and his dad made a green bean casserole. He and AJ made the pumpkin pie. Marcella chopped vegetables for the salad. His uncle and aunt joined them along with his cousin who lived nearby, bringing a pasta salad.

"Since you're the most religious one in the family, would you say the blessing?" his dad asked him.

They held hands around the table. He squeezed Marcella's

hand as he thanked God for bringing all of them together. When he said amen, he looked around the table feeling gratitude. He might not have blood ties to any of them, but they were his people, his family.

# Chapter 26

$M$arcella woke to a blanket of white covering her backyard. Time to get out the fat tire bike. It would be a slower commute to work, but she still intended to exercise and enjoy the fresh air. The deep tissue massages she gave her clients provided a good upper-body workout, but her legs would suffer if it weren't for biking. She packed leftover quinoa salad, carrot sticks, and hummus for lunch and checked the time. She'd have time to get to Shear Delight by bike, especially now that the bridge had been lowered for the winter and she could ride across on smooth pavement, rather than the lower metal-grate deck. After pumping up her fat bike tires, she was on her way.

As she was crossing over the bridge, her phone rang and she let it go to voicemail. When she reached the other side, curiosity got the best of her. Who even calls anymore? Even her dad texted her. She stopped to check, half hoping it was Drew. She hadn't seen much of him in the last week since they'd returned from downstate. She pulled the phone from the pocket of her backpack. Not Drew. Her dad.

He'd left a message. "Hi, Marcella. Call me when you have a minute. We have unexpected news."

She had a sinking feeling in her gut. Now what? She

tried to let go of the anxiety, but it gnawed at her as she biked through downtown Douglass. She breathed deep, cold nipping at her cheeks, willing her mind to unwind as her feet circled over the brick-paver road. At work, she wheeled her bike into the storage room and wiped it down before preparing for her day. Two clients in the morning, then a lunch break, followed by three in the afternoon. It would be a full day.

On her lunch break she sat at a café-sized table in the small kitchenette next to the storage room. As she munched carrots dipped in her homemade hummus, she checked her phone. Another voicemail from her dad.

"Just trying to reach you," he said.

And a text from Drew. She felt anticipation as she opened his message. She had to admit that if it weren't for her concern for AJ and his obvious resistance to the idea of his dad dating, she might be open to more than friendship.

*Have a four o'clock meeting and Patty is sick with a stomach bug. Would you be able to watch AJ?*

She'd be happy to help, but she wouldn't be home until four. The last time she'd watched AJ, he'd arrived at the house at three thirty. She texted back.

Her phone dinged a minute later. *He should be fine. He's almost old enough to stay alone but doesn't have a key. I'll call the school and let him know he should go home and wait on the porch until you get there.*

Marcella bit another carrot. She'd feed AJ carrots and hummus for an after-school snack. She was still harvesting them from her garden. She and Mom had found the best way to make them last was to leave them in the ground until needed. Maybe if AJ didn't have too much homework, they'd pull up the rest, because it was early December and soon the ground would be hard and there'd be too much snow. She'd store the rest in a plastic tub of moist sand in the basement. She enjoyed sharing her passion for growing things with AJ, passing along little tidbits of knowledge she'd learned from her mom.

Later that afternoon, she found him waiting on the front porch as planned.

"Hi, AJ."

"Hi." He scowled.

"What's wrong?"

He shrugged.

"Were you waiting long?"

Another shrug.

"Should we make tea?" she asked.

His face brightened. "Okay. It's cold out here."

AJ wasn't a big fan of the hummus, but he ate the carrots and drank the tea. His mood seemed to improve after eating.

"Do you have homework today?"

He nodded, opening his backpack. He removed his candy bar fundraising box, which was looking somewhat bedraggled. "Dad and I went around the neighborhood yesterday and I sold twenty. Do you want to buy any more?" he asked with puppy-dog eyes.

"I'll take five," she said. "I don't need the sugar, but it's for a good cause." She opened her purse and handed him a five-dollar bill. "So what do you have for homework?"

"Math and English." He pulled a book out of his backpack, along with a notebook and pencil. "I need to write a book report."

She dropped her head to read the title. "*Wonder.* I love that book."

While he worked on his homework at the kitchen table, she took her phone to the living room and returned her dad's call.

"Hey, Marcella. I wanted to let you know that we have an accepted offer on the duplex."

"Oh." She felt like she'd been hit in the gut. She'd thought once the snow came, she was safe until summer. People didn't like to move in the winter. She sighed. Her rent would likely go up. Her budget would be tight if her rent was the same as Drew's. She should probably look for a one-bedroom once the college students left for the summer and places opened up.

"The offer's contingent on an inspection, but the new owner would like to occupy the upper flat at closing. It could happen as early as the end of January."

"What?" Marcella wanted to cry. "Then where will I live?" She couldn't believe her dad and Kandy were doing this to her.

"We have a vacancy in the Smelter Street apartment building. I know it's not ideal, but I'll hold it for you in case you want to live there until something better opens up."

"Okay." She sank onto the couch. She dreaded the thought of moving there. The units were ugly—bare bones with industrial carpet. The places took a beating, so Dad didn't put money into them. No private green space.

"Marcella." AJ entered the room holding a textbook.

"Dad, I need to go."

"Okay, we'll talk later."

"Are you okay?" AJ asked.

She straightened on the couch. "Yeah. I'm fine."

"I forgot my protractor at school and I need it for my math homework."

"Oh, bummer. I don't think I have one."

"We have one downstairs. Can you unlock our apartment so I can get it?"

Marcella hesitated. She always gave the required twenty-four-hour notice to tenants if she needed to access the apartment, but in this case, she wouldn't be going in. It was AJ's home, too. "Okay."

They went down the back stairway, and she waited outside while he went in. She looked out the window next to the back door. A sense of loss washed over her. She'd miss her garden. She'd miss her trees. She'd miss her home. She'd miss her neighbors. She'd miss Drew.

After a few minutes of waiting she called into the apartment for AJ. "Are you coming?" Maybe he'd gotten distracted playing on his iPad.

He came to the door with a protractor in one hand and several sheets of paper in the other. He held up the papers. "This doesn't make any sense."

She glanced at the paper with a pie graph. "More math?" She wrinkled her nose. "I may need to read your textbook to help you. It's been a few years." Math hadn't been her strongest subject.

"No. It's not homework. I was looking for the protractor in Dad's desk drawer, and this was on top of it. The results from that ancestry test that Dad and I did."

"Oh." Marcella attempted to keep her voice even. "That's what you're looking at?"

"Yeah. I have Scandinavia, Finland, and Iberian Peninsula, whatever that is." He stumbled over the word *Iberian*. My mom's Finnish—I know that—but my dad has Ireland/ Scotland/Wales, Europe West, and Great Britain. That's what I don't get. How come we're completely different?"

*Oh boy.* She had screwed up big time letting him in when Drew wasn't home. She had been flustered by her dad's phone call and hadn't been thinking. She exhaled. "Why don't you ask your dad about it when he gets home? Let's see if we can get your homework done before he gets here."

# Chapter 27

"Is AJ okay? Are you okay?" Drew grabbed his keys and headed for the door after Marcella called him sobbing and not able form a complete sentence. "Should I call 911?"

"No."

He understood that. She mumbled something else.

"I can't hear you."

"I'll text you," she said.

He stopped in the hallway and spun around. He couldn't leave his computer logged on. He headed back to his office to shut down and grab his laptop.

His phone dinged when he reached his desk.

*I'm so sorry. I wasn't thinking. I let AJ into your apartment to get a protractor. He found the ancestry results and wants to know why you don't have any ethnicities in common. I said he'll have to talk to you about it when you get home.*

He sat back on top of his desk. She let him into the apartment? Not how he wanted this to go down. He felt a twinge of irritation. He'd printed the results with the intention of talking again to the lawyer, but then had rethought the impulse. AJ was turning eleven in February. Only seven years away from adulthood. Perhaps it was best to do nothing unless Danny pushed it, and Drew was hoping he wouldn't. But why hadn't he shredded those papers or taken them with him? He pounded his desk with his fist.

"Are you okay?" Senja called from the next cubicle.

"Yes," he said, more sharply than he intended.

She rounded the cubicle wall and studied him. "You don't look well."

"I need to go home. I'll finish up that report tonight and get it to you before morning."

"No problem. I hope everything's okay."

"I hope so, too."

The ten-minute drive had never seemed so long. As he crossed the bridge, he prayed. *God, help. I have no idea what to say to my son.*

He parked the truck and took the stairs two at a time up to Marcella's apartment. She met him at the door with a tear-stained face.

"It'll be okay," he said.

She bit her lip.

AJ came up behind her. "Marcella's sad because she's going to have to move," he volunteered.

"What? Really? Did the duplex sell?"

She managed a nod. "The new owner wants to occupy the upper flat when they close. It might be as soon as January."

"I'm sorry." He gave her a hug. "We'll help you look for something else, right AJ?"

"Yeah. We'll help you move your stuff."

"Thanks, guys," she said, managing a half smile.

Downstairs, AJ seemed like his normal self as Drew threw frozen chicken nuggets and French fries into the oven. AJ disappeared into his bedroom, and when Drew peeked in, there he was on his iPad. Normal AJ behavior. Maybe he had forgotten about what he saw.

But later, when Drew was cleaning up the kitchen, AJ brought it up. "I saw the results of that ancestry test we did. I have them in my backpack." AJ retrieved the papers and Drew leaned against the kitchen counter, bracing himself.

"Why don't you and I have any of the same ancestry? Was I adopted?"

"No." He gulped. "Do you understand how babies are made?"

AJ shrugged.

"Let's sit down."

They sat at the kitchen table. Drew took a deep breath and gave a brief explanation. He'd been planning on having the talk with him over the summer before middle school, but apparently now was the time.

When he was done, AJ frowned. "But I should still have some of your ancestry, right?"

For a split second, Drew was tempted to lie. *Maybe you just got Mom's.* That might smooth things over now, but down the road it would make them worse.

"Mom and I were married when you were born. I'm your dad on your birth certificate." He looked down at the floor and took a deep breath. "It's likely that your biological father was someone else. Neither Mom nor I made the best decisions about sex when we were young."

AJ studied the floor. "So my whole life's a lie?" he said finally.

"I didn't lie, bud. I didn't know."

"You knew." AJ narrowed his eyes. "You had the test results."

"I didn't know until I got them a couple weeks ago. I was trying to figure out what to do, what would be best for you. I love you, AJ."

"Don't call me that. I'm not your junior. I'm somebody else's kid." Light dawned in his eyes. "Danny was mom's boyfriend." He suddenly looked terrified. "Does he know?"

"I don't know. I think he suspects. I don't think anyone knew for sure."

"Mom knew. She had to know, right?" His face contorted in anger. "I hate her! I hate her!" He ran to his bedroom.

Drew followed him and sat on the bed while AJ sobbed. Drew had never seen him so upset—not when his mom died, not when they moved. It was as if all the sadness and rage of the last two years was finally coming out. If only kids came with a manual. He was at a loss. All he could do as he sat there was to pray, for AJ and for himself. It seemed like an eternity before AJ's cries subsided.

AJ turned his head to look at him. "Are you still going to be my dad?" The look on his face made Drew's heart ache, AJ's eyes asking, "Do you still love me?"

"Always," Drew said, laying a hand on his son's shoulder. "I love you, Andrew."

"Andy," his son corrected. "I'm Andy." He sat up.

Drew pulled him into a hug. "I love you, Andy."

Later that evening, Drew said goodnight to Andy—the new name was going to take some getting used to—before going down to the basement to do laundry. He started a load of towels in the washer, removed the load of whites he'd left in the dryer, and placed the pile on the folding table.

As he matched up and folded socks, he had to look twice to determine which white athletic socks were his and which belonged to his son. There wasn't that much difference between them. He couldn't remember how big his feet had been at that age, but his son's feet seemed large for a ten-year-old. Danny was taller than Drew, so it made sense AJ—that is Andy—had bigger feet.

It would take time to adjust to his son's new name, but he didn't mind it. Drew had always been Andrew at home, but in grade school he was Andy. In eighth grade, Mandi Hansen, the cutest girl in his homeroom class, said she wouldn't go out with him because a couple having rhyming names was too corny. When he said he'd go by Andrew, she agreed to be his girlfriend. The relationship didn't last long, but it sparked the change and he firmly claimed Andrew as his name by the end of the school year. The following fall, within the first few weeks of high school, his buddies shortened it to Drew.

He figured he shouldn't take it too personally that his son wanted to pick his own name. It was probably good for him to feel a sense of control in the whole mess. No one wanted to be called junior forever. Drew had tried not to let on how much finding out they weren't biologically related affected him. He didn't know his bio roots going backward, but having that connection going forward had been more important than he realized. With three socks left, he matched the final pair and threw the unmatched single on top of his pile of folded clothes. How did that happen every time?

He moved to his weight bench and loaded up the barbell with discs. He exhaled as he lifted, then held the bar above his head, feeling his core activate. It felt good. His body wasn't designed to sit at a desk all day. He lowered the bar and stood up and stretched. His back still wasn't great, but the exercise helped.

As he sat for a second set, a zinger shot up his back. He stood and bent over, reaching toward his toes. His hamstrings were tight. He bet another massage would help, but his last massage with Marcella had been awkward, and it would be even more so now that their relationship had deepened beyond attraction. And it would be awkward to get a massage from someone else. It was too small of a town. She'd probably find out and be offended. He'd just have to deal with the discomfort.

# Chapter 28

$M$arcella removed the cheesecloth from the top of the jar of sauerkraut that sat on her kitchen counter. She was eager for her new batch to be ready, having eaten the last of what was in her fridge. It had been six days since she started the fermentation process, and it had been twice as long since she spent time with Drew. Since the day she screwed up, they hadn't said more than hi as they crossed paths in the hallway. She wondered how things were going with AJ. She'd grown to care about him and was concerned. She wanted to ask, but it wasn't the type of conversation to have in passing, and Drew didn't seem to be in a disposition to chat. She wondered how long he'd be upset with her. She wished she had his friendship, his listening ear, his support. She was still reeling from finding out that the duplex sold.

As she removed the jelly jar of water she'd used to weigh the cabbage down in the mason jar, she noted that brine still covered the purple veggies. She reached a spoon into the jar and tasted the mixture of purple cabbage and apple. Tangy, still crunchy, and almost sour enough. She replaced the jelly jar and fastened the cheesecloth with a rubber band. A couple more days and it would be perfect.

If she were going to move in a month, she had a lot to do. She still hadn't found a place to live, and it wasn't likely anything would open up in the weeks before Christmas.

There were several nice luxury town houses on the canal, but they were out of her price range. The other options looked as rough as her dad's building. Places would open up in the summer, but what was she to do until then? The closing date on the duplex had been set for January 21, so she was trying to brace herself for a move to the armpit of Douglass. It wouldn't be that bad, she told herself. There were people in the world who lived in shacks. But ugh! The only vacant apartment in the building was in the basement. It would be temporary, just until summer. When the college students left, she'd find something better. Her pep talk to herself wasn't working. She sighed as she looked out the window into her snow-covered backyard.

She also needed to figure out what to do about Christmas. Dad had called, inviting her to come to Madison. In past years, she celebrated with him and Kandy at the lake house. She'd spend a few hours there on Christmas Day. They'd eat dinner and open gifts. If she were to spend Christmas with them this year, it would require a longer visit. One she wasn't sure she had the energy for.

She needed to talk to a friend. A couple weeks ago, Drew would've been the one she turned to, but things had changed between them.

She didn't have anyone else. She didn't want to burden Louisa. Marcella's problems were miniscule compared to a terminal disease. She'd been spending more time with Beth but wasn't comfortable confiding in her.

Drew had been concerned about Andy's ability to make friends, and he mentioned something about that being a problem for those who lose mothers at a young age. Was that her issue? For the last few years, she'd considered Achara her best friend, but the language barrier made it difficult to have deep conversations. There was little risk of her getting too close, which was probably why it had been so easy to hang out with her.

She'd planned to use the morning to start packing a few things in boxes, but when she turned on her phone, she had a text message from the receptionist at Shear Delight asking if she wanted an eleven o'clock. She agreed. She could use the money.

She checked her client schedule and stared at the screen. Her eleven o'clock was Drew Smith. She wasn't sure how she felt about that. She walked to her bedroom to get ready for the day. His back was probably hurting again, and she'd focus on helping him heal. She was a professional. She could do this.

After kicking through snow, she opted to drive to work. Winter was here to stay, and she wouldn't see grass again until April. In her SUV, she turned on the radio and immediately turned if off. It was the season for Christmas music. December always brought back memories.

When Marcella was a kid, she and Mom tromped through the bush, collecting pine, balsam, and fir branches in a sled. Then they made swags and garlands to decorate their house and the nursing home where Mom worked. Dad would join them in the woods on a Saturday to find the perfect tree. A tree might look great in the woods, but once it was set up in the house, bare spots stood out. Mom and Marcella would stand back and direct as Dad turned the tree in the stand until the homeliest side faced the corner.

They'd watch *Charlie Brown's Christmas Tree*, and when she was older, *It's a Wonderful Life*. Mom played Christmas music all month.

Caroling was one of the highlights of the year. Mom always organized a group from church to sing for the residents at Ridgeview Nursing Home. Marcella loved seeing the joy on the residents' faces when the group sang and visited with them.

For the past few years, Marcella had hosted Christmas for her international tenants so they could experience American Christmas traditions. She took the Puntasrimas and a couple of their friends to cut down a tree from the woods by her dad's house. They had a tree-decorating party, watched *It's A Wonderful Life*, and ate Achara's delicious Thai food. She missed her friends.

After pulling into the parking lot behind Shear Delight, she turned off the engine and took a deep breath, trying to snap out of her funk. She should have ridden her bike, even with the snow. The exercise would've done her mood good.

She got out of her vehicle and walked up the side street to Avery Avenue. Before turning the corner, she looked back to the canal, which was the only blue in a landscape of white. With the temperature dropping, it would likely freeze over within a week. Snow accumulated on the ski hill, adding to the artificial base the operators had been making. She looked forward to snowboarding. She hoped to take AJ. He'd enjoy that. With the snow coming down, she could barely make out the gray steel mine hoist that sat atop Quincy Hill. She stuck out her tongue and caught a snowflake. She breathed in the winter air and exhaled. Ready or not, it was time to work.

She felt more like herself as she readied her room for the day and did her stretches. She started harp music on her phone. A few minutes before eleven, she went to greet Drew.

He smiled broadly. "Hi, neighbor."

Not for long, she thought. His innocent greeting had her fighting a lump in her throat. She clasped her hands tightly together. "I'm ready for you."

He followed her through the salon to the dimly lit room where she left him to undress.

Several minutes later, she knocked on the door before entering.

When she pulled back the sheet and ran her hands over his back, she could feel inflammation. "I'd like to try eucalyptus oil," she suggested. The essential oil had analgesic and anti-inflammatory compounds.

"Sure," he agreed.

She added a few drops to the carrier oil and massaged it into his swollen muscles.

"How have you been?" he asked.

"Fine." She worked her way up to his shoulders. She felt a twinge in her own shoulder, and she pressed on the same spot under Drew's clavicle. His muscle was like a rock.

He winced. "That's a tight one."

"Too much pressure?" she asked.

"No, it needs to be loosened up. Too much sitting and stress."

She wanted to ask how things were going with AJ, but it was not the time or place. He was here for treatment.

"So have you had any luck with the housing hunt?" he asked when she moved down to his legs.

Well, that was personal. "I haven't," she said simply.

He lifted his head and craned his neck to look at her. "Are you okay?" He said the words compassionately—like he really wanted to know. As if he really cared.

"Not really." Her eyes began to sting.

"What's going on?"

The tears overflowed, and words tumbled from her mouth. She told him about the awful apartment she was going to have to move into and the sadness she always felt at Christmas, missing her mom. "I'm sorry," she said when she finished. "That was unprofessional."

She'd melted down with a client, which completely violated her professional training, crossing personal and work boundaries. It sometimes went in the other direction as friends came for treatment and clients became friends. She didn't mind listening, but she'd never dumped her problems on her clients. "I think we're done for today, and there's no charge," she said.

Concern showed on his face. "I'd give you a hug, but I'm in my briefs."

She stepped out and pulled herself together. When he came out of the room, she handed him her coworker's card. "Becca and I sometimes trade massages. She's great. Next time, schedule with her."

# Chapter 29

*D*rew pulled shopping bags out from under his bed. He'd purchased a bunch of small items to make the gift opening last longer—a board game, a puzzle, and a young reader novel that Brooke Davis, a teacher who attended Faith Church, had recommended. Earlier that evening, Drew had unpacked the Christmas tree from its box, and he and Andy decorated it. Now that his son was sleeping, it was time to get presents under it. Drew reached far under the bed to fetch the big gift, which was wrapped in a bedsheet—a snowboard. When you live in snow country, you either need to embrace the six months of winter or go crazy.

Marcella had promised to give Andy snowboarding lessons over Christmas break. Drew sighed. He was still getting used to the name change. AJ was now Andy, and Marcella might not be a part of their lives anymore. He was in shock over her abrupt dismissal of him the other day, and he wasn't sure what he'd done wrong. But she'd made it clear. She wanted nothing to do with him. It made him realize he needed to find more friends. He had his in-laws, but they didn't hang out. They were Andy's grandparents, not his friends.

He unrolled wrapping paper, put the puzzle on top, and sliced off a sheet.

He usually chatted with a few folks at church on Sundays. Most of the people who sat near Ron and Patty were older, except for Brooke, who sat a few rows ahead of them. She was always friendly when he checked Andy into Sunday school at Faith Church. Although she taught at the elementary school all week, she also volunteered as a Sunday school teacher on the weekend. He figured she must really like kids.

It was hard to be a single dad in a small town. He needed to make an effort to put himself out there, to get involved in the community. There had been an announcement in the church bulletin that the worship team was looking for volunteers. That might be a good way for him to plug in and get involved, and there were people his age on the team—Brooke, for one, and a young father named Devin on drums. He should call the church to see if they wanted another guitar player.

Drew finished wrapping Andy's presents and pulled out the trinkets he'd bought for Ron and Patty. An electric back massager for Ron—he had also ordered one for himself—and a wall calendar filled with whimsical artwork for Patty. He had continued Kristine's tradition of giving her the calendar, and when she received it the prior Christmas she'd expressed appreciation—the only time that had happened since Kristine's death. He wrapped those gifts and picked up one other item he'd ordered. A box containing tea infusers with garden-themed charms. A dragonfly, a butterfly, and a ladybug. They hadn't been expensive, but they seemed like something Marcella would like. He pushed the box back under his bed.

He put the other presents under the tree before turning off the Christmas tree lights. As he moved to lower the window shade, Marcella pulled up in her SUV. He watched from the darkened living room as she walked to the front yard and wrapped her arms around the oak tree. She stood there in the frosty night for at least a minute. He considered inviting her in but decided against it. He would give her space and let her reach out. As he closed the shade, he said a prayer for her.

Drew dropped his son off at Patty and Ron's before heading to the church for his first worship team practice.

Brooke crossed the sanctuary when he came in the door with his guitar. "Hi, Drew. Glad you could join us." She squeezed his arm, a big smile across her face. She was energetic for nine o'clock on a Saturday morning.

"Thanks." He sipped his coffee.

"Our new guitar player's here," a woman at the piano called. "Welcome, Drew. I'm Nancy." She pointed to the other members of the worship team. "Devin's on drums. Bruce is our lead guitar. It looks like you already know Brooke. She's our vocalist."

Bruce lifted his hand in a wave and quickly pulled it back as Drew moved closer to shake his hand. "I've got a bad cold here. I don't want you to get this bug." He said the words with a nasal tone, and his nose was red.

Drew pulled his guitar from its case and gave it a quick tune.

After they had run through several Sunday morning Christmas songs, Bruce stopped and loudly blew his nose. "You know, I'm struggling here. I think I'll go home and get some rest before tonight." He paused, looking at Drew. "Or, maybe you'd be able to fill in tonight?" He looked at him hopefully.

"What's going on tonight?"

Brooke bounded to Drew's side. "Caroling. I'd love for you to come. We meet at the church at five and then go to a couple places to sing. The kids get a sleigh ride, and we can carpool. AJ would love it."

"Yes, he would." He found himself agreeing. It would be a good activity for him and Andy, a distraction from the holiday reminders that Kristine was not with them.

"If you're free after rehearsal, you and I can review the carols and figure out what key to play them in."

"Sure. I could stick around."

After three more songs, Nancy, Bruce, and Devin left, leaving Drew with Brooke.

She pulled up a list of songs on her phone. "Should I text these to you? If you don't mind giving me your number." She smiled and winked.

Drew liked her sense of humor. "I'm going to need chords, too."

They worked together to find each of the songs on the internet and took time to practice them. Drew was familiar with some of the tunes, but he hadn't learned to play any of them. Brooke was great though, patient in teaching him the songs. She did have a beautiful voice.

"I look forward to seeing you and AJ this evening," Brooke said after they'd finished running through each of the carols.

"Thanks. He wants to be called Andy now." Drew put his guitar back in its case.

"I suppose there's a lot of options with a name like Andrew. He's your junior?"

Drew hesitated.

Brooke studied him with a perplexed look.

"Yes. He's my junior. Andrew Richard Smith, Junior."

Back at home, Andy was excited to hear they'd be going on a sleigh ride. "Is Marcella going?"

"No."

"Why not?"

"This is a Faith Church activity."

"She could still go, right?"

"I don't think she'd be interested."

# *Chapter 30*

$M$arcella brushed snow off her SUV and started it up to melt the ice off the windows. She went back in the house to grab a quick bite while her vehicle warmed. She'd spent much of her Saturday sorting stuff into piles—donate, storage, and what she'd need in her temporary housing. She put a few crackers on a plate, along with smoked Lake Superior trout from the local fish market.

She sat at the table with her dinner and a cup of peppermint tea as she searched Craigslist for rentals on her phone. No new listings since she'd checked earlier in the day. She sighed. She rinsed her dish and cup and put them in the sink before gathering her things and heading out. She paused in the yard, breathing in the crisp air, enjoying the serenity of her backyard. Live in the moment, she told herself. She'd love her little space while she still had it. She climbed in the SUV and headed to Ridgeview Nursing Home to give Louisa a massage. She found her in her room, sitting in her wheelchair with her head drooping to one side.

"Are you sleeping?" Marcella asked softly.

Louisa lifted her head and opened her eyes. "Hello." Her voice was garbled, but Marcella could still understand her if she listened carefully.

Louisa was too frail to be transferred to the massage table, so she remained in her chair while Marcella did what she could. After hanging Louisa's urine bag on the side of the wheelchair, Marcella tilted her seat back to elevate her feet. She pulled up a stool and massaged the edema out of her feet using a jojoba oil mixed with lavender and frankincense essential oils. She gently moved up Louisa's legs, which were now little more than bony sticks. So much muscle had wasted away, she thought sadly. Marcella worked on Louisa's belly, using the tips of her fingers to massage the small intestines in clockwise motions around her navel. Then she worked the large intestine, hoping to stimulate movement.

"It would've been nice to be constipated at the wedding," Louisa said quietly. She managed a chuckle. "I appreciate your help. And it seems I breathe a little easier after you do that belly massage."

"I'm glad." Marcella felt a renewed sense of purpose as she continued the massage.

Beth arrived midway through the hour. "Hi, Marcella." She leaned down and kissed Louisa on the cheek. "Hi, Grandma."

Beth pulled up a chair. "So, I had a doctor's appointment yesterday, and I wanted to show you some pictures." She was glowing as she opened her purse. "Here's baby." She held the pictures up so Louisa could see.

Marcella moved closer to take a look. "Aah."

"I'm so excited. I feel the baby move, of course, but seeing our little peanut's head and hands makes it feel so real." Beth sat back.

"Do you know if it's a boy or girl?" Marcella asked.

"We decided we're going to be surprised."

"I can't wait to meet the baby," Louisa said softly.

Marcella felt a lump in the back of her throat. She hoped Louisa would still be with them in late April. Marcella would do what she could to help her hang on. If Louisa thought the belly massage helped her breathing, she'd make a point to do it regularly.

"Oh," Beth said, turning to Marcella. "I wanted to invite you to join us for Christmas dinner and see if you'd be willing to help Grandma get to her house again."

Anticipation flickered in Louisa's eyes.

"I'd love to come, and I'd be happy to help." Marcella felt a sense of relief. She wouldn't be going to Madison because she'd be helping Louisa. A very good excuse.

"How are you doing, Louisa?" a nurse's aide said after poking his head in the room.

"Fine," Louisa said, barely above a whisper.

The man smiled with a slightly pained expression, as if he didn't understand. He knelt down near Louisa's head. "Could I get you anything?"

"I could use water. I feel dehydrated."

"What was that? I couldn't understand what you said."

Louisa sighed. She must have had to deal with that often as her slurred speech was difficult to understand for most, except for those who had been with her through the whole journey.

"She wants water," Marcella said.

"She's dehydrated," Beth added.

"I'll be right back." The aide left.

"I can't stay long," Beth said as she pinned one of the pictures to Louisa's bulletin board. "I need to get ready for Danny's work party."

"Have fun, my dear," Louisa said.

Beth kissed her grandma again. "I'll come by for a longer visit tomorrow." She straightened. "See you, Marcella. Thanks for coming today."

"Bye." Marcella finished the massage, returned Louisa to a seated position, and then sat in the chair that Beth had vacated, leaning back and crossing her legs. She had no plans for the evening, and no real desire to get back to her packing. She had accomplished enough for one day. "Should I go see if I can find hot water for tea?" she asked. The aide hadn't yet returned with water.

A smile lit up Louisa's face. "I'd love tea, even if that aide brings me water."

Marcella walked down the hallway toward the kitchen. In some ways, Ridgeview felt like a second home. She had spent a lot of time there as a kid when Mom was the activity director. She'd get dropped off by the bus after school and do her homework in Mom's office until she finished up her workday. If Marcella had time, she'd go find someone in need of company.

In the kitchen, a sign was posted with the monthly activities. They still used the same Word template her mom created with the same corny clip art, and it was posted in the same place. And there was caroling tonight. A sense of nostalgia washed over her, and Marcella was surprised by her feeling of gratitude. She wasn't feeling the prick of sadness that often accompanied her memories of Mom.

She checked her phone. Caroling would begin in an hour. She filled Styrofoam cups with hot water, grabbed a straw, and headed back to Louisa's room.

She put a spoonful of dried peppermint leaves in each of two infusers she'd previously brought to Louisa's room. She dropped them in the cups to steep. "Christmas carolers will be here in an hour. Do you want to go listen to them?"

"I'd love to. How are things going with Drew?" Louisa's eyes twinkled.

Marcella sighed, her shoulders slumped. "Well, you know I went downstate with him for Thanksgiving."

"Mmm-hmm." Louisa smiled.

Marcella pulled the infusers from the cups. "And then I screwed up and let AJ into his apartment."

"I remember."

Marcella held the straw to Louisa's lips. "I've been having a hard time reading him since then."

Louisa took a sip. "Why's that?"

"I don't know. I don't think he understands that we're just friends."

"But you want more."

Marcella opened her mouth, then hesitated. She gave Louisa another sip and then sat back in her chair.

After some time passed, Louisa said, "I take that as a yes."

"It's complicated."

"My dear Marcella, I'm afraid I've spent too much time listening to people, content to watch their lives play out and letting them discover the consequences to their actions."

"You've always been a good listener." Marcella sipped her tea.

"But I don't have much time left. And I've seen this play out in your life for too long. You need to hear this."

Marcella swallowed hard. She knew Louisa was speaking from love, but she had never heard her give such a stern introduction.

"You need to trust people. You need to let people in." Louisa was emphatic and spoke more clearly than she had in the past month.

"Oh, I trust Drew." Marcella leaned forward.

"I mean trust him enough to be vulnerable and love him."

"I'm not concerned about that. I just don't want to do to AJ what Kandy did to me."

"Then do it differently, but don't let AJ keep you from loving Drew. You're afraid to love Drew because you fear loss. And you think that you can't lose what you don't love."

Marcella was stunned. She had never heard her friend, her mentor, so riled up. Louisa might be on to something, but maybe Marcella was better off without the drama. She was happy with her little life. "What if it's a risk I don't want to take?"

"Because love's so much greater than loss." Louisa closed her eyes as if weighing her next words. "Loss isn't just a risk. It's a certainty. But you must move forward to stay alive, pursuing something of value to transcend a life of suffering. You're a courageous woman, and you need to trust people as a manifestation of your courage and their potential to love. And only through love can we know our creator."

"Yeah. I thought I knew God. But how could he let my mom suffer like she did?"

Still with her eyes closed, Louisa laid her head back on the headrest. She looked exhausted. Maybe she didn't have an answer for that. They sat in silence for some time, and Marcella sipped her tea.

And then in a whisper, as if talking to herself, Louisa said, "Good and evil. Light and darkness. Love and loss. Joy and suffering. We'd never know one without the other. But through it all, the love of God weaves its way into eternity."

Marcella sipped her tea and Louisa drifted to sleep. As Louisa napped, Marcella thought about her words. Maybe she was right. Maybe the only thing that kept her from loving Drew was fear. She felt courage build within her.

Drew and Andy arrived at the Faith Church parking lot, where a farmer had two draft horses harnessed to a wagon with rubber wheels. A Quincy streetlight illuminated snow falling out of the dark sky. An inch had accumulated in the parking lot.

Drew expected the sleigh to have skis, but the farmer explained that a sleigh with skis gains too much momentum and would be difficult to stop. They talked to the farmer about the horses, and he gave Andy treats to feed Star and Sassy. Andy climbed into the wagon with a few other kids. Hay bales lined the sides and back of the wagon bed.

"Hi, Miss Davis." Andy looked past Drew.

"Do you want to ride, too?" Brooke asked Drew, putting a foot on a wheel.

"I thought the sleigh ride was for the kids. Aren't we carpooling?"

"It looks like there's room for us." She threw her leg over the side and stepped in.

Drew grabbed his guitar. He sat in the back, with Andy on one side and Brooke on the other.

"There are blankets up here," the farmer called back. "It'll get cold once we start moving."

Drew crawled to the front and pulled a blanket from the stack under the farmer's seat. He covered himself, Andy, and Brooke.

The farmer rattled the reins and barked a command. "*Kävellä.*"

The wagon lurched forward. Bells jingled as the horses pulled it through downtown Quincy. As many times as Drew had driven through the town, he hadn't ever really noticed its charm and character. He was usually sitting in the driver's seat of his truck looking out in front of him, but the view was different as he leaned back on a bale of hay, looking up at ornate embellishments on the facades of nineteenth-century brick buildings. Even the newer buildings, the ones built in the 30s, 40s, and 50s had a certain small-town charm. Large, plate glass windows were lettered with the businesses' names.

After crossing through an intersection with a blinking red light, the farmer yelled *ravata* to his horses, and they began to trot down North Canal Drive, bells jingling all the way.

At Ridgeview, they gathered in the community room, where a number of residents were already seated in rows of folding chairs, and others were parked in their wheelchairs. Drew looked around, wondering if he'd see Louisa. He hadn't seen her since the wedding.

He pulled his guitar out of the case and tuned it, while Brooke corralled the kids and directed everyone into position. As Drew gently strummed the first three chords of the first carol, he saw her. And not just Louisa, Marcella too. They both looked so happy. Drew raised his hand and nodded hello. Marcella waved back, then looked away. She was such a beautiful woman, way out of his league. He'd been fooling himself to think he had a chance with her.

Drew kept an eye on Brooke, following her lead in the songs. Whenever he felt unsure, he stopped strumming altogether. She had such a strong, beautiful voice that he wasn't really needed. But she was right about Andy loving it.

After singing the songs, Andy dashed to Marcella's side. "Dad said you wouldn't want to come."

She gave him a hug. "I've missed you, AJ."

"Andy. I'm Andy now."

Drew listened in on the conversation as he put away his

guitar, and then he joined them.

Marcella smiled. "Hi."

Drew hesitated. "Hi." He wanted to hug her as his son had, but he resisted the impulse. Instead, he knelt by Louisa's side. "How are you doing?"

"I'm well," she mumbled.

"That's great. You look well."

"Good job, Andy," Brooke said, approaching them.

"Thanks, Miss Davis."

"You too, Drew."

Drew stood. "Thanks, Brooke. Do you know Marcella?"

"No." She extended her hand. "It's nice to meet you."

Marcella shook her hand. "Likewise. I'd best get Louisa back to her room. It was nice to meet you. See you guys."

Drew watched as she drove Louisa's chair down the hall, wishing he'd taken the opportunity to try and reconnect with her.

After she left and Andy ran off, Brooke asked, "Are you guys dating?"

"Me and Marcella?"

Brooke nodded.

"Oh, no. She's my landlord. Why would you think that?"

"I just thought…" Brooke shrugged. "Never mind."

"I'm hopelessly single," Drew said.

"Me, too." Brooke blushed. She looked at him and smiled. "Or maybe we're not hopeless. Do you want to have coffee sometime?"

# Chapter 31

*M*arcella set a terra-cotta teakettle on the antique wood-stove in Louisa's kitchen. "The wood heat feels good, hey?"

Louisa, reclined in her wheelchair, smiled. "It's warming me to my bones."

"Tea tastes better when it's heated by a wood fire." Marcella sat at the table along with Lorna and Senja. "You've always told me that."

It was time to relax now that she and the sisters had the potatoes peeled and boiling on the electric range. Beth was at the counter snapping green beans, and her mother, Rebecca, was making sauce from whole, frozen cranberries. The turkey had already come out of the oven and was resting, and in its place were Lorna's pecan and apple pies. Danny, Mak, and Beth's father, Oliver, were hanging out in the living room.

Marcella buttered a slice of sweet cardamom bread. "Do you want some *nisu*?" she asked Louisa, holding it up. "Something to take the edge off?" She moved to feed her a bite, but stopped when Louisa spoke.

"Incline me so I don't choke."

Marcella pressed a toggle switch, and Louisa's seatback moved forward. Marcella gave her a bite, cupping a hand under the bread to catch the crumbs.

"Mmm." Louisa looked absolutely contented.

"It's good to be back in your house, isn't it?" Marcella was delighted to see the joy on Louisa's face.

"Yes." Louisa nodded slightly. "And it's good to be with family and friends."

"Mom," Rebecca said, "I think you'd be much happier here than at Ridgeview."

"Help isn't easy to come by." Louisa's words were difficult to understand.

Marcella repeated Louisa's words, translating her garbled speech. She suspected she was the only one close enough to hear her over the clamor of the room.

"Elizabeth, weren't you lining up help?" Rebecca asked.

"Grandma's right. I could barely find enough help to cover the days, much less the nights."

"Now, now." Louisa was looking much less contented.

"We should save this for another time," Senja said.

"I'm shocked at how far—" Rebecca's voice broke, and she wiped her eyes on the back of her sleeve. She left her pot on the counter and ducked out of the kitchen to the living room.

Louisa let out an exasperated breath.

"Ooh, *nisu*," Mak said as he entered the kitchen with Danny, presumably so Rebecca could talk to her husband in private.

"And tea's brewing on the stove," Danny said. "It's like old times, Grandma Lou."

The smile returned to Louisa's face.

"How are the book sales, Mak?" Marcella retrieved the kettle from the stove and set it on a trivet on the table.

"Ahh." Mak flapped his hand.

"Not good?" Danny laughed.

"It's going great!" Lorna exclaimed. "*The Child of Rumspringa* reached number twelve in its category on Amazon."

"Amish, Texas, Western romance?" Danny asked.

"No. Number twelve in historical romance." Lorna said

the words proudly.

"It's trash." Mak, seated at the table, buttered a piece of bread. "One reviewer even said that. One star. Trash. That's all she said."

"It's not." Beth rested her hands on her belly. "I read the manuscript. It was a sweet story."

"Hardly original." Danny scoffed.

Mak took a bite of his bread. "I couldn't believe it myself. I had to purchase a Kindle version of my own book. Da publisher rewrote the manuscript without my permission. She took an innocent scene where I allude to activity in the hayloft and turned it into Amish erotica. It's indecent."

"You're a prude." Lorna slapped his bicep with the back of her hand.

Mak grunted. "I'd prefer to leave da details to the reader's imagination. I wasn't writin' an R-rated book."

Danny laughed so hard he snorted. Louisa chuckled.

"It's not funny. Da publisher didn't have a legal right to do it. She claims she did it under da revision clause, but da revision clause is only for future editions of da book. It wasn't being revised, because it wasn't even published yet, and da contract gives *me* artistic control over everything in that book."

"But it's selling well?" Marcella asked as she gave Louisa a sip of tea.

"It's selling so well the publisher wants Mak to finish *The Child of Rumspringa Returns*," Lorna enthused.

"Good grief." Danny threw up his hands. "Do you not have a single original idea?"

"Could you publish with somebody else?" Marcella asked.

"She has da right of first refusal."

"So you're going to do it?" Beth asked.

"It's not my name on it anyhow. It's makin' me money. And unlike makin' wood and plowin', once it's done, it's done. I don't have to do anything else other than write another 20,000 words." Mak finished his bread and licked butter off his fingers. "It got me thinkin', Marcella, are you still seeing that Drew guy? I want to talk to him."

"I was never seeing him."

"But he's your tenant, right?"

"Not for long."

"Why's that?"

"My dad sold the duplex. The owners want to occupy the upper unit, so I need to move."

"Where are you going to live?"

"In a basement unit of the Smelter Street apartments."

"Ewww," Senja said. "That's rough."

"My dad owns the apartments. They're horrible, but he said if he put any money into them the students would trash them anyway. But it's temporary. It's something until summer."

"Move here," Louisa said.

"What was that?" Marcella wasn't sure she'd heard her correctly.

"Move into the farmhouse."

"Seriously?"

"Sure. It would be better for the house to have somebody here."

"I don't know what to say."

"Say yes."

Rebecca returned to the kitchen. "Okay, Mom. It's settled. I'm taking a leave of absence from work so I can come and care for you in your own house."

Marcella felt her heart sink into her stomach. The relief she had felt when she thought she found housing was short-lived, but it was better for Louisa to have her daughter with her.

"That was an ironic turn of events." Mak stood. "You can't make this stuff up. I have to get my journal."

"That's not irony," Beth said. "That's an unfortunate coincidence."

"Grammar Nazi," Mak said under his breath as he stepped out of the kitchen.

"What's an unfortunate coincidence?" Rebecca asked.

"Louisa just offered to let Marcella live at the farmhouse," Danny said.

"That's perfect," Rebecca said. "Maybe you could help with Mom's care?"

"I'd love to. I had already offered to help." Marcella's relief returned. She loved the farmhouse and was honored to help with her dear friend's care.

"Thank God," Senja said. "He's got everything under control."

Marcella cringed and looked out the window so as not to display her emotions. It was comments like that that kept her away from church. It grated on her when people talked about God like he was some kind of puppet master pulling strings, micro-managing the world, as if all the suffering were somehow part of his divine plan.

# Chapter 32

*D*rew ran a razor over his cheeks, even though the stubble hadn't grown much since he shaved that morning. As he leaned in close to the mirror, he caught a glimpse of Andy peering at him from outside the bathroom.

"Why are you getting all dressed up?" he asked.

"I'm going out." Drew grabbed a hair sticking out of one of his nostrils and yanked it out.

"Is that why I'm going to Grandpa and Grandma's?"

"You're going over to Grandpa and Grandma's because they invited you to stay the night. And I figured since you're going over there, I might as well go out."

"Are you going out with Marcella?" The tone of Andy's question conveyed a sense of anticipation.

Drew studied Andy's smiling face. "Unfortunately not."

The smile disappeared. "Then with who?"

Drew adjusted his collar. "With a friend."

Andy gave a quick nod and retreated to his room. The poor kid had withdrawn back into his shell since Marcella set definite boundaries for the relationship. It showed how much he needed a woman in his life. Maybe Brooke would be that woman. It was hard to say how well they connected, even after several rehearsals and seeing her at Sunday morning worship services. She'd suggested coffee the night they'd gone caroling, but he played it cool, not wanting to look desperate.

That was probably his mistake with Marcella. He came on too strong. That only worked in high school and college. You tell a buddy who tells some girl who tells her friend you like her, and the relationship blooms within the day, then fizzles just as fast. But mature women want relationships to evolve organically.

"Are you ready?" Drew called to Andy, pressing a button on a key fob to remote start his truck.

"Yeah." Andy threw his duffel bag over his shoulder and followed Drew outside.

The Keweenaw was blanketed with another couple inches of snow. Drew tried to recall the last day it hadn't snowed. Maybe a few days after Christmas, but he was pretty sure there'd been snow every day so far in January. Now it was the middle of the month and the banks were already a foot high.

Drew opened the driver's side doors and Andy crawled in the back. Drew grabbed a snow brush to sweep the windshield and hood. He looked up to the second-story unit. All the windows were dark, and he hadn't seen or heard much life upstairs in well over a week. He suspected Marcella had already moved without telling him. He would've helped her, but she had probably recruited Mak and Danny to do it on a day when he was at work.

After dropping Andy off, he headed back down the hill to the bottom of Quincy. Brooke lived in a town house right on the canal.

She invited him in. "I'm just about ready."

While Brooke disappeared into another room, Drew looked around from where he stood near the door. A modern kitchen with stainless steel appliances and quartz countertops. A vaulted ceiling over a living room with a wall of windows. He could see faint lights through the falling snow on the other side of the canal. There was a collection of framed photographs of sailboats on another wall.

Brooke reappeared with a bright smile and her handbag tucked under her arm. She was a pretty woman, wearing a floral blouse and straight-legged pants. She didn't have the ethereal beauty Marcella possessed, but she was certainly attractive.

"Nice artwork," Drew said, motioning to the collection of sailboat pictures.

"Thank you." She smiled. "I took those."

"Really?" He looked at them more closely. The center photo was a close-up of a red sail and mast. It had an artsy feel to it. "I like that one. You're talented."

"Thank you. It's a good hobby for me, especially in the summer when school's out."

"This place is great," Drew said. "Do you rent or did you buy it?"

"Ha." She pulled boots out of the front closet. "I'll never complain about getting the summers off, but I couldn't afford this on a teacher's salary. My grandparents own it. They live in a house overlooking the big lake, and they have this for the boat slip. My grandpa developed these units, and he kept one to dock his boat. They might move here someday when they need to downsize. In the meantime, they let me live here so I can keep an eye on the place while I save money to buy something." She grabbed her coat. "Ready, Freddy?"

"Sure, Betty." Drew laughed. "I used to say that to Andy all the time, but he started getting irritated with it."

"I used to be irritated when my dad said it, or at least I pretended to be." Brooke took Drew's arm walking to the truck.

Drew opened her door and helped her in. After he came around the truck and got in, he asked, "What are you in the mood for tonight? I have reservations at La Cocina, but we can do the Cornucopia, or Chinese or even sushi. It's hard to believe we have so many choices in such a small town."

"I love Mexican, so La Cocina's great."

The two settled into a booth in the brightly colored restaurant which was decorated with paintings of agave farms and other scenes from the Mexican countryside. A waiter dropped off menus and glasses of water, and then took their drink orders—a margarita for Brooke, and for Drew, root beer.

"You don't drink?" she asked.

"Not anymore." Drew opened a menu. "It was getting a bit out of control, especially for my wife, and I kept hoping she'd follow my lead. She never did. And then she died in the car crash."

"That was the reason for the accident?" Brooke closed her menu and set it on the table. "I didn't know. I'm sorry."

"I don't know for sure. She was drinking..." Drew bit his lip as he shrugged. "But she might have swerved to avoid a deer, or she hit an ice patch. I never had a chance to ask her."

Brooke looked around the restaurant. "Do you see our waiter? I'll cancel my drink order."

Drew waved his hand. "No. No. Don't worry about it. It doesn't bother me in the slightest if other people drink. And I'm not an alcoholic or anything like that. I just stopped drinking. It was more of a lifestyle choice."

Brooke settled back in her seat. "Is that why you moved to the UP? Lifestyle choice?"

"I needed help raising Andy. Being a single parent's hard, especially without support. I have friends in Wausau, but nobody I could count on."

The waiter came back with their drinks, dropped off a basket of chips and salsa, and took their food orders.

"And how has it worked out?" Brooke sipped her water.

"Better than I expected. My landlord really helped draw Andy out of his shell."

"Your landlord's Marcella?"

"Yeah. You're good with names." Drew dipped a chip in salsa and popped it in his mouth.

Brooke grabbed a chip. "I have practice memorizing thirty names every fall."

"Now I'll be getting a new landlord, because her dad sold the duplex."

"You don't look too happy about that."

Drew shrugged. "We haven't been talking anyway." He took a sip of his pop. "It's really too bad for Andy. The loss of his mother's been hard on him. He needs a woman in his life."

Brooke took another sip of her water, leaving her margarita untouched. "It must've been hard on you too, to lose Kristine."

"It was two years ago, last week." Drew twisted the ring on his finger. "I'm not sure if it's something one ever gets over. But at this point, I try to focus on happy memories." The conversation with Brooke was too focused on him. He'd made that mistake with Marcella. Brooke was good at probing him, but he should reciprocate. "So, are you from the area?"

"Yep. I went to college in Marquette and worked there for a few years, but it was a little too far from family. And then a teaching position opened at Quincy at the same time my grandpa built the town houses. Everything kind of fell into place."

"Dad?"

Drew looked up at his son standing next to the booth. "Hey, buddy."

Ron waved from a table on the other side of the restaurant while Patty looked down at a menu.

"Hi, Andy," Brooke said.

"What are you doing here?" Andy asked in an accusatory tone.

Brooke recoiled.

"She's my friend," Drew said. "What are you doing here?" He matched his son's tone in jest.

"Grandpa said he was cooking tonight." It was the sort of thing Andy would typically repeat with a smile, but he remained stone-faced.

"Tell Grandpa not to burn the tortillas." Drew didn't get the slightest smile out of Andy for that one.

Andy walked back to the table, and Drew nodded a hello when Patty looked up, but she diverted her eyes.

"Is Patty okay?" Brooke asked.

"She's never forgiven me for Kristine's death, but I don't know what she thought I could've done—told her she couldn't leave?" He dipped another chip and took a bite.

"I'm sure she's still grieving. Sometimes it hurts less to be angry than sad."

"There's truth in that." He could see that playing out with Patty, Andy, and even Marcella in her relationship with her stepmother. His own grief had been mostly sadness, and any anger he had was directed toward Kristine. "How did you get so wise?"

Brooke shrugged. "You learn that type of stuff in child development classes. I don't see too much of Andy, but it seems like he's doing well."

"He is now, or at least he was. He seemed angry with me, but then he was doing better, thanks to Marcella. She has a way with him. But then—" Drew sipped his soda. There he was going again, making it all about himself.

"You're not over her yet, are you?"

"The ring? I just like wearing it."

"I don't mean Kristine. I mean Marcella."

"I don't think you should go out with Brooke," Andy said as soon as he climbed into Drew's truck the next morning. "She's a teacher at my school. That's just awkward. And what about Marcella?"

"You didn't want me to date Marcella, either." He understood that Andy didn't want more changes in his life. Drew got that, but it had been two years since Kristine died, and one thing her death had taught him was how uncertain life was. You couldn't put life on hold.

"I didn't say I didn't want you to date Marcella."

"Yeah, you did, at Granny and Pop's." He'd never forget the look on his son's face when Andy had found the two of them on the couch, or the look of horror on Marcella's face.

"I didn't say I didn't want you to date. I just wanted to know what was going on. You never tell me anything."

"Well, Marcella's not interested."

"Why not?"

Drew shrugged. "I can't answer that."

# Chapter 33

"*D*ad, do you know what pigs and heat are?" Andy fiddled with a piece of paper.

Parenting win, Drew thought. He'd gotten through the sex talk, and now Andy was coming to him with more questions. "Well, when pig farmers are ready to breed more pigs, they need to wait for the sow to be in heat. That means she's ready to get pregnant, and then they bring in a boy pig. I shouldn't say boy pig. We talked about that. Wait until you're a man, and married. But pigs don't get married, so the farmer selects a man pig. A boar, whatever. Anyhow—"

Andy stared at Drew with a look of befuddlement. "No, Pigs-n-Heat is a hockey game. You know who the pigs are and who the heat are?"

"Oh, the cops and firefighters?"

"Yeah, there's a game this weekend. Danny's playing. The kids at school said he's really good."

"Of course he is."

Andy held up a flyer. "Can we go?"

Drew let out a deep breath. "I don't know."

Andy crossed his arms. "So, you're never going to let me see him again?"

"I didn't say that." He'd been trying his best to avoid the issue.

"We stopped going to Pinehurst. You won't let me go to Trailblazers anymore."

"I'm looking out for your best interests."

"But you haven't asked me what I'm interested in. You never ask me. You treat me like a kid."

"You're ten."

"I'm almost eleven."

"Okay, you're eleven, but I'm the adult here, and I'm worried about you."

"You're worried about me? Or are you worried about you?" Andy stared him down.

"Fine, we can go."

It was for a good cause, Drew told himself, as he paid for their nominally-priced tickets. The money would be used to help crime and fire victims. Besides, they could easily go unnoticed in the 4,000-seat arena, and Andy would be busy with his buddies. He'd brought his mini-stick, planning to play floor hockey in the hallways between periods.

"Should we get popcorn?" Drew asked.

"Yeah!" Andy agreed.

At the concession stand, Drew ordered nachos, popcorn, and two hot chocolates.

"Hey, guys," Beth Johnson greeted them when he turned around with his drink tray in one hand and nachos in the other.

"What number is Danny?" Andy asked, already with his hand in the popcorn box.

"Sixteen." Beth stepped aside to let the guy behind her order at the counter.

The sight of a very pregnant Beth brought back memories of Kristine when she'd been pregnant with Andy.

Beth put her hands on her stomach. "You're wondering

how far along I am, but you're afraid to ask."

Drew smiled. "I've learned never to ask."

"Peanut is due in April."

"Wow."

"Wow like I don't look it, or wow like I'm already huge to have a couple more months left."

"Wow, like you look great."

"Good answer." Beth laughed. "Have you talked to Marcella recently?"

"Not for a while."

"You should give her a call."

"I don't think she wants to hear from me."

"Why would you think that?"

Drew shrugged.

"I've never seen Marcella so happy as the time when she was dating you."

"We weren't dating," Drew said. "We were just friends."

"Danny and I were just friends, but he kept pursuing me."

Mak came up from behind her and guffawed loudly. "He didn't pursue you. He let you leave for California, and then he sat around and moped about it until you couldn't take it anymore."

Beth laughed. "Hey, don't sneak up on a pregnant woman like that. You could send me into labor."

"*Hyvää päivää,*" the man greeted her with the Finnish good day. He looked down at her belly. "Wow! You're ready to pop."

His wife Lorna sidled up and slapped his belly with the back of her hand. "Hi, Beth. Hello, Smith boys."

"*Hyvää päivää,*" Drew said.

"Ooh, the Irish boy speaks Finnish." Mak snickered

"Of course," Drew said, "I married a Finn."

"Can you guys wait a minute? I'd like to sit by you." Beth stepped back in line. "But first I'm going to order a giant pickle. Cliché, I know."

"Can I get one, too, Dad?"

"I'll get you one," Beth said.

The group found seats a few rows up from the bench where the cop hockey players sat. As soon as Danny came off the ice after warming up, Beth got his attention. He did a double take, seeing Drew and Andy there with her.

After the first period, it became clear to Drew that the fire-fighters were outmatched. Of course, Danny was the all-star on the police team. Yet another reason for his son to idolize his bio-dad. Granted he was younger than the old-timers on the other team, but sheesh, was there anything the guy couldn't do?

After the game, Andy took off to hang out with his friends, while Drew visited with Beth as she waited for her husband. He could see the awkward conversation coming, but he couldn't avoid it forever.

Danny showered quickly and went to find Beth. He wanted to get right home so they could get to bed. She was needing more sleep lately, and he was exhausted. His body had taken a beating, and he'd pay the price tomorrow. When he hit thirty the year before, things started taking longer to heal.

Outside the locker room, kids were playing with mini-sticks at the end of the hallway. He remembered doing the same thing as a kid, not long after the arena was first built. He squinted, and his heart quickened. One of them was AJ.

At the top of the steps on the concession level, Beth was talking to Drew. He swallowed hard. She'd been bugging him for months to face the situation head on. Just have a conversation with the guy. Call him up. Invite them over. Whatever. He was reluctant to press things, and she eventually dropped it.

Drew looked up when Danny was a few feet away. He couldn't help but think Beth had a hand in cornering the poor guy.

"Hey, man." Danny stood in front of him.

"Oh, I have to use the ladies room." Beth disappeared.

Drew took a deep breath and let it out slowly.

Danny put out his hand. "We should clear the air." The encounter was uncomfortable, but they wouldn't be able to avoid it forever.

Drew shook his hand. "What do you know?" His voice was laced with apprehension.

"I know your son looks like me, when I was his age, and I was with his mom eleven years ago."

"And what do you want?"

It suddenly clicked for Danny. The man who stood in front of him looked like a deer caught in the headlights. He was scared. Afraid that Danny was going to try to take his son? He couldn't even imagine the trauma that would cause AJ. "I'd like to watch him grow up. I want him to do well in life."

"He *is* doing well."

"I'll leave it up to you and him if you want to have any contact with me. I don't want to come between you two."

Drew didn't relax.

Danny continued, "You know when I think about who I was a decade ago, I think, what would've I done if I'd known? Would I have married her? I honestly don't know. I wasn't walking with God, and I was an immature kid. I wasn't ready to be a father or a husband."

"I wasn't much of a husband at twenty-one, but I can't imagine not being AJ's dad. I mean, Andy's dad. He wants to be called Andy now. He said he's not my junior."

"Whoa. Dude, that had to hurt."

Drew's shoulders relaxed slightly. "Yeah. He's just trying to exert control."

"Beth's been bugging me to invite you guys over for dinner. Maybe you can leave it up to him if he wants to do that or not?" he asked hopefully.

"Good game, Danny!" Andy bounded over, running ahead of Beth. "You were great tonight."

"Thanks." He high-fived him.

"Hey, buddy." Drew put his arm around Andy. "Do you want to go have dinner with these guys? I bet Beth has jars of pickles."

# Chapter 34

"*T*hanks for letting me use your skis again," Marcella said as she tucked the laces under a Velcro flap on a ski boot.

Louisa displayed a facial expression that usually accompanies a shrug, but her shoulders remained motionless under the afghan that covered her. "Have them."

"You don't want to give them to Rebecca or Beth?"

"I have no use for cross-country skis in California," Rebecca said, reclined back in the La-Z-Boy, "and I can't imagine Beth would be interested."

"She tried skiing," Louisa said.

"At the end of my ski, I'll stop by Beth's to see her new nursery." Marcella put on her ski jacket, gloves, and *chook*. "She told me earlier she was making another batch of *riisipuuroa* today, so I'll see if she has any I can bring home for you."

Louisa smiled. With Rebecca's insistence, she'd gotten a feeding tube. It had done her a world of good, giving much-needed nutrients. Her speech had even improved. She was still able to eat for pleasure, particularly moist food that didn't require chewing. The traditional Finnish rice porridge was exactly the type of thing she enjoyed.

At the base of the porch steps, Marcella clipped her boots

into the ski bindings and skied across the plowed area to the open field. There had been enough warm days in March to compact the snow and form a base for skiing under the couple inches that had fallen that day. Even though she'd lived on the Keweenaw her entire life, she was still amazed by the amount of snow that fell. It wasn't even shaping up to be a record year, and they'd already received 250 inches.

She made a loop around the old, broken-down barn, picking up her tracks on the second and third times around. It was good to get exercise. The last few weeks had been stressful and exhausting, though she had a deep sense of purpose as she cared for Louisa. Rebecca was doing the nights, for the most part, and Marcella was on duty most evenings. Beth came over frequently to help out, although she was very pregnant and less able to do the heavy lifting, so Senja and her sisters ramped up their support.

Marcella stepped out of her tracks and headed toward the little blue house. She appreciated the longer days of sunlight, although she knew winter was far from over. The last of the snow probably wouldn't melt until mid-May. She stuck each of her skis into a snowbank next to the stoop and hung the poles on the tips.

Beth answered the door. "Oh, Marcella." Her voice held an element of surprise.

Marcella hugged her friend. "I was out for a ski, and I thought I'd pop over to see the nursery."

"Welcome!" Danny called, coming out of a back room. "Oh, Marcella."

Marcella laughed nervously. "Did I catch you at a bad time?" She didn't think it would be an issue considering they were neighbors and saw each other practically every day, albeit at Louisa's house.

"No. It's fine," Beth said. "We have dinner company coming. We have a few minutes before they show up."

"Maybe I should come another time." Marcella took a step back toward the door.

"Yeah, please stop by tomorrow, anytime." Beth leaned back into Danny as he held her from behind and rested his chin on her head.

"I told Louisa I'd see if you made *riisipuuroa*." Marcella could smell the creamy, cinnamon dish either in the oven or fresh out of it.

"I'll bring some over in the morning."

Marcella opened the door to leave. "Drew!"

He was standing on the steps with his hand poised to knock. "Marcella?"

"Marcella!" Andy leapt over the threshold and wrapped his arms around her.

She squeezed him tightly. "I think you've had a growth spurt since I last saw you."

He stepped back, grinning. "A couple inches. I'm eleven now, and I'm five-two-and-a-half." He had grown since she'd seen him, a gap showing between his pant legs and his ankles.

"Eightieth percentile," Drew said, stepping in. "He'll be as tall as Danny."

"Welcome." Danny extended his hand to Drew.

Drew shook his hand and told Beth, "You look wonderful."

She laughed with a hand on each side of her large belly. "I'm so ready." She winced. "This baby's quite the kicker."

"Our little soccer player," Danny said.

Marcella stepped around the men. "I should go."

Drew looked at her with pleading eyes, but didn't object.

"You don't need to go," Beth said. "We have plenty of food if you want to stay for dinner."

Danny whispered something in Drew's ear, and Drew nodded.

"Hey, Andy," Danny said, "do you want to go play pool or foosball?"

"Yeah!" Andy headed for the basement stairs, obviously already familiar with the house.

"I'll take you guys on in foosball." Beth walked after them, waddling a bit.

"Two on two." Danny laughed.

"He's still going by Andy?" Marcella asked Drew, taking off her *chook*. She remembered how the boy corrected her when she called him AJ at the nursing home.

"Yeah, when the whole thing blew up, he decided he was Andy." Drew took off his jacket.

Marcella squatted and untied her ski boots. "And I take it you've been here before?" She stood and kicked off the boots as she slipped out of her jacket.

"One other time, at the end of January. We worked things out. It's good for Andy." He grabbed her hand. "Do you want to go sit down?"

"Sure." She followed him to the couch, her hand in his. It felt so natural to be holding his hand. She remembered the feeling of laying her head on his chest that night at his parents' house. She'd been so distracted with life she hadn't realized how much she missed him.

Drew sat in the center of the couch, still holding her hand as she sat next to him. He peered deep into her eyes with an intensity that broke down her defenses. It looked like he was weighing his words. How did things come to this point? What had it been? Three months since they'd talked. It was after that massage.

"I'm sorry," Marcella began.

"No, no." Drew's face relaxed, and he took a deep breath. "You don't need to be sorry for anything. I thought about us over the last few months, thinking maybe I was just pushing for a relationship because I don't like being single, and I want Andy to have a mother figure in his life. Maybe that's a little bit of what I was thinking, and it wasn't fair to you, but I realized I don't want just anybody. I want you. You make me a better person, a better father. You're good for Andy, and he wants you in his life. I should've reached out to you sooner, but I'd been drowned in grief for so long before you pulled me up for air. When you left, I fell right back into it."

Marcella's eyes filled with tears, blurring her vision. She squeezed his hand. "I'm sorry."

Drew smiled. "We've already been over that. Just say you'll go out with me. Let's see if we can make it work."

She squeezed his hand. "Yes, I'll go out with you."

# Chapter 35

"I'll go up again so Brett can show you how it's done." Drew stepped up to the rock-climbing wall at Douglass State. "On belay."

"Belay on." The staff member reviewed the instructions with Marcella as Drew slowly climbed the red route.

They each had been up the wall on a beginner's green route, with the college student belaying. Marcella was almost ready to be certified, so they could continue their first official date without an audience.

About halfway up the wall, Drew reached for a stone. As he shifted his center of mass toward that hand, he lost his grip. The weight of his body coming down jarred his other hand free. "Falling," he yelled.

Brett lowered him to the ground.

"What was the rating on that one?" Drew asked.

"That's a five-nine." The staff member removed the knot from his harness.

"Really?" Drew looked up at the section of wall that should not have been that difficult with his climbing experience. "I've gotten out of shape over the last year."

Tethering Marcella to the opposite end of his rope, Drew

reviewed how to tie the climber's knot. He measured out a length of rope from his outstretched hand to his chest, made a figure eight, and ran the tail along the same path to double the knot. "Now you try it."

She measured out the rope, and he guided her hands as she made a figure eight. "You're not wearing your wedding ring," she said softly. "Did you take it off for the climb, or is that permanent?"

"Climbing with a ring on is a good way to lose a finger."

A look of disappointment flashed across her face.

Drew helped her cinch the knot. Maybe it *was* time he stopped wearing the ring. He could see how it would send the wrong message. He should've told her the ring was off permanently. He'd need to set things straight later, when they didn't have an audience.

Brett coached Marcella on the process of managing the rope as Drew went up the red path again, this time with a bit more ease.

"Lower me." Drew rappelled down as Marcella let out rope.

After she practiced belaying a couple more times, Brett certified her and left them alone.

"Are you ready to climb again?" Drew asked Marcella.

She looked up. "I guess so."

"I think you can manage the blue route," Drew suggested. "The green's too easy for you."

She stepped up to the wall. "On belay?"

"Yup, that's the command." He tightened the rope. "Belay on."

She grabbed a blue stone. "Climbing."

"Climb on."

She lifted her knee almost to her chin, skipping a lower hold and placing her foot on a stone chest high. She pulled herself up and climbed the blue path like it was a ladder. About halfway up the wall, she stopped.

"You're doing great," Drew called up to her.

She looked back down with a smile before looking back up

the wall. She reached over to a red stone on an adjacent path. She crossed her other hand in front of her face and grabbed the same stone. She suspended her body by her fingers and let her legs swing down before securing a foothold on another red stone. From there she continued to scale the wall on the red path. She seemed to know intuitively which way to turn her body, keeping her weight centered. She climbed to the top of the wall as nimbly as a mountain goat.

"Lower me," she called down.

"Lowering," he replied.

Back on the ground, her face was aglow. "I could get into this."

"You're amazing." He impulsively pulled her into a hug. He wanted to talk more about the ring, but not there. The mood had shifted to lighthearted fun. "Do you want to try again? You could try the black route."

Marcella glanced up the wall. "The one with overhangs?" She laughed. Turning back to him, she asked with a twinkle in her eye, "Do you remember the night you told me you'd teach me to climb?"

"That was unforgettable." He laughed, remembering his surprise to see her underwear hanging on his weight bench.

After they each climbed a few more paths, they cleaned up in their respective locker rooms. He studied his reflection in the mirror. Why hadn't he simply and immediately told her he was done wearing his wedding ring? That was dumb. Now he had to bring up the topic.

At Chen's Wok in Douglass, a waiter brought hot tea, pouring each of them a cup, and took their orders.

Drew took a sip before broaching the subject. "I didn't mean anything by wearing the ring. I'm just used to having it on, but now it's off."

"For the climb, or for good?" She raised an eyebrow.

"Yes and yes, but I'm hoping to replace it with a new one someday." Why had he said that? Good way to scare her off on their first date. He slapped his forehead. "That was a stupid thing to say."

"It's okay." She sipped her tea. "I'd like to date you. We have time to figure things out. It'll be seven years before Andy's an adult."

*Seven years?* He tried to hide his reaction. "Right," he said in the most measured tone he could muster. He'd have to take what he could get.

After the meal, the waiter brought the bill and fortune cookies.

She opened hers and read it aloud. "The flexible shall not be bent out of shape."

Drew laughed. "That's fitting, considering your climbing skills."

"Your turn."

He broke his cookie and pulled out the paper. Reading it, he smiled.

"Read it to me," she encouraged.

Feeling his cheeks warm, he handed her his fortune.

She read it aloud. "Love, because it's the only true adventure."

"Hopefully that's true, too," he said.

She reached across the table and squeezed his hand.

He felt like he was flying.

# Chapter 36

$M$arcella clapped after the fifth-grade choir's final song of the Quincy Elementary Spring Program. As the choir teacher directed the kids off the risers and Andy walked with his class out of the gymnasium, the principal thanked all the parents for coming and reminded them of the procedure for checking out their kids if they wished to have them leave with them. Drew reached over and grabbed Marcella's hand after the final applause, and they remained on the bleachers as the audience began to clear out. She noticed Ron and Patty talking with another older couple. Patty looked in her direction, doing a double take. Marcella waved to her with her free hand.

"I was thinking we should take another road trip," Drew said. "Easter weekend."

"Sure." Keeping hold of his hand, because the feeling was still so novel, so comforting, she used her other hand to pick up her phone from the bench beside her. She looked up her work schedule. "I have one regular client scheduled on the Monday after Easter. I'm sure she won't mind if I reschedule her for later in the week. If you can get off work, then we could have a little more time with your parents."

"Actually, I was thinking we should go to Madison."

She recoiled, pulling her hand away. "Why?"

"You've met my parents. I'd like to meet your dad and his wife."

She hesitated. "I don't think they have room for all of us."

"Andy and I will get a hotel," he countered.

"It's kind of far to go for a weekend."

"A minute ago you were fine driving ten hours downstate. Madison's only six."

"I don't know." She sighed. "I need to think about it."

He grabbed her hand again. "I want to take things to the next level."

She drew in a deep breath. What did he mean by that?

He continued, "I want us to share our lives. I want to meet your dad, Marce."

Marce. He was calling her Marce. The nickname Dad gave her. It made her miss him. Her heart softened. "I'll think about it."

"I don't want it to be too much for you. I'll get a hotel room for you, too. And we can make it easy on them by taking them to an Easter brunch someplace nice."

Marcella shook her head. "If we visit them, Kandy will want to cook. She loves it, and she's good at it," she admitted grudgingly.

"The line at the checkout station is probably short by now." Drew let go of her hand and stood. "Should we go get our boy?"

Marcella cringed at his choice of words and then followed him off the bleachers. She wouldn't presume Andy was *her* boy. They were both her guys, but Drew was making it sound like they were a family.

In the lobby, Marcella saw Ron and Patty again, and she stepped over to say hi to them as Drew requested that Andy be released from his classroom.

"It's impressive to see all the parents and grandparents here," Marcella said.

"And girlfriends," Patty said. There was an edge in her tone.

"Patty," Ron said, "for goodness sake."

Marcella didn't know what to say. She felt like pulling her

head down into a shell.

"Hey, guys." Drew came up alongside Marcella, putting his hand on the small of her back.

Patty turned her back to them, looking down the hallway.

Ron shook Drew's hand. "The boy can sing."

"He doesn't get that from me." Drew laughed nervously, probably realizing the sad truth of the statement.

"Kristine had a beautiful voice." Patty faced them.

"Yes, she did," Drew agreed. "And here he comes."

Andy slogged down the hallway caring a heavy backpack. He picked up his pace when he saw them, and then came up alongside Marcella. She gave him a one-armed hug.

"Don't you have a hug for your grandparents?" Patty asked pointedly.

Andy shrugged, dropped his backpack, and stepped toward her.

"Wonderful job." Patty hugged him and kissed him on top of the head.

Marcella thought about the Madison trip while they walked home from school with Andy. She'd go to Madison, and she'd get her own hotel room. She was a twenty-eight-year-old adult woman. She could make the visit on her own terms.

"Andy, would you want to go to Madison with me and your dad?"

"Yeah, do we get to stay in a water park?"

Drew mouthed a thank-you to Marcella, and then told Andy, "Not on this trip."

"Ahh."

"But we'll make sure to get a hotel with a pool," Marcella said, as she dialed her father.

"Marce, it's good to hear from you," he enthused.

"Hi, Dad." The moment she heard his greeting, she was glad she'd called. "I was wondering about Easter. I'd like to come to Madison."

"Really?" He sounded surprised. "You don't know how happy that makes me. We'd love to have you."

She could hear the smile in his voice. "I'd like to bring a friend—two friends actually." She winked at Andy. "We'll stay in a hotel."

"I'm having lunch with Kandy here. Let me tell her the news."

Marcella heard muffled conversation for a moment.

"Kandy suggested we check with our concierge," her dad continued, "and see if we can rent the guest unit in the building. She'll pray it's available. I'll call right now." He disconnected the line, not giving her a chance to object.

During the rest of the walk home, Andy told her about Grand Lodge, his favorite water park in Wausau. She was surprised by how calm she felt about the trip. Having Drew and Andy going with her was a big part of that. She looked forward to swimming in the pool. Relaxing in the hot tub. Eating at restaurants. And even the family dinner would be fine, now that she was no longer the third wheel, but an adult woman with her own guy, or rather, guys.

Besides, it would be good to get away from the cold and the snow. By mid-March, the streets and the sidewalks were bare, but the banks were still high and there was still plenty of snow in the yards and fields. Madison was far enough south the weather should be decent.

As they reached Drew and Andy's apartment—it still felt strange to go back to the place she had once called home—her dad called her back. "I'm sorry. It's booked for Easter weekend."

"That's okay. We're looking forward to getting a hotel, anyway." Maybe they'd get adjoining rooms or a suite.

"Kandy said she'll pray something will open up here. I'll let you know."

"Okay, whatever, Dad. We'll come down on Friday and head back on Monday morning."

"We can't wait to see you, Marce. And meet your friends."

# Chapter 37

*M*arcella threw her bag in the back of Drew's pickup truck and climbed in to the front seat, eager for their mini-vacation to begin. "Hi, guys."

"Good morning, beautiful." He called her beautiful like it was her name, reaching over and touching her shoulder.

She reveled in his affection. She turned her head toward the back seat where Andy sat playing on his iPad. "Hi, Andy."

He kept his head down, silent.

"You didn't say hi to Marcella," Drew reprimanded.

"Hi." Andy grunted, his eyes glued to the screen.

She looked at Drew questioningly. He smiled at her. Either he was ignoring Andy's bad mood or he was oblivious to it.

"Hey, Andy." She turned around as they crossed the lift bridge. "Ninety-nine bottles of beer on the wall," she sang playfully, hoping he'd snap out of his funk and join in.

He glared at her with the crabbiest look she'd ever seen on his face.

She turned back around. This was what she'd been afraid of. They were taking things to the next level, but Andy wasn't on board. Maybe he was okay with her being with his dad, but he probably hadn't realized that meant expanding his world to include her family. Especially on a holiday. She got it, but Drew wanted more. She did too, she had to admit, but not at Andy's expense.

Drew turned on the radio, then reached over and grabbed her hand, caressing it gently with his thumb. That simple, intimate gesture stirred longings in her. Longings that would likely never be fulfilled, she thought soberly. Thankfully, her phone rang, and she used that as an excuse to pull her hand away.

"Guess what?" Kandy bubbled. "I got a call from the concierge. The guy who was going to stay in the guest condo broke his leg and cancelled, so you and your friends can stay here. How's that for divine timing? A real answer to prayer." Leave it to Kandy to see someone else's broken leg as God's intervention in the world.

"Thanks, but we'll stay in a hotel all the same," Marcella said.

"Nonsense," Kandy said. "The guest condo is nicer than any hotel you could find. And it's only $75 per night."

"Thanks anyway, but Andy's looking forward to swimming in the hotel pool."

"Andy? You're bringing a man?"

"A man and a boy. Drew and his son Andy. They rent the lower flat of Dad's old duplex."

Kandy asked for details about his age and interests.

"Andy, my stepmom wants to know if you like Easter egg hunts."

"Yeah," Andy perked up. "But I haven't done one since Mom died."

Drew shook his head. "Parenting fail," he said softly.

Marcella chatted with Drew for the next two hours, occasionally trying to draw Andy into the conversation, but he wasn't having it. A couple hours later, they stopped for fast food in Rhinelander. Andy sat in the booth next to his dad, and Marcella sat across the table from the guys.

Andy took a sip of his drink. "Do you want to see our old house?" he asked Marcella. His voice held a challenge. "It's on the way."

"Yes. I'd love to see the place you called home for so many years."

"I told you she'd want to," Andy said.

They both looked to Drew.

He looked exasperated. "I suppose we can drive by. We can see the front yard anyway."

Andy's face broke out in a smile, and he remained in a decidedly better mood. Drew, however, was quiet as they continued on to Wausau.

They drove into an early to mid-century neighborhood with low-numbered avenues and streets named after trees. The grassy strip between the narrow street and sidewalk was lined with evenly spaced Norwegian maples. Drew slowed and pulled to a stop in front of a Craftsman-style bungalow. Marcella rolled down the window, and Andy leaned over her to take a picture with his iPad.

"That's my old bedroom." He pointed to an upstairs dormer window.

A car pulled into the drive, stopping short of the garage that was tucked behind the house, and a gray-haired woman got out. She crossed the lawn to where they were parked on the street. "Can I help you?"

"We just stopped to see the house," Marcella said. "This is where he grew up." She motioned back to Andy, who had shrunk back on the jumper seat.

"Oh, so you're the Smith family?"

"*They* are," Marcella said. "I'm just a friend."

"Do you want to come in?" The woman smiled warmly.

"Yes," Andy said before Marcella or Drew could reply.

They followed the lady around the back of the house and through the kitchen entrance.

Andy pointed to a Dutch door that separated the kitchen from the dining room. "That's where I played fishing when I was little. I had a broom with a string and a clothespin on it. I held it over the door, and Mom clipped stuff to it and said I caught something. I caught socks, napkins, spoons. Sometimes she puts candy on it."

"That's a fun idea," Marcella said, painfully aware he'd slipped into the present tense.

Drew stood by the front door, his eyes glassy. "I'm going to wait outside." He stepped out. Marcella began to follow him and then hesitated, glancing back at Andy.

"Can I show her my room?" Andy asked the new owner.

She nodded. "Which one was yours?"

"The blue one."

Marcella drew in a breath. She'd give Drew a hug later. Right now, Andy needed to show her these remnants of his early childhood.

The woman led the way upstairs. "I painted it, but it's still blue. Blue with a little gray in it."

Andy surveyed the room. Two sets of wooden bunk beds took up most of the floor space. "It's smaller than I remember it."

"I have four grandsons," the woman explained. "I have them over for sleepovers."

He stepped forward and touched the white doorframe. "That's where Mom marked how tall I was every year before school started. It's painted over now."

Andy walked slowly back through the house. He pointed to a corner in the living room where a recliner sat. "That's where we put the Christmas tree." He nodded to built-in shelving under the stairwell that was now the home to books and knickknacks. "That's where I kept my Lego creations."

Back in the truck, Andy asked if they could play the alphabet game.

"Sure," Marcella agreed. They took turns spotting the letters as they drove out of Wausau, but Drew didn't join in, his face somber as he gripped the steering wheel. She reached over and rubbed his shoulder.

Drew was glad that stopping at their old home improved his

son's mood, but it brought back memories he would rather have left in the past. He'd always cherish the good times. Holidays. Birthday parties. Andy's toddler years. His first day of school posing on the front steps. Drew and Andy wrestling on the living room carpet.

But there was pain, too. The drinking. The arguing. The blow-ups, which resulted in Kristine leaving more than once. And not all of it was her fault. He hated remembering what he'd been like then, how he would explode in anger when he got frustrated.

Apparently, Andy remembered the good, and for that Drew was thankful. He glanced back at his son in the rearview mirror.

"W," Andy crowed as they approached West Hanover Road.

"I'll find X at the next exit." Marcella rested her hand lightly on Drew's shoulder.

He could feel her empathy. He loved her. He needed her. He vowed to himself to do things differently. He liked that they didn't fight or even so much as argue. Well, there was that time she was weird after the massage, but he let it go, and it ended up working out. He was ready for another relationship. He was older. More mature. More seasoned. It helped that he didn't drink anymore. And finding faith taught him to overlook others' faults, to look more at himself and what he could do better.

She might want to wait until Andy was an adult before moving the relationship forward, and he could live with that. He didn't like the thought. He'd rather marry her sooner and maybe have another kid.

He and Kristine never planned on having another baby. First Drew had to finish school, and then he was starting a job while they were settling into their first house. Kristine seemed to resent the whole thing. Of course she loved AJ, and she was a good mom, but she'd make snide comments about the best years of her life being ruined. She wanted to have fun. Travel. Buy nice things.

He could only pray for her. He tried to change her, but

she needed to want something better for herself. He wished he could say she moved in a positive direction, but their last conversation ended in another heated argument. And just like that, she died. If there was anything Kristine's death taught him, it was that life was fragile and unpredictable. Time was limited.

"Z, in construction zone," Andy yelled as they passed an orange sign.

Marcella reached back and gave him a high five.

They both needed her. He grabbed her hand and held it for the rest of the drive to Madison.

The GPS on his phone guided him to the high-rise condominium.

"This is nice," he said, looking at the steel and glass building.

Marcella stared across the road, toward the lake.

He looked back in the rearview mirror at Andy. "Ready, Freddy?"

"Sure, Betty."

"Earth to Marcella." He touched Marcella's shoulder, and she jumped. "You okay?" he asked.

She took a deep breath. "Here goes nothing."

Andy pulled his backpack from the truck bed. It might've been the first time he was able to reach in from the side by himself. He was getting so tall. Drew locked their luggage in the truck's cab.

In the lobby, a man in a polo shirt sat behind a granite counter. "Can I help you?"

Marcella didn't answer so Drew took the initiative. "We're here to visit Larry and Kandy Seppa."

The concierge offered a smile. "May I tell them who's here?"

After phoning, the man buzzed them through a door. "The elevators are around the corner to the right. Sixteenth floor, unit 1604."

A sixty-something woman dressed in slacks and a silky shirt met them at the elevator bank. "So these are your guests."

She smiled broadly, her tone warm and welcoming. "I'm Kandy."

Drew smiled and gave a quick nod.

Marcella stiffened as she awkwardly exchanged a hug with her stepmother. "Is Dad here?"

"He's still at work. He'll be home shortly."

Marcella grabbed Drew's hand. "This is my boyfriend, Drew Smith, and his son, Andy."

Kandy squealed and covered her mouth.

Drew couldn't hold back a smile. He liked the sound of that introduction. It was the first time he'd heard Marcella refer to him as her boyfriend.

Kandy directed her gaze at Marcella. "You didn't tell us you were dating."

Marcella straightened. "I just did."

Drew held out a hand to Kandy. She took it and then pulled him into a firm hug.

Kandy turned to Andy. "You can call me Grandma Kandy. All the kids at church do."

"Okay." Andy shrugged.

"I can tell already that we're going to be pals." Kandy stepped forward and hugged him. "Grandma Kandy and Andy. I'm a poet and I didn't know it." She laughed as she stepped into the elevator and held the door open for them.

"Welcome, welcome." Kandy led the way down the hall into the condo. The open-concept design made the unit feel spacious, and the finishings were luxurious with a glass-tiled backsplash behind granite countertops, stainless steel appliances, and gleaming hardwood floors.

In the living room, Andy stood in front of the sliding glass doors that opened to a balcony with a lake view. "That's nice."

"The lake is the reason we want to live here." Kandy opened the door to the balcony. She motioned for Drew and Marcella to follow as she and Andy stepped outside.

On the balcony, Kandy was saying something to Andy about fireworks and sailboats. A brisk wind blew off the lake, whipping Marcella's hair into disarray. She shivered. Drew put his arm around her and pulled her close, her hair tickling his nose.

"And if you come back this summer when it's warm, we'll rent kayaks," Kandy concluded with a flourish of her hands. "Come inside, and I'll get you some lemonade and we can play a game. Do you know how to play Uno?"

Andy nodded.

Kandy clapped his shoulder with the palm of her hand, and they went inside.

Drew hung back with Marcella. She stood against the railing, facing the lake. Even with a pensive look on her face, she was decidedly beautiful.

"There she goes," Marcella huffed, "trying to insert herself into his life. Did you hear her? Grandma Kandy?"

Drew looked down over the railing at the traffic passing below, trying to consider her point of view. He turned and looked through the sliding doors. Andy and Kandy sat at the kitchen table with glasses of lemonade. Kandy shuffled a deck of cards as Andy talked, his hands animated. Kandy burst into laughter and Andy followed suit. "I don't think Andy minds."

Marcella viewed them through the window and then spun around and clenched the railing. "I don't know. Maybe it's just me."

Drew put his hand on top of hers, caressing her fingers. Her hand was cold. "Come here," he said, wrapping her in a hug.

"All these years, I thought Kandy was awful. She said things that hurt me." She hesitated. "Andy seems to like her, though."

"He barely knows her," Drew countered. "If she's that bad, she won't be able to hide her true self for long."

Marcella sighed. "She's not that bad. I guess as far as Kandy goes, in my eyes, she can do no right. I'm ashamed of how I feel toward her, but…" She shrugged. "There it is, the ugly truth of who I am."

He squeezed her, silently praying she'd find resolution, peace. As he prayed for her, he realized he too needed the same. Being in his old home had pulled at scabs of wounds he thought had healed. "We're quite the pair," he said, brushing her hair from her face.

# Chapter 38

$M$arcella sat in her hotel room in a wing chair next the window. The capitol building lit up the night sky on the isthmus between Lakes Mendota and Monona, her dad and Kandy's condo building in the foreground. She lifted her mug. The peppermint tea from the hotel lobby wasn't as potent as what she had at home, but it was still a good way to unwind before bed.

Dinner at the condo had gone well. Kandy made lasagna and a chopped salad. Conversation was pleasant, and her dad and Drew seemed to connect. Her dad even took him to his office to show him a project his company was rolling out soon. While Marcella helped Kandy clean up, they discussed plans for the next day. They'd visit the indoor section of the botanical gardens and go shopping. Both ideas appealed to Marcella.

She'd recently been doing most of her shopping through an old classmate's online and pop-up stores. She liked the Bohemian-style clothing, but she needed new summer sandals. The selection was limited in the Copper Country. She also hoped to get Andy new clothes without stepping on Drew's toes. She still wasn't sure how to broach the subject. She could measure the boy's growth spurt by the distance from his shoes to the hem of his pants. He definitely needed pants, but she didn't want to be intrusive.

Later, swimming in the hotel pool had been just plain fun. She raced Andy across the pool, and he beat her twice. The boy was a fish. Then she and Drew sat in the hot tub, scoring Andy's cannon balls. It had been a good day. She loved being in their lives.

She heard a knock and opened the adjoining door.

"Hey, beautiful," Drew said softly. "Andy's asleep."

"Do you want to sit for a few minutes?"

He nodded and followed her across the room but didn't sit down. They stood near the window, taking in the view together. Drew pulled her close, and she leaned her head against his shoulder. He turned toward her, cupping her face with his hand, and drew her lips to his. They kissed, tentatively at first, and then the passion between them built until Drew pulled back. "It's a good thing Andy's with us to chaperone," he said softly. He sat in a wing chair.

"Yeah," she agreed, plopping down in the other chair but unable to take her eyes off his. She took a deep breath.

"I like your dad, Marce," he said.

She smiled. "I'm glad." She hadn't realized how important that was to her.

"You doing okay?" he asked her. He leaned forward and touched her knee.

"Yeah," she said. "Things are going well, hey?"

"Very well." His eyes twinkled as he leaned back in the chair. He patted his thigh. "Come here, beautiful."

She rose and sat in his lap, her arms around his shoulders as they kissed their good-nights once again.

The next day, they all strolled through the Botanical Gardens conservatory, a glass pyramid filled with exotic plants and flowers, complete with fragrant orchids and free-flying birds. Dad and Drew chatted about business and politics, while Kandy enthusiastically guided Andy. Marcella took the time to commune with the plants. It was in gardens such as these where she felt closest to God, where the spark of divinity in man brought order out of chaos.

They drove to the mall, Andy riding with Kandy and Dad, and met at the food court. The group got food from different restaurants and found a table. Marcella stabbed a forkful of salad. "The conservatory was a great idea, Kandy. It was beautiful."

A smile lit up Kandy's face. "I thought it would be right up your alley. You'll have to come back in the summer when we can tour the outdoor gardens." She turned to Drew. "You and Andy, too. If you let us know in advance, we can book the guest condo in our building."

After lunch, Kandy took charge. "How about Marcella and I take Andy to the department store and get him pants?" she suggested.

"Kandy!" Marcella cringed at Kandy's impertinence. "It should be up to his dad to buy him clothes." She looked to see how Drew would react to the interference.

He shook his head. "Parenting fail," he mumbled.

Andy seemed oblivious to the conversation as he sucked up the last of his giant milkshake through a straw.

"I'd be happy to buy him pants," Kandy said. "That's what grandmas do."

"You're not his grandma." Marcella knew her tone was sharp but she couldn't stop herself.

"Kids can't have too many grandmas."

"But it's not up to you to insert yourself into his life."

Kandy recoiled, her face showing the pain of past conversations she and Marcella had years before. "I know I'm not his real grandma."

"I like having you as a grandma," Andy said.

Marcella felt hurt that her little guy sided with Kandy. "Drew, help me out here."

"I don't mind, and he does need new pants." He dug his wallet out of his back pocket. "Let me give you some cash."

Dad flapped his hand. "Keep your money. We can afford to buy Marcella's favorite boy pants."

"Do you even want pants?" Marcella addressed Andy, not

sure why she was arguing against it.

"I'd love pants." Andy agreed happily. "The kids at school have been teasing me about my high- waters."

"Kids can be so cruel," Kandy said.

"I took him to Shop-Mart," Drew said, "but they didn't have anything there that fit him. It was all pretty picked over, and they were just getting in their summer shorts."

"So Dad said I'd have to wait for back-to-school shopping." Andy slid his chair back and lifted a foot. "I've been wearing my soccer socks so my legs wouldn't show."

Drew shook his head again, with that familiar look of defeat on his face. Marcella grabbed his hand.

"Larry, should we go to the bookstore and get some coffee?" Drew stood, keeping hold of Marcella's hand with tender affection. "Do you want to come with us, Marce, or go with Andy and Kandy?"

Marcella sighed. "I should go with them."

After sending Andy into the dressing room with a stack of jeans and khaki pants, Kandy looked to Marcella with sad eyes. "I did a number on you, didn't I?"

Marcella shrugged, not sure how to respond.

"I recognized it then," Kandy continued, "and I tried to pull back, but I don't think I ever said I'm sorry."

Marcella's eyes began to sting, and she blinked back tears. She didn't want to cry in front of her stepmom. "You said some hurtful things, like you would've never been able to marry my dad if my mom hadn't died."

"I said that?"

"Yes, and you're always saying stuff like that, like God's making all these horrible things happen so he can answer your prayers. Like that poor guy who broke his leg. That was your answer to prayer so the guest room opened up." Marcella's anger adequately suppressed her tears.

"God doesn't make bad things happen, but he allows them."

"Ahh." Marcella turned her back to Kandy. "That's a copout. I'm so tired of hearing that."

The conversation fell silent, and a short time later Andy came out of the dressing room with his head hung low.

"Did any of them fit?" Marcella forced herself to use a pleasant voice.

"No. The waist was too big on all of them."

"That's because you just had a growth spurt. Now you'll start filling out your frame, so it's good your pants are a little big in the waist. We'll get you a belt. Go back in and try them on again. I want to see them with a belt."

After Andy went back in, Kandy said, "You make a very good mother."

"I'm not his mother." Marcella took a camouflage belt off the rack near the entrance to the dressing room.

"He needs one."

"I didn't need a mother when you showed up. I needed a dad, but he was too busy with you."

Tears filled Kandy's eyes.

Marcella regretted her words. "I'm sorry. That was harsh."

"No, you're right," Kandy said.

"Here's the first pair," Andy said, holding the pants up with one hand on the waist. "Are you okay, Grandma Kandy?"

Kandy wiped her eyes. "I'm fine."

Marcella inspected Andy's pants, pulling the waistband out to see how big they were. "You're going to fill these out soon." She threaded the belt through the loops and cinched it tight.

"They look very nice," Kandy said.

"Let's see what else fits using the belt." Marcella directed Andy back into the dressing room.

"Well," Kandy continued their conversation, "we might need to face the real possibility that I'll always be a horrible step monster, so I just ask for your forgiveness and grace."

"You're not a step monster. I'm probably not being fair to you. I don't know. I'm pretty screwed up myself."

"I love you, Marcella." Tears flooded Kandy's eyes. "I wish I was better at showing you."

Marcella put her arm around Kandy's shoulder. "You do

fine," she said. "I love you," she added, realizing it was the first time she had said so, and it was true. She lowered her voice. "The idea of trying to be mom number two to him terrifies me."

"You'll do fine." Kandy said.

Back at the condo, Kandy had a crockpot of chili ready for dinner. She brought up the plan for Easter Sunday. "If we go to the early service, then we can do the Easter egg hunt before dinner, otherwise we'll do it after dinner. The ham will be ready at about one o'clock."

Marcella felt her stomach tighten. They hadn't discussed Easter services.

"What time are your services?" Drew asked.

"Nine thirty and eleven o'clock," Dad said.

"We can do the 9:30 service," Drew said cheerily. "That's 10:30 Michigan time. Besides, we're all early risers anyhow. Right, Marcella?"

She took a deep breath. "Right."

# Chapter 39

*T*he vibe at Downtown Church reminded Drew of the church he had attended in Wausau, but on a larger scale. There were parking attendants waving folks in, a coffee bar, and an auditorium with a black, steel-rafter ceiling. He settled into his seat between Andy and Marcella in a row with Larry and Kandy. Announcements by way of short video clips were projected on three screens turned at different angles above the stage.

A guitarist began to play a riff on his electric guitar, and the rest of the worship team rushed on stage. The leader motioned for all to stand, and Drew placed his coffee on the cement floor under his chair.

"He is risen," the worship leader proclaimed.

"He is risen indeed," Drew called back along with the others in the auditorium.

"Let us rejoice," the worship leader shouted, and the lead guitarist morphed his riff into the melody of a new song Drew had recently heard on Christian radio.

He clapped along to vibrant, polished music—something found in larger cities, he thought appreciatively—as Marcella stood next to him, sipping tea. After a number of rousing songs, the congregants took their seats.

A guy wearing a polo shirt and khakis stepped to the mic. "Welcome. I'm Pastor Dave. We're so glad you could join us for Resurrection Sunday. First off, we're going to hear some stories about resurrection in the lives of ordinary folks who have found hope in Christ."

A video—obviously done in house, as Drew recognized the background from the lobby—featured a young couple and their beautiful, adopted eighteen-month-old daughter. They took turns sharing about their struggles with infertility. They kept their faith in God, and their prayers were answered, but in a way they didn't expect. Next up was a middle-aged couple sharing their story of an affair. They had been on the brink of divorce, but then the husband repented, his wife found grace to forgive him, and they both found healing in Christ. Lastly, a woman talked about being healed from cancer. The doctors had found a tumor in her brain. It was terminal. The tumor disappeared, and there was no scientific explanation.

Marcella sat stiffly, looking down at her lap. Drew grabbed her hand.

"God so desperately wants to bring healing in our lives," the woman on the video concluded with a gentle smile.

When the congregation burst into applause, Marcella pulled her hand away and stood. She exited the sanctuary.

"Stay here with Kandy," Drew told Andy, and walked after Marcella. He found her outside, leaning against a tree near the parking lot. "Do you want to go sit in the truck?"

She nodded and followed him to the vehicle.

"You okay?" Drew started the truck to warm the cab, taking the edge off the gray, forty-five-degree day.

She shrugged. "I'm not a big fan of churches like that."

"It was the cancer story, wasn't it?"

She nodded. "Not just that, but yes. Sometimes there aren't happy endings."

"Don't you think a lot of it is up to us, how we respond to tragedy? You're one of the kindest and most empathetic people I know, and I think some of that is because of what you went through."

"I don't believe it's worth it. My mom suffered and died young so I could be a better person?" Her voice had an edge to it. "And so Kandy gets to marry my dad?" she muttered under her breath. She straightened. "Just because good comes out of a bad situation doesn't mean it was meant to be."

"I don't really understand all that theological stuff. I just know my life was transformed by faith. When I found Jesus, my priorities changed. I became much less argumentative. Kinder. You wouldn't have liked me before. And I know I couldn't do this parenting thing on my own."

Marcella sighed. "I know faith is important to you, but it's easier for me to accept the suffering in the world if I leave God out of the day-to-day happenings. I have a hard time understanding why God would pick winners and losers."

Drew frowned. He was at a loss for what to say, or more like at a loss for how to say it. He wanted to say she was being too negative, blaming God for the bad and not giving him credit for the good. But he didn't want to be critical of her. "Could I pray for you?"

She shrugged and crossed her arms. "You can pray in your head, because I don't want to hear it."

"In that case, I'll go back in." Drew wanted to hold her, but she was shutting him out again.

"I'll wait here till you're done." She laid her head back and closed her eyes. "With videos like that, I don't think I can handle the sermon."

Drew left the truck running and went back into the auditorium. He understood she struggled with her faith, but she was raised in the church and had the values and love espoused by Jesus. He thought they could find common ground, but maybe there was too great a gulf between them.

Marcella survived the day wearing mostly a pleasant face. Andy loved the Easter egg hunt, and Kandy cooked a wonderful meal. Drew and Dad continued to build a rapport. They were alike in many ways, including being oblivious to where she was emotionally and the kind of support she needed from them. She was glad the day was done and they were back at the hotel.

She sat in the wing chair sideways, with the small of her back against one armrest and her feet tucked up against the other, sipping tea. So much had happened over the last year, and even more in the last few weeks. It had been an emotional roller coaster. In many ways, life had been easier when she had her routine of biking, working, and gardening. Now she felt as if she were being pulled by a fast-moving river. Drew was at her side, not noticing she was drowning.

He knocked on the adjoining door, and she got up to open it. She resumed her position in the chair, while he sat in the other.

He patted his lap, but she was comfortable where she was. "Andy went right to sleep," he said. "He had a great day."

She looked across the lake to Dad and Kandy's condominium. Some lights were still on, but she wasn't sure which unit was theirs. Dad had moved on quickly after her mom's death, and now he had moved further, both physically and emotionally. She wondered if he ever thought of her anymore, of his wife of eighteen years.

"Tonight you're looking at the skyline more than you're looking in my eyes." Drew leaned forward and touched her ankle.

Marcella shrugged.

"You're still upset about the video?" he asked.

A tear rolled down her cheek. The video might've pulled the plug on her downward spiral, but it was more than that. It was another gut punch. It had been a long year of emotional gut punches.

"Are you going to shut me out again?" Drew asked.

Marcella brought the tea to her lips and sipped, as her eyes followed the lines of white streaks in the night sky from spotlights that lit the capitol dome. She remembered nights when she drove herself to the state park at midnight to watch the aurora borealis. Life was simpler then.

"Nothing to say?"

"I'm too messed up for a relationship," Marcella said.

Drew folded his arms.

She could feel the negative energy three feet away. "Things have been moving too fast. I think we should take a break."

"Do you want to break up?" he asked.

Marcella didn't want to break up. All she wanted to do was slow down. They should give each other a little space. But apparently Drew only thought in absolutes. "If that's what you want," she said, through clenched teeth.

"This on-again off-again is too hard on Andy," he said.

"And that's what I've been most afraid of, how this would affect him." She finally looked at him, but now *he* was staring out the window. "My mom's death rocked me to my core, but my dad wasn't there for me when I most needed him."

"I'll be there for him."

"There's also the issue of faith. I know it's important to you, but I struggle with it. I do believe in God and Jesus, but I can't understand why he allows good people to suffer. Why he ignored my prayers but answers others. And every time I go to church, I'm reminded of how mad I am at him. I know you want to raise Andy in the church, and I think that's good, but I don't know if I can be a part of it."

Drew sat silently with his chest slowly rising and lowering.

Now was probably the time to say it. To get it over with. With resignation in her voice, she said, "It probably would be best if we broke up."

He swiveled his head with his eyes narrowed. His jaw dropped open as if he was about to say something, and then he pressed his lips together and breathed out slowly through his nose, as if he was willing himself to be calm. "Andy loves you. I love you."

"Oh, don't say that. That would make it all the harder if this doesn't work out."

"So you do want to make this work?" He leaned forward. "I'm getting mixed signals."

"I can't handle this emotionally. And I don't want to risk hurting Andy."

"This will crush him." Drew stood with his shoulders slouched and head down. "I'm not going to say anything to him. He'll be busy with school and he'll have the Mackinac Island trip to look forward, so hopefully he won't notice we're not seeing each other anymore. And maybe you can make an effort to see him this summer."

"So that's it?" Marcella realized she had hoped for more of a fight from him, for him to fight for her.

"Unless you tell me to stay and that you'll try to make this work." He lifted his head and looked into her eyes.

She wasn't ready to say that. She averted her eyes back in the direction of the artificial aurora. She wasn't ready to commit, but they had become too comfortable too quickly in each other's presence. She needed time to think it through. She wasn't sure she believed all she'd said, and she wanted him to help her make sense of it all.

"That's what I thought," he said, and then left the room, closing his adjoining door behind him.

"Stay," she whispered as a tear rolled down her cheek. "I'll try to make it work."

On the ride home, it was Marcella's turn to be glum. Andy was exhausted enough from the trip that he slept most of the way home, and Drew engaged him in conversation when he was awake. Drew mostly ignored her but was polite the few times he did need to speak to her.

# Chapter 40

*B*efore getting Andy from Ron and Patty's, Drew swung by the co-op to pick up deli food for dinner. It wasn't home cooking, but he felt better about it than frozen pizza or hotdogs.

"Hey, Patty," Drew said, bumping into his mother-in-law in the snack aisle. "Where's Andy?"

"He's with Ron. I'm on my way to a meeting," she said, scanning the shelf of chips. "Andy said that you broke up with that Marcella."

"I don't know why he would've said that. I didn't say anything to him."

"He said you don't tell him anything." She glanced at him with a look of disdain.

Drew felt socked in the gut. Andy had leveled that concern before. Maybe it was time to be more open with him. He was obviously old enough to figure out things on his own.

"I can't say I'm unhappy about it," Patty said.

"What do you mean by that?" Drew was sick of her snide comments.

"Andy doesn't need another mother." She tossed a bag of root chips in her handheld basket. "For a while, she was all he talked about."

"What's wrong with that?" Drew felt the need to defend Marcella, even though their relationship was over.

Patty squared her shoulders. "She's nothing like Kristine."

"Of course not."

"And she doesn't deserve him," she said.

"But he deserves her."

Patty turned her back to him and walked down the aisle. "You never deserved Kristine."

He walked after her. It was time to call her on her hostility toward him. "Hey, I loved Kristine, and it tore me apart when she died."

Patty spun on her heels and jabbed a finger into his chest. "Then you shouldn't have killed her."

He stepped back. "Killed her? I didn't kill her."

"You kicked her out of the house."

"I did not. She left of her own free will like she did all the other times. What was I supposed to do? Lock her in a room?"

"Well," Patty said, crossing her arms, "you made life unbearable for her."

"We had a good life, and sure we had our disagreements, but what was unbearable was her choosing to get so hammered that she was still half drunk and unable to get up in the morning when I needed to go to work."

"I doubt that's true."

"You only ever heard one side of the story, and she only ever called you when she was mad at me."

Patty averted her eyes.

"You may never like me, but I want you to be part of Andy's life. I don't want him to forget about his mom, but he needs to move on with life, and so do you."

Tears rolled down Patty's cheeks, and her shoulders began to shake. Drew put his hand on her shoulder, but she shrugged it off and turned her back to him.

Drew could see the same rage in Patty that Kristine possessed. They fought in similar ways, but he nonetheless had empathy for the woman. She was hurting, and her grief was manifested through anger at him. He wasn't going to be able to change her heart or mind, but he'd had enough of her behavior. "If you're going to undermine me in my efforts to help Andy heal and have a happy childhood, then I'll cut you out of his life."

Drew turned toward the deli, where Mak stood at the end of the aisle scribbling in his journal. "Hi, Mak."

"*Päivää päivää,*" the man muttered with his head still down. "So you broke up with Marcella?"

"Did you hear that?"

"I heard it all, champ." Mak tapped his pen on his journal. "Although yous were talkin' too fast for me to keep up."

"Oh, great."

If Drew wasn't going to have the support of his in-laws, and without Marcella in his life, maybe it was time to look for work in the Detroit area before Andy got too settled and made more friends. He'd let Andy finish out the year at Quincy Elementary, especially because he was looking forward to the Mackinac Island trip. Drew would at least have a chance of getting a decent reference from Janet if he quit Douglass State in the summer when things slowed down.

Marcella put clean sheets on the massage table and went up front to meet a first-time client—someone she would've never expected—Toivo Maki.

"He said he needed to run to his truck to get something," the receptionist said.

Marcella pulled a tissue from a box behind the counter and turned her attention to the jade plant near the lobby window. She wiped a film of dust off the rubbery leaves. "Breathe, little plant."

"*Hyvää päivää,*" Mak barked upon entering.

"Oh, you have a copy of your book there."

"Yah." He held a copy of *The Child of Rumspringa.* He followed her through the salon. "I thought you might want a signed copy."

"Thank you. Are you going to sign it from Iris or Mak?" She stopped short of her room and motioned him ahead of her.

"I already signed it, from Iris, of course." He handed her the book. "I can't have any hard evidence out there that I'm behind this phenomenon." He stepped into the room.

She laughed. "I'll give you a minute to get under the sheet. You can hang your clothes on the hooks."

On the cover of his book was a smiling young woman in a period dress and bonnet in front of a field of golden grass under a blue sky. On the title page, Mak had written in flourishing, beautiful handwriting *Love & Grace, Iris MacDowell.* That was sweet, Marcella thought. She turned the book over. For the author photo, he had used an image of his wife, Lorna. She laughed again.

When Marcella entered the room, Mak lay face up on the table wearing a long-sleeved T-shirt and the sheet pulled up to his belly. "You didn't want to take off your shirt?"

"I don't have anything on underneath it."

"That's generally the idea."

"I'm new to this. First time I got a massage."

Marcella set the book on her table. "You have beautiful handwriting."

"I don't. I'm da only one who can read my handwritin'. Lorna signs all da books."

Marcella checked if he'd object to a pine essential oil. It was typically a favorite among the old Finns, and he did indeed like it. She squirted jojoba oil in the palm of her hand, followed by a dab of pine oil, and worked them together. She lifted the sheet at his ankles to get a sense of where to start. "And you're still wearing your long johns?" She worked the oil into his feet.

"Yah, it's all connected."

"I've never seen anything like that, for adults anyway."

"Lorna calls it my onesie." He snorted a laugh. "But I hate that draft up my back when I'm shovelin' or makin' wood."

"That's all right. I can work through the fabric, but I won't be able to use the oil." She held his ankles up, sensing tightness in his hips and lower back. "So what brings you in today?"

"I'm here doin' research. Google's great, and I's watchin' massage videos on da YouTube, but I figure I'll write more authentic if I actually experience a massage."

She smiled. The man took his craft seriously. Marcella massaged up his leg, eventually working her way to the front of his thighs.

Mak winced.

"Too much pressure?" she asked.

"No, no. Feels good. Just a tight spot."

After kneading his quadriceps, she lifted his knee, pushed it partway across the other leg, and worked his IT band.

With a strained face, Mak asked, "What are you workin' on now?"

"Your iliotibial band. It can get tight from doing a lot of sitting."

"Yah. I'm spendin' more time at my desk writin'. My publisher's driving me to get this new book finished by June so we can get through da editin' process and have it published in time for Christmas."

"What's the book called?"

"*The Child of Rumspringa Returns.*"

"Another Amish romance?"

"Yah. Da child's father has a love interest who's a masseuse."

"We kind of prefer 'massage therapist' these days."

"Yeah, I read that. But back then they called them masseuses."

"Did the Amish even have masseuses?"

"Da Amish and da Mennonite were into all sorts of holistic medicine."

She set his leg back down and moved up, driving a fist into the front of his hip.

He grimaced, and she let up on the pressure.

"What's that you're workin' on?" Mak asked.

"Your hip flexors."

She continued to work his hip until she was back to the

initial level of pressure, but without him showing signs of pain. "Are you ticklish?"

"I don't think so. Not anymore."

She dug her fingers under his hip bone. "Lift your ankle up a little bit."

As he did so, she felt for the muscle and pressed into it hard.

"*Makkara, makkara, makkara.*"

Marcella laughed at the old man using the Finnish word for sausage like a swearword. "Yeah, it's pretty tight."

"Whatcha workin' now?"

"Still the hip flexors. What you're feeling is your psoas."

"How do ya spell that?"

Marcella spelled it out for him. "I'm not sure massage practitioners from the time period you're writing about would've been familiar with the psoas muscle."

"Good point, but that's not all I'm doin' research on. I's workin' on finishin' up da rough draft now, tryin' to figure my way out of da dark moment."

She moved around to his other leg, starting again with his calf.

"He loves her. I can tell. And he thinks she's da best thing for his kid, but they stopped talking, and he says she's shuttin' him out."

The story was sounding too familiar. He was fishing. "Have you been talking to Drew?"

"I get inspiration from many places, and any resemblance to actual people is purely coincidental. I need to understand her motivation. Let's say, hypothetically, da man and the boy is da best thing to happen in her life."

Marcella shorted her work on his calf and promptly moved to his quadriceps.

Mak winced. "Why would you think she rejected him?"

"Maybe being Amish is important to him, but she has too many scars from her past to embrace the lifestyle." She kneaded the muscle. "Maybe he's so focused on what's good for him and the kid that he's not attuned to her needs."

"This book's going to be a BS," he said exuberantly.

"Huh?"

"A BS. A best seller. This is good," he said, seemingly oblivious to the pressure she was exerting on his hip flexors. "Now, how do they resolve it? How do they get back together?"

"Maybe they don't."

"We need to have a happy ending. My readers demand it." His face was again showing signs of strain.

"Life isn't fiction. It doesn't have happy endings."

"Ya know, I started writin' romance because it sells. But now, I'm startin' to like da genre because ya see how strong love is. My first book showed that love is stronger than shame. This book I'm workin' on is about love being stronger than blood ties, but I'd say love's also greater than hurt, anger, grief, even doubt. Don'tcha think?"

She shrugged.

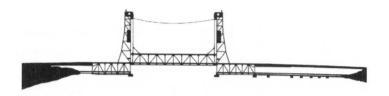

# *Chapter 41*

*M*arcella sat with Louisa in eager anticipation of word from the hospital. Beth had gone into labor the prior evening, and in the morning, Rebecca went to the hospital to await the birth of her grandchild.

In recent weeks, Louisa had been drifting in and out of sleep throughout the day, rarely awake for more than ten minutes and unable to sleep for more than a half hour without pain medication. And with the opioids, her breathing became frighteningly shallow. She'd been reduced to little more than a thin layer of skin over bones, except for the swelling in her extremities. She had somehow maintained her ability to talk, although it was little more than a whisper, and only single words and short sentences.

Rebecca had said that each time her mother woke up the night before, she looked to her inquisitively, and when Rebecca said there was no news, she closed her eyes again. In the morning, Louisa refused her medication, perhaps in an effort to remain more alert and despite the anxiety she experienced when her breathing would catch or she'd get phlegm in her throat. With Louisa reclined back in her wheelchair, Marcella massaged her feet.

Louisa mouthed something, and Marcella drew near.

In a faint whisper, she said, "Birds."

Marcella knew what she was asking. She sat her up and moved her into the kitchen, reclining her again with her head turned left toward the window where chickadees fed at the bird feeder.

"I think I'll make peppermint tea," Marcella said, and the corners of Louisa's mouth pulled up slightly.

A fire was still smoldering in the antique kitchen stove, so Marcella added a few pieces of hardwood to the firebox. While the stove roared to life, she filled a ceramic teakettle with water and set it on the stove. Louisa had always said tea tastes better when heated on a wood fire. Marcella believed that was true. It activated more than the taste buds. It stirred the soul.

Marcella sliced a small piece off a loaf of cardamom bread.

"Would you like *nisu*?" she asked Louisa.

Louisa rocked her head back and forth no more than a quarter of an inch, and Marcella understood that as a no. Of course she wouldn't want it. She hadn't eaten anything by mouth for a month or more, but it seemed the polite thing to ask. She buttered the small piece and popped it in her mouth.

Two robins danced in the backyard, which was now clear of snow. The plowed banks and deep drifts at the edges of the field had yet to melt, and Marcella knew all too well that another heavy snow could still fall in April or May. Nonetheless, it felt like spring.

"The robins are back," Marcella said.

Again, the corners of Louisa's mouth pulled up into a partial smile.

The kettle whistled, and Marcella steeped the loose-leaf tea. She thought back to the many times she'd visited with Louisa after giving her massages. She and Louisa shared a love of tea, and it had been Louisa who inspired her to grow her own peppermint leaves and dry them.

Marcella poured them each a cup. She doubted Louisa would take it with a straw, as she hadn't done so in the last couple weeks, but maybe she'd appreciate a spoonful.

Marcella sipped her tea. It was still a bit hot. She watched Louisa, who had now been awake longer than she'd been for the last several days. The hospice nurse speculated she could go at any time. Rebecca and Marcella agreed it was best not to tell Beth how poorly Louisa was doing. She certainly didn't need the added stress at the end of her pregnancy, especially not while she was giving birth.

With the tea cool enough, Marcella picked up a spoon and offered some to Louisa. "Would you like a spoonful?"

Louisa moved her eyes up and down, her way of nodding yes.

Marcella inclined her backrest and fed her a teaspoon of the peppermint tea.

Marcella's phone dinged. It was a text from Danny, a picture of Beth holding a pink-capped baby.

"Louisa, it's a girl." Marcella showed the picture to Louisa, and Louisa's eyes sparkled.

Another text came in. *Mom and baby are doing great. They should be released tomorrow morning.*

Louisa fell asleep as soon as Marcella reclined her chair. She laid the afghan over Louisa's thin body, pulling it over her feet. Her breathing became shallow, and Marcella grew concerned. She wondered if she should text Rebecca at the hospital, but Rebecca was in the middle of one of the happiest moments of her life, and Beth and Danny couldn't very well leave, either.

Marcella kept a watchful eye on Louisa as she added more wood to the fire, keeping the kitchen warm for her.

A couple hours later, Louisa stirred and opened her eyes. "Read," she said in barely a whisper.

"Sure," Marcella agreed. "What do you want me to read?"
"Bible."

Marcella recoiled, but remembered the peace that came over her mother when Marcella read Scripture to her in her final days. "Okay," she said. "I'll go get a Bible."

She went out to the garage where she had her boxes and furniture stored. She remembered which box the books were in, and she opened it to find her mother's Bible, with its tattered, leather cover.

Back in the kitchen, Louisa was sleeping again. Marcella made herself a light lunch of *makkara*, cheese, and Swedish hardtack with butter.

Louisa opened her eyes, looking toward the chickadees.

Marcella opened the Bible to pages filled with yellow highlights, underlined passages, and notes in the margins. Her mother had loved this book. Marcella turned to Psalms and read until Louisa fell asleep again.

"Louisa." Marcella tenderly ran her fingers through Louisa's hair.

She opened her eyes.

"Beth texted," Marcella said. "They're on their way home from the hospital. They're going to stop here with—" Marcella caught herself. Beth had asked her to keep the name a secret. "They're going to bring the baby to meet you."

"It was a girl?" Louisa mouthed the words.

"Yes."

Half a smile crossed Louisa's face, and her eyes drifted shut again. Marcella massaged Louisa's feet. She didn't know if it made much difference at this point, but it was something she could do. Rebecca was sleeping upstairs, exhausted after having been up with her mother the night before and at the hospital the prior day.

Louisa opened her eyes again. "Thank you for coming," she mouthed, as if Marcella had just arrived. Louisa's jaw cramped and she looked panicked.

Marcella moved to massage Louisa's jaw.

"No, no," Louisa said softly, her breathing labored.

"Should I play for you?" Marcella offered, hoping to ease Louisa's anxiety.

"Yes," Louisa mouthed, the look of panic still in her eyes.

Marcella lifted her guitar from its case and played *Amazing*

*Grace*, the old hymn her mother had loved. A song from her childhood. She knew all the words by heart. When she reached the end of the third verse, "And grace will lead us home," Louisa seemed to relax.

Marcella sang the final verse. "When we've been there ten thousand years, bright shining as the sun, we've no less days, to sing God's praise, than when we've first begun." As she sang, she realized that in her heart of hearts she believed there was a heaven. Even though it seemed incomprehensible that God would sit idly by while his people suffered, she somehow found herself holding on to hope that in the end, in the very end, all would be well.

Louisa's breathing evened.

The door opened and Beth and Danny came in, Danny holding a car seat with a light blanket laid across the top. Beth kissed her grandmother and gave Marcella a hug.

"Hey, Grandma Lou. Marcella." Danny set the carrier on top of the table.

"Oh, that makes me so nervous," Beth said. "Put her on the floor."

Louisa smiled, and Marcella chuckled for her.

Beth bent to unstrap the baby from the carrier. She carefully lifted the newborn infant out and held her close as she made her way to Louisa. "Grandma, I want you to meet your great-granddaughter, Louisa Grace Johnson."

Tears filled Louisa's eyes as Beth held baby Louisa next to her grandma's chest. Louisa Herrala's mouth moved, and Marcella realized she was silently singing *Jesus Love Me*. Marcella picked up her guitar and strummed the chords softly. Louisa looked to Marcella, asking with her eyes if she'd sing. So she did. "Jesus loves me, this I know, for the Bible tells me so."

All three verses came back to her, because that too had been a song of her childhood. "When at last I come to die, he will take me home on high," she sang the simple words. Even with all her unanswered questions and doubts, she still loved Jesus.

When the song ended, Louisa Herrala studied the face of

Louisa Grace and then closed her eyes.

"We should get you home," Danny told Beth. "Let Grandma Lou sleep, and you should get a nap, too, before I go to work."

After they left, Marcella sat strumming chords while Louisa slept. At one point, Louisa mouthed something. Marcella wasn't sure what she said. She leaned closer.

"It's beautiful here." The words were louder, clearer than Louisa's speech had been all day.

Marcella ran to the bottom of the stairs. "Rebecca, come quickly," she called.

Rebecca and Marcella held tight to Louisa's hands as she crossed the bridge.

Pinehurst Church looked much the same as the last time Marcella had been there when she was a teenager, except the balsam firs on either side of the building were taller and paint had peeled off the red metal roof. She arrived for the visitation before Louisa's funeral service.

A pianist played hymns while the attendees queued to pay their respects. A spray of daisies sat atop a closed casket near the front of the sanctuary, next to a large framed photo of Louisa. Marcella drew in a breath. She had almost forgotten what the before-ALS Louisa looked like, when her face was full and round, her eyes smiling. A sob coursed through Marcella's body. It was just like Mom, she thought. Dying was so hard. Death so cruel.

Marcella made her way through the receiving line of family. She hugged Rebecca and offered her condolences to her husband and Louisa's son, both of whom she recalled seeing at Beth and Danny's wedding.

"I'm so sorry," she told Beth, who looked as exhausted as sad, with baby Louisa in a car seat on the floor behind her.

"I'm sorry for you, too." Beth pulled her into a tight hug. "I know how much you loved her."

"Yes, I did," Marcella said. "In a lot of ways, she was family to me." Her own grandmas had both died when Marcella was a young child.

"She was like a grandma to many people. Danny always called her Grandma Lou."

Marcella hugged Danny, who then introduced her to Beth's brother and sister-in-law.

The receiving line grew longer, and seats began to fill. Marcella scooted in next to Lorna and Mak.

His eyes were glassy. He took a red handkerchief out of his pocket and blew his nose loudly. "I'm gonna miss that lady." He sighed.

Marcella patted his arm.

The sanctuary was filling with familiar faces. Louisa's dear friend Senja sat next to Lorna. Aimee and Russ were there in the row behind them, along with Aimee's mother and her boyfriend.

Ten minutes before the service was to begin, the pastor walked to the podium. "Many are still on their way in. If there's room in your pew, please move to the middle so others can find seats."

Marcella shifted over, along with others in her row.

Drew squeezed in next to her, putting his arm over her shoulder. "Hey, how are you doing?"

She burst into tears, leaning her head against his shoulder. After composing herself, she said, "Thanks for coming."

The funeral director wheeled the casket down the side aisle and out of the sanctuary, marking the end of the visitation before the service. Mak excused himself and exited, along with Russ, Danny, and Beth's father, brother, and uncle. Beth pulled baby Louisa from the carrier and followed her family out.

At the top of the hour, the funeral director called out, "Please rise."

The piano fell quiet, and everyone stood in somber reflection.

Mak and the other pallbearers wheeled the casket back down the center aisle, with the rest of the family following behind. The congregation remained standing until the casket was in place and the family was seated.

The pianist began to play again, and the congregation sang, "Oh, love of God, how rich and pure! How measureless and strong! It shall forever more endure. The saints' and angels' song."

So fitting, Marcella thought as she joined her voice with the many who had loved and been loved by Louisa.

At the end of the service, the pallbearers wheeled the casket back out of the sanctuary and lifted it into the back of the hearse. The burial would need to wait a month until the ground thawed.

Drew gave Marcella one last hug and left with little else said. He was a good man.

# Chapter 42

"Time to get up." Drew shook Andy's shoulder.

He stirred and groaned.

"Are you still feeling sick? Do we need to stay home?"

Andy sat up with a start. "What time is it?"

"It's three thirty."

"I can go. It must've been something I ate. I feel fine." Andy lay back down. "I'll just sleep a little more." He was out within seconds.

Drew jumped in the shower, relieved the Mackinac Island trip was still a go. It would've crushed Andy to miss it. He'd been looking forward to it all year, and he worked so hard selling those candy bars. But the night before the big event, he hadn't felt well. He went to bed early, and Drew hoped he'd sleep it off. Just in case, Drew had given the lead teacher a heads-up that they might need to back out. Drew would be the chaperone for Andy and two other boys. They'd share a hotel room, and Drew would follow the group around the island. If he and Andy had to stay home, the other two boys would be split up and assigned to another chaperone, which would make for a tight squeeze in the hotel rooms.

Drew put granola bars in his pocket for breakfast. He put

on a baseball cap and carried his and Andy's duffel bags out to the truck.

At ten to four, he shook Andy's shoulder to wake him. It seemed even harder to wake him than the first time, but once Andy realized it was time to leave, he dove out of bed. Drew had set out his clothes the night before, and Andy slipped into a clean T-shirt and sweats. They were out the door a few minutes before the hour to catch the bus at the elementary school, which was scheduled to leave at 4:30 a.m. Insanely early, but Quincy Elementary had the timing of the trip down to a science after two decades of the tradition.

On the bus, some of the kids were surprisingly energetic for it being the middle of the night, but Andy went back to sleep, resting his head on his balled-up jacket against the window. An hour south of Douglass, after rounding Keweenaw Bay, the bus screeched to a halt. Kids screamed. In front of the bus, a deer stared into the headlights before scampering off the road in the twilight of early morning.

Andy was roused by the commotion. "Dad, I'm going to throw up." Andy began to heave.

Drew grabbed his baseball cap off his head and held it in front of Andy. There it was, coming out into the cap.

The kids in front of them poked their heads over the seatback. "Ewww!" They scurried to seats farther up.

The news of the incident must've rippled like a wave to the front of the bus, because in no time Brooke Davis came back armed with a garbage can and a roll of paper towels. Drew threw his hat away, and he cleaned up Andy, the seat, and the floor.

Andy went back to resting with his head against the window. Poor kid.

They were on a tight timeline to get to Negaunee for a special before-opening tour of the iron museum, so the decision was made to push on. It was one of a few stops on the way to Mackinac Island in an effort to break up the long trip, and everything was planned down to the minute. Besides, there was a chance Andy had motion sickness. Drew prayed he'd snap out of it.

Andy slept most of the way to the iron museum, and when he woke he seemed fine, but once he got out of the bus he threw up again. It was looking like a bug. Andy's teacher talked to Drew and pressed him for the only decision that could be made. Andy would have to go home.

Drew broke the news to his little guy, and Andy sobbed. He insisted he'd be fine, but they both knew it wasn't wise for him to be traveling with all the other kids when he had an active bug.

Drew called Patty, but she didn't pick up her phone. It was still early, before seven in the morning. The kids were already pouring into the museum. Drew wondered if Patty was screening her calls, as they hadn't talked since the co-op confrontation. But Ron should be home, and he wasn't picking up either. Maybe they couldn't hear their home phone from the bedroom. He tried their cell phones, but his calls went straight to voicemail.

Drew sat with Andy while the other kids toured the museum, trying his in-laws periodically. The tour would soon be over, and the other kids would get on the bus. Who else could he call? He dialed Marcella. It might be awkward, but he had no one else.

"Oh, Andy." Marcella felt so bad for him.

"Don't get close. You'll get sick."

"I'll take my chances." She squeezed his shoulder.

"Thanks for coming." Drew grabbed their duffel bags.

Andy crawled in the backseat and sat in the middle. He put on the lap belt, loosened it, and lay across the seat. He slept for most of the ride back.

As they approached Douglass, Drew clutched his stomach. "I'm going to be sick."

Marcella stopped the SUV, and Drew managed to make it to the ditch where he vomited.

At their home, Marcella stayed to nurse the guys. Andy seemed to be feeling better and played on his iPad for the rest of the morning, while Drew took a nap.

Marcella surveyed the contents of the fridge and cupboards, looking for what might appeal to an upset stomach. She cooked a batch of rice and flavored it with salt, pepper, and lemon juice.

She poked her head into the living room where Andy lay on the couch. "Do you want to get something in your stomach again?"

Andy agreed and joined her in the kitchen.

"They're visiting the island today." He stared at the table. "God must hate me."

"What?" She sat next to him.

"He controls everything. So why did he make it so I got sick on the Mackinac Island Trip?"

"I don't know." Her heart ached for him. "All kinds of bad things happen to people, and we don't know why, but God is love, so I'm sure he doesn't hate you." She offered him what she had trouble claiming for herself, but she believed it for him. She remembered Louisa's words. "Good and evil. Joy and suffering. We'd never know one without the other." She reached over and squeezed Andy's shoulder. "I'm sorry you didn't get to go to Mackinac." Her heart filled with love for the boy as the realization dawned on her. It was as Louisa had said—love was weaving its way into her life. She prayed the same would be true for Andy.

Drew woke the next morning feeling like a new man. He'd slept on and off the day before, thankful Marcella had cleared her schedule to watch Andy. When he came out of his room, Marcella was sleeping on the couch. He slipped into the bathroom and then tiptoed across the floor to the kitchen to brew a pot of coffee. He grabbed the coffee out of the cupboard and filled the pot with water.

"Do you have any tea?" Marcella asked, standing in the doorway.

"Good morning, beauti—" Drew put his hand to his mouth. "I'm sorry. I wasn't thinking."

Marcella smiled. "I like hearing it, even if you're lying through your teeth."

"No lie, beautiful." Drew pulled a box of assorted tea bags from the cupboard. "Andy used all of the peppermint tea he made with you."

"That'll be fine." Marcella filled a small pot with water and set it on the stove. "Someday I'll teach you all about loose-leaf tea."

"Really?" Drew pulled a chair from the table and motioned for her to sit. "So we have a future?"

"Do you want a future?"

"Of course."

"Then why didn't you pursue me?" Marcella asked the question with sadness in her eyes.

"Pursue you? That's what I was doing."

"No you didn't. We had one argument, and you threw in the towel."

"You made it pretty clear where we stood."

"I was trying to figure things out, and I needed you to help me through it. But apparently you're conflict avoidant."

"Conflict didn't work well for me in my marriage."

"I'm not Kristine."

Water boiled as bubbles popped and sizzled against the inside edge of the pot. Marcella poured hot water into a cup and steeped a bag of green tea in it.

Drew's coffee was brewed, and he poured himself a mug. "So, what did you have to figure out?"

"If love is worth the risk."

"Is it?"

"I think so. Even if it means I might have to live through losing you one day, I want you, both of you, in my life.

Drew slid his chair over and grabbed her hand.

"But," Marcella hesitated, letting the word hang in the air, "as much as I want to be there for you, I need to know that you'll be there for me."

"Always." Drew nodded.

"None of this running from an argument."

"You got it. We'll fight every day if you want."

Marcella laughed, placing her hand on his chest and pushing him away in jest.

"I'm going to kiss you now." He leaned in.

"Oh, no you're not." She stiffed-armed him. "Not until you're bug-free for twenty-four hours."

# *Chapter 43*

$M$arcella sat in the enclosed porch on Louisa's old rocking chair, surveying the yard and the field beyond. Apple blossoms called to her, and she rose, went outside, and crossed the yard. She stood under a tree. Lifting her nose to a low hanging branch, she breathed in the sweet scent. Bees buzzed overhead. She savored the glimpse of heaven on the warm evening in early June.

She walked to the garden she'd planted with Beth the prior week. The sun had baked Marcella's skin as she dug the ground, planted seeds, and watered herbs, bok choy, carrots, beans, and peas. Beth helped as much she could but spent half the time fussing over Louisa, who sat in a stroller. Beth shooed any blackfly that dared to invade her baby's personal airspace.

They might not be able to enjoy the fruits of their labor now that the house had cleared probate and Rebecca and her brother were ready to list it with a realtor. Marcella initially didn't want to bother with the garden, and she hadn't even started plants indoors. But Rebecca had encouraged them to go ahead, because houses in the Copper Country could take months or even years to sell, and she welcomed Marcella to stay there rent free until then. She only needed to pay utilities.

However, Marcella didn't plan to stay past August. She'd have to secure a place before the students arrived. She didn't want a repeat of trying to find an apartment in the middle of the winter.

Marcella knelt and plucked persistent weeds that had re-appeared near her germinating seeds. Planting a garden was the best way to usher in summer, and she was glad she did the work no matter how things turned out. Now she wished she had started the plants indoors, but what a chaotic spring it had been caring for Louisa in her final days.

The last few weeks had been unseasonably warm, so she might not have lost much time. She should be able to harvest the peas, at least. By the time the house was listed—by the time an offer was made, the inspections were done, and the closing scheduled—yeah, the peas would have enough time to come up. She might even be able to get some bok choy. Now that she was thinking of an early harvest, she should plant spinach.

A horn honked, and Drew's truck pulled into the driveway. She waved. Drew parked. Andy climbed out of the cab and jumped into the truck bed. Drew met Marcella in the garden.

"Hi, love." She hugged him.

He pressed his lips against the top of her head. "Hey, beautiful."

"Is he okay?" Marcella looked to the truck.

"Andy? Yeah, he's fine. He's just waiting for us." With an arm over her shoulder, Drew looked toward the old bro-ken-down barn in the field, past a swath of purple lupines. "It's really something in the spring."

"Yeah," she said. "And in the summer, fall, and winter."

"It would kill me to lose this view." He looked down into her eyes with a certain intensity. "And you."

"That's sweet." She kissed him.

"It'd be a shame for you not to harvest the garden you planted."

"I was just thinking about that. But planting it is half the fun."

"I've got some good news." Drew ran his hand down her

arm and held her hand. He faced her and grabbed her other hand. "I just heard this house sold. Rebecca accepted an offer."

"What?" Marcella stepped back. "Beth didn't tell me. I thought they were going to list it next week."

"It just happened. A private party bought it before they listed it."

"Oh." She cringed. "When do they want to close?"

"As soon as possible. The guy has cash in the bank from a house that already sold."

"That's not good news. It's horrible." She looked to the ground, shaking her head. "Well, it's good for Rebecca and Scott, but I won't even be able to enjoy my peas, and I haven't even started looking for a place to live."

"Whoa, whoa." Drew pulled her back in. "I said good news, and I meant it."

"The buyer wants you to stay in the house, because he doesn't want to move in until he's married."

"When's he getting married?"

"I don't know." He held her close. "When do you think he should get married?"

"Drew, you're not making any sense."

"It doesn't matter for your living situation, anyway, because he wants you to stay, especially after the wedding."

Marcella arched back to look up to his face, as he held the small of her back. "Are you...?"

Drew dropped to one knee. Holding her hand, he held a ring up with his other hand and asked, "Will you marry me?"

"Is that—" Marcella recognized the ring. It was her mother's. "How did you get that?"

"Your dad gave it to me. By the way, he said if you said no, I have to give it to you anyway."

"Yes!"

Drew slid the ring on her finger. He stood and wrapped her in a hug.

"Did she say *yes*?" Andy called from the back of the truck.

"She said *yes*," Drew yelled back.

Andy jumped out and ran to them.

Understanding fully descended on her. "You. This house. Us." Her eyes filled with tears.

Andy ran up, hugging them both from the side.

Marcella squeezed her guys tight.

She and Drew agreed they didn't want to wait long. They just had to figure out where to have the wedding.

They could have it at Faith Church, where she now attended with Drew and Andy. Patty had been advocating for that location and was even planning to host a bridal shower tea there. She was glad Patty had warmed up to her, and Marcella felt at home at Faith Church, but for years she hadn't pictured herself having a church wedding. Kandy had suggested the botanical gardens in Madison. Marcella checked out pictures of the outdoor gardens online. It was a stunning setting for a wedding. The farmhouse was another option. Aimee's wedding had been simple yet beautiful.

As Marcella pored over the current issue of *Modern Bride* magazine, she realized even a simple wedding was too much. Her heart wasn't in the planning. Maybe it would have been if her mom were still alive.

One afternoon, when she and Andy were biking along the canal, he made a comment about missing out on the Mackinac Island trip. An idea came to her. During the next week, she made a few phone calls to inquire about wedding packages. She booked one in which everything was arranged, and all she and Drew had to do was write a check and show up.

When she called Dad to invite him and Kandy, he insisted on paying for the wedding. "You're my only daughter," he said. "It's something I want to do."

The next day, Kandy called to offer help so Marcella and Drew could have a mini-honeymoon. "After the wedding, we'd like to take our new grandson to a waterpark so you and Drew can have a few days together."

Less than a month later, Marcella, Drew, and Andy spent a

couple days together camping near Mackinaw City. They took a ferry to the island, biked around it, visited Fort Mackinac, rode in a horse-drawn carriage, and popped in and out of numerous shops. Marcella ate more fudge than a bride-to-be should ever eat, and then on the big day, she checked into a quaint, historic inn on the island.

Marcella examined her reflection in the floor-length mirror of the bridal dressing room.

"That's a beautiful gown," Beth said, standing behind Marcella. Beth tucked a stray hair behind Marcella's ear and adjusted her veil.

Marcella ran a finger across the smooth pearl button at her neck. "I love it." She blinked rapidly to ward off tears. Wearing her mother's vintage wedding dress made it feel as though Mom were a part of the special day.

There was a knock at the door. "Ready to go?" the wedding coordinator called.

Beth let her in, and she presented Marcella with a bouquet of sunflowers.

Marcella inhaled sharply. "Those are perfect." The half-dozen, large, golden flowers were tied with a lace ribbon. She turned back to the mirror. The bouquet and the dress each possessed a rustic elegance.

Beth hugged Marcella. "I'll see you outside."

Marcella met her dad on the back porch of the inn.

His eyes glistened. "Oh, Marce, you're just as beautiful as your mother was when she wore that dress. Thirty years ago next month." He held out his elbow for her to hold.

Marcella clutched the bouquet as she walked carefully down the stone staircase to the garden. She caught Drew's eye. He looked at her lovingly, his face tender. Next to him Andy stood solemnly. She flashed him a smile, and his face brightened.

A harpist played while she and Dad crossed the lawn.

Those in attendance rose from their chairs. Kandy. Drew's parents. Beth and Danny, holding baby Louisa. Even Ron and Patty had made the trip.

When they reached the fountain, Dad kissed her cheek and joined her hand to Drew's. She stood next to her guys as they faced the gray-haired minister.

After Drew made his vows, it was her turn. "Andrew, I give you this ring, as a symbol of my love and as a reminder that I have chosen you to be the one to share my life." She slid the gold band on his finger and then looked down at her own finger. Her mother's solitaire ring and the diamond band Drew had picked out fit together perfectly. Her heart overflowed as the minister pronounced them husband and wife, and Drew leaned in to kiss her.

# *Epilogue*

*A*ndy walked into the woods and surveyed the platform that would be the floor of his deer stand. A tree supported the stand on one side. The other side was supported by two, sixteen-foot posts. He climbed up a ladder to the platform and lay back, looking up at the treetops swaying in the breeze. Clouds moved above him, but it felt like he was moving, as though he were on a boat.

He'd taken gun safety training over the summer, and then he, Danny, and Dad began work on the stand as the last project before school started. It needed sides and a roof, but Danny said that could wait until after youth deer hunting season in September, when he'd teach Andy how to hunt. Dad said he was going to learn to hunt too, but he'd have to wait until November.

Andy sat up. He'd better go light the sauna stove. His best friend, Austin, would be coming soon, along with the other guys for Trailblazers.

He packed the bottom of the stove with newspaper and then placed kindling and small logs on top of that. He struck a wooden match on the concrete floor and lit the paper in a couple places. Once that was burning well, he added larger logs into the firebox. When he closed the door, he could hear the fire die down, so he opened the fresh-air damper, and it roared back to life.

He headed to the garden to see what veggies he might want for a snack. Maybe he'd pick something to add to their dinner before Trailblazers. In the garden, Beth knelt between lettuce rows while little Louisa toddled around nearby.

"Hi." Andy snapped a bean off a vine and popped it in his mouth.

Beth looked up and smiled. "I'm glad you're here. Louisa's trying to eat everything except the vegetables." Beth motioned to her half-full bowl of lettuce leaves. "I'm not making much progress here. Maybe you could watch her so I can finish up?"

"Sure." He turned to Louisa, crouching with his hands out like claws. "Hey, Lou-Lou, I'm gonna get you."

Louisa squealed in delight and toddled away. He chased after her and scooped her up. She giggled and held on to his neck as he bounced her. It was pretty amazing to feel so loved by such a little person. He looked into her eyes, seeing the same dark brown color as when he looked in a mirror.

Beth finished collecting lettuce and stood, wiping her hands on her jeans. "Thanks, Andy."

"Mama." Louisa pointed at Beth and then looked to Andy for confirmation or praise.

"That's right, smart girl." He buckled Louisa into the jogging stroller.

She waved to him while Beth pushed her down the path back to their little blue house.

Andy pulled a handful of small carrots from the ground for Marcella. She'd taught him how to thin the crop so that some of the carrots would grow larger by late fall. He walked to the Herrala farmhouse—actually it was the Smith house now. Although he'd lived there for more than a year, he didn't always think of it as his home. He still had fond memories of Wausau, and he missed Mom, but life was pretty good, and it hurt less and less to think of what he'd lost as time went on. Marcella told him that hurting less didn't mean he was betraying his mom. He'd been thinking about that, especially when Louisa called Beth *Mama*.

He found Marcella cutting up chicken in the kitchen, where he put the carrots on the counter.

"Thank you." She set the knife on the cutting board and went to the sink to wash her hands, stretching to reach the tap over her expanding belly.

Andy laughed. "Wow, you're huge. Do you have twins in there?"

"Hey, mister." She smiled. "Just for that, you get to clean the carrots."

He didn't mind, because he'd get to snack on them before they were cooked. As he rinsed carrots, he decided to tell Marcella what was on his mind. "I was thinking that when the baby comes, it might confuse him if I call you Marcella."

"Confuse *him*?"

"Yeah, because it's a boy," Andy said. "Anyway, I'm thinking I should call you Mom."

Marcella leaned against the counter. Tears filled her eyes. "I'd be honored to have you call me Mom, but only if *you* want to."

"I'd be cool with that."

She eyed him seriously. "I'll never try to replace your mom."

"I know you're not my mom-mom, like Danny's not my dad-dad, but you're something else." He shrugged. "And I'm okay if you want to call me your son."

Her face broke out in a smile.

"Hey, there's my three favorite people." Dad stepped into the kitchen and set his briefcase on the table. "Come here and give me a hug."

# Acknowledgments

Thank you to my editing team—Alexandra, Andrea, Cyndi, Dan, Jana, Steve, Susan, Todd, and Mom. We did it again! Thank you for making *Across the Bridge* a better story.

Isaac and Sara, without you I wouldn't have been able to write AJ. I'm so thankful to be your mom.

Explore Copper Island and
find discussion questions at
**KristinNeva.com**

### *Snow Country*

Jilted three weeks before her wedding, Beth Dawson escapes sunny California for the snowy Upper Peninsula of Michigan, where State Trooper Danny Johnson challenges her to let go of her rules for Christian courtship. Her domineering mother chides her to stay single and wants her to talk her ailing grandmother into moving to Los Angeles. Grandma resists moving, but the shocking diagnosis changes everything.

### *Copper Country*

Aimee Mallon wrestles with faith, family, and forgiveness as she pursues her dreams. She's navigating a difficult relationship with her father, who's oblivious to the pain he's caused the family. She loves her boyfriend, Russ Saarinen, but he has his own hang-ups, which have led him to a rustic lifestyle in an off-the-grid cabin. Will bitterness keep Aimee and Russ from merging their life paths when forgiveness seems unmerited?

If you've been introduced to Copper Island through *Across the Bridge*, you'll enjoy reading *Snow Country*, where the series began.

Get to know Louisa before the diagnosis. Danny meets AJ at Kristine's funeral. Mak starts to mine the lives of Beth and Danny for what will become his first book, *The Child of Rumspringa*. And of course, Beth and Danny fall in love.

Preview the prologue and first chapter on the following pages.

# SN❄W COUNTRY

## *Prologue*

*B*eth Dawson checked her email. *Can we do lunch today? We need to talk.*

It must be important. Her fiancé knew how busy she was. Maybe Alan had found a vacation rental for their honeymoon. They would drive down to San Diego. Not exotic, but relaxing. She smiled at the thought and typed a reply. *I'll pick up food. Love you.*

She'd always dreamed of a Christmas Eve wedding, but now the timing seemed crazy. Between planning for that and the Family Resource Center's Christmas festivities, she'd barely seen him the last couple of weeks, except for dinner with his mom over Thanksgiving. It would be good to connect today. She turned her attention back to the flyer she was creating. The Christmas party was always fun for the tutors and kids. Christmas cookies. A Nativity play. Angel Tree gifts for all the kids. She clicked print and checked off another item on a long to-do list. She grabbed her purse.

"I'm glad I caught you." Her boss stood in the doorway. "I know you're busy, but would you mind driving the van tonight? Mark went home sick."

Beth grimaced at the thought, but caught herself. "Sure,

Gary."

She stepped out into a 70-degree day in the parking lot. Through the gate, she walked beside a fence topped with barbed wire. The neighborhood was a concrete jungle, except for a few palm trees next to an overpass. Beth wouldn't venture out by herself after dark, but during the day it was safe. Down the sidewalk of the busy street, she passed the Resource Center's thrift store where graffiti covered its metal donation bin. At the bus stop, she chatted briefly with a mother of two kids who came to the tutoring program. She ventured on to Restaurant *El Corredor* and purchased burritos.

She met Alan in his office where she pulled up a chair across from him.

"We've got to call off the wedding." He pushed papers off his desk into a drawer.

"It'll come together." She laughed as she took the burritos out of the bag and set them on the desk. She pulled the foil wrapper off her burrito. "I know it's hectic, but you know how much I wanted a Christmas Eve wedding, and we don't want to wait another year." She shot him a flirtatious smile.

He looked at her blank-faced. "You don't understand. We need to call it off permanently."

Was he serious? She sat frozen, blinking. "Why?" She barely got the word out.

Alan unwrapped his burrito.

"Why, Alan?" She couldn't believe this was happening. Three weeks before the wedding.

He met her gaze for a moment and then looked past her at the wall. "It's not you. It's me." He mumbled the words.

*So cliché.* Her mind raced with so many thoughts. The non-refundable deposits. The apartment lease they had signed. Gifts they had already received. What would she tell the teen girls she mentored? She had talked about her engagement with them, using it as a model of how life works when you wait on God. What had gone wrong?

Something clicked. The dinner. "It's your mother, isn't it?"

"It's not her. It's not you. It's me." He squeezed a packet of hot sauce on his burrito.

*Of course it's you, you spineless weasel.* She didn't say it. Instead, she clenched her teeth. She had done everything right.

He bit into the burrito, and his jaw worked as he stared at her dumbly.

Why were they having this conversation in the middle of the day? At work? He couldn't wait until the end of the day or the weekend or better yet, why not months ago? Her chin quivered. Anger rose in Beth's throat. "You think this is a conversation to have over lunch?" She spit out the words and slapped her burrito on his desk.

"We can still be friends." He wiped his desk with a napkin.

Well, I like my friends so that's not going to work, she thought. "Let me help you clean that up." She swept both burritos into the garbage can.

"Hey, I was going to eat that."

"I was going to marry you." She plunked the can down next to him. "Go ahead. Eat it." She twisted the engagement ring off her finger and was about to throw it at him, but then thought better of it. She stuffed it in her pocket and left.

# Chapter 1

*Five Weeks Later*

*B*eth strained to see beyond flashing red lights into the dark past an ambulance parked on the shoulder. A car lay upside down in the snow-filled ditch. She gasped. *God, help them.*

Intermittent wiper blades swept melted snow from her windshield. Her headlights illuminated the side of a sheriff's car, and on the other side of the accident, another vehicle blocked the road. No other cars on the road for over an hour, and now this.

She'd witnessed many accidents in LA, but somehow this one unsettled her. She shivered. She had never seen such darkness as on those country roads on the way to the Upper Peninsula of Michigan.

She checked her phone. Two bars. She'd call Mother.

"Hello, this is Rebecca Dawson."

"Hi, it's me."

"You made it. How's Grandma?"

Beth moistened her lips. "I'm not quite there. There's been an accident—"

"Oh, no. I told you it was too dangerous to drive across the country," Mother scolded.

Beth sighed. Why had she even called? "I didn't get into an

accident. I'm just stopped at one."

"They probably hit a deer. Why are you still on the road? I told you to get an early start from Minneapolis so you wouldn't be driving at night. What took you so long to leave?"

"I don't know." She scrambled for an excuse that would satisfy Mother but came up empty. "I guess it just took a while to get going."

"You must learn to keep better track of time. It was bad enough you drove across the country, but the roads are dreadful there in the winter. It's dangerous driving with all that snow."

The drive had been pretty in the daylight, but it got dark quickly. Mother was right. She should've left earlier.

"How much farther do you have to drive?"

"My GPS says I'll be at Grandma's in a half hour."

EMTs appeared from the ditch, bright reflective stripes and patches on their jackets. They were pulling something. A sled with somebody on it. They lifted the person up and onto a gurney.

That looked rough. *God, I pray he's alive.*

"When you get in, be sure to talk to Grandma about coming to California. Show her the pictures I sent with you."

"Yes, Mother." How many times had she said that phrase? She might have called her *Mom* when she was a young child, but for as long as Beth could remember, her mom was *Mother*.

"It's not safe for her to be in that house by herself out in the country. I want you to talk to her about it tonight."

"Yes, Mother."

Mother droned on about her battle to get Grandma to move.

Grandma had fallen a week before the wedding—well, a week before the canceled wedding. She had still planned to fly out to LA for Christmas, but with the fall wasn't up for traveling. Beth decided to visit her instead. Besides, she needed time away to pick up the pieces. When Mother finally came around to the idea of her driving to Michigan, it was clear she had another agenda. She wanted her to convince Grandma to return with her to LA.

The EMTs loaded the patient into the back of the ambulance.

Beth straightened in her seat, put her foot on the brake, and shifted the car into drive. "I've got to let you go now."

"Call me tonight after you talk to Grandma."

The ambulance sped off with sirens blazing. The cops left, and Beth drove on—the sole car on the road—even slower than before the accident.

She gripped the steering wheel and leaned forward as she struggled to see the snow-covered centerline. She made her way across the Lift Bridge and onto Copper Island. As she drove down Main Street in Quincy, Douglass's twin town, cars passed her. Another driver tapped his horn.

Red lights reflected onto her dashboard, and a siren chirped. He couldn't be pulling her over. Her speedometer read fifteen miles per hour. She slowed to ten, hoping the vehicle would go around. Sirens blared as she drove through town in a slow-speed chase.

In the rearview mirror, headlights blinded her. A truck? She looked for a lit parking lot. Men had been impersonating cops and raping women. That was LA. *This is small-town America, but you never know.* She pulled into a gas station and parked in full view of the cashier. A blue SUV parked behind her. Instead of a bar of lights on the roof, there was one large, old-fashioned, red light. It looked like something anybody could rig up.

A man approached her Toyota Corolla and, with a thick knuckle, rapped on the window.

She cracked it open. "Who are you?" She looked for an actual metal badge, instead of the embroidered emblems on his jacket and tight, black stocking cap.

"Who am I?" he barked. "I'm a trooper with the Michigan State Police. Why didn't you stop?"

She gathered her courage. "How do I know you're a real cop?"

"Ma'am, you can't fake being a cop in a town this small."

He unzipped his jacket to reveal his badge. "Call 911 if you want. They can verify."

She looked in her rearview mirror. "But you're not driving a real cop car."

"We drive trucks. I need to see your driver's license, registration, and proof of insurance."

She rifled through the glove box and slipped the documents through the crack.

"Los Angeles, California, hey."

Beth was silent.

"Ma'am, that was a question. You from Los Angeles, California?"

"Oh, yes, I didn't know that was a question. You didn't upspeak."

"Huh?"

"You didn't use upward inflection of the end of your sentence so I would know it was a question."

"You're a schoolteacher, too, hey."

"Was that a question?" She frowned. "No, I'm not a schoolteacher. I'm a youth worker. Well, I'm nothing, now. Are you going to give me a ticket? I wasn't speeding."

"You were obstructing the flow of traffic, going too slow. How many drinks have you had?"

Beth gasped. "Drinks? None. I'm accounting for road conditions, sir."

"This fluff? This is a dry, January snow. These are not dangerous road conditions."

"I just passed an accident on the way into town." Mother was right. She shouldn't have come here.

"I was there. She didn't go off the road because of the conditions. She was drunk." He shook his head. "What are you doing in Michigan?"

"Visiting..." Tears stung her eyes and she blinked them away.

"Oh, now don't cry." The trooper's tone softened.

"I'm not," Beth snapped. She just wanted the whole ordeal to be over so she could get to Grandma's. "Just give me the ticket."

"I'm not gonna give you a ticket."

"Why? Because you thought I was going to cry?" Instead of holding back like usual, she let loose. "What kind of cop are you if you don't follow through on your threats?"

"I'm a trooper, not a parent. I'm not even married."

"What did you mean by that? Why would you think I'd care about your marital status?" She scowled. "That's so unprofessional."

The trooper cocked his head. "Are you okay?" He stared into her eyes.

She seethed. "You are *not* my therapist."

He shrugged and chuckled. "You might need a better one. Look, ma'am, pick up the pace, or at least stay in your lane."

She clenched her jaw.

"And welcome to God's country." After handing the documents back to her, he walked back to his truck.

Beth regretted her terseness. He was just doing his job, and he had gentle eyes. He didn't deserve that. She put her head down on the steering wheel and sobbed, stress overcoming her. It had been a rough five weeks. Get a grip, she told herself as she pulled a package of tissue from her purse and blew her nose.

Up Quincy Hill and a few miles past town, a pickup truck passed heading the opposite direction, leaving in its wake a short-lived blizzard that both mesmerized and frightened her. She turned down a country road flanked with trees. Even with the snow, it looked the same as it did on her many childhood visits, every summer with her parents. She hadn't been back for years, not since Grandpa Sam's funeral. When was that? He had died the summer after her freshman year of college. Had it been seven years?

Past red pines that lined the driveway, the headlights flashed on a woodshed, sauna, and on banks of snow as she turned her car toward an old, gray stucco farmhouse. She drove through a few inches of fresh powder and parked near the front steps. The porch light was off, but a light inside the house burned brightly.

She turned off the car and sat in silence for a minute, composing herself. As she got out, she slipped and grabbed the car door to steady herself. Beth walked with short strides to the house. She locked the car behind her, and the Corolla chirped.

Inside the enclosed porch, a few pieces of firewood were stacked in a hopper to the right of the main door. Two rocking chairs sat to the left of the door with a small table between them. Beth had played at the feet of her grandparents who sat in those chairs, her grandma drinking tea and reading a book and her grandpa drinking coffee and reading the newspaper.

"Grandma," she called, as she entered the warm house. Hit with the scent of cardamom bread, she inhaled, closed her eyes, and tilted her head back. Ahh, *nisu*. The scent brought her back to her childhood. Eating the sweet, hearty bread in Grandma's kitchen. "It's me."

"Coming," Grandma called. Moments later, she enveloped Beth in a tight squeeze. She was a small woman, not frail, just petite. She had gained a bit of weight since Beth last saw her, but she carried it well. "I'm so glad to see you. I guess I fell asleep waiting for you. How are you, dear?"

"It's good to get away." She bit her lip. Away from all the drama—seeing Alan every day at work, returning wedding gifts, canceling reservations—while he went on as if nothing happened.

"I can't believe that boy. Three weeks before the wedding. So fickle." Grandma shook her head. "Now, don't just stand there. Come have something to eat."

Beth kicked off her boots, hung her jacket, and followed Grandma down the hall. A fire was burning in an antique kitchen stove, and a pot simmered atop a modern cooking range.

"How was your trip?" Grandma pulled a bowl from the cupboard. "Such a long drive from California. Good thing the snow was light tonight."

Beth thought sheepishly about her encounter with the police officer. She brushed it off. It didn't matter. The important thing was that she had made it. Safe and sound.

"Come sit down. I have stew on the range, and I made *nisu*."

"I'd love that." Beth sat at the oak table that stood against the wall under a window. A floodlight lit up the snow-filled back yard. The cardamom bread lay sliced in the center of the table. Next to it, a knife rested on the edge of a saucer beside a stick of butter. She buttered a slice of the bread.

Grandma set a bowl of stew in front of her. "Would you like tea, dear?"

"Please."

"Tea tastes better when it's heated by a wood fire." Grandma set a ceramic teakettle on the old stove.

Beth put a spoonful of stew in her mouth and closed her eyes, savoring the garlic, basil, and vegetables. Happy memories from summer visits at the farm flooded her mind. Helping Grandma weed and water the garden. Digging fresh carrots and eating peas and beans right off the vine. The Upper Peninsula—or the UP as the locals called it—was earthy, real. Like Mother, she was concerned about Grandma living alone in the country, but she wasn't convinced she should leave. "This is delicious. Thank you for having me."

"I'm glad to have you. With Sam gone, this house is too big for me." Grandma leaned against the counter.

"I'm sure it's a lot of work to keep up the farm." Beth tried to get a sense if their concerns were justified.

"There's nothing left of the farm, other than my garden. I kept the goats and chickens for a while because your grandpa liked to watch them, but I got rid of them after he died."

"Are you doing okay here by yourself?" She asked the question tentatively. She didn't want to be in the middle of things between her mother and Grandma. She had come here to escape drama.

"I do just fine on my own," Grandma said sharply. "I didn't give up the farm because I'm incapable of managing it. I gave it up because I'm too busy. But if your mother is worried, tell her Danny, my neighbor boy, checks in on me most nights.

He makes sure my wood hopper's full. I have petroleum, of course, but with the cost, I try to use wood as much as possible, at least during the day."

"I can haul your firewood," Beth offered.

"So can I. I like doing it, in fact, but I also like Danny's company. While you're here, I want you to relax. Get some rest." The teakettle whistled, and Grandma picked it up by its bamboo handle and set it on a woven reed trivet on the table. "I'll make us chamomile tea, if that's all right with you. I dried flowers from the garden last summer. It's so calming before bed."

"That sounds great."

While Grandma stuffed the tea ball and dropped it into the kettle to steep, Beth finished her stew. She pushed the bowl aside. Grandma served two cups of tea and sat across the kitchen table from Beth, who dipped the bread in her tea—something she hadn't done since she was a kid. That's how Grandma taught her to eat it.

"Hello?" A call came from the front hallway, and Beth jumped in alarm.

"That's Danny."

"He doesn't knock?"

"That's the Yooper doorbell—open the door and yell. I'm glad you'll get to meet him. He's about your age. Come on in, Danny." Grandma went to greet him. "Don't worry about your boots just yet. I'll get a towel you can stand on."

Danny stepped into the kitchen still dressed in his State Police uniform. He pulled off his stocking cap revealing short, dark hair. A smile emerged on his angular face.

Beth wanted to hide under the table.

17479813R00187

Made in the USA
Lexington, KY
19 November 2018